D1527067

NEVER BORROW A BARONET

Published by Edwards and Williams
Copyright © 2018 by Regina Lundgren

Printed in the USA.

Cover Design and Interior Format
© THE KILLION GROUP INC.

FORTUNE'S
BRIDES
BOOK
TWO

Never Borrow a Baronet

REGINA SCOTT

*To my mother, for her unfailing patience,
and to the Lord, the author of all patience*

CHAPTER ONE

Essex, England, March 1812

My, but life could be unpredictable.

Patience Ramsey peered out of the window of the elegant coach, gaze on the greening fields they passed, hand stroking the fur of the grey-coated cat in her lap. Raised in the country, spending the last three years as companion to the sickly Lady Carrolton, she had become accustomed to routine, solitude. A genteel lady fallen on difficult times could expect nothing more. At least, that had been her impression until she'd met Meredith Thorn of the Fortune Employment Agency, and Miss Thorn had introduced her to Miss Augusta Orwell.

"Gussie," the tall, spare daughter of a baronet had proclaimed the moment they'd met at the family's London town house on Clarendon Square. "Everyone calls me that. Well, everyone I like. And I like you. You have presence."

Patience still wasn't sure why the older woman had said that. She had never noticed a particular attitude when she looked in the mirror. Her long, thick, wavy hair could not claim the glory of gold nor the biddable nature of brown, and it was hardly visible in the serviceable bun behind her head. Her brown eyes could never be called commanding. And while her curves might be a tad more noticeable than Gussie's, she was in no way approaching the status of an

Amazon. Besides, a presence was not required to serve as a companion. Lady Carrolton would only have seen it as an impertinence.

But, before she was even certain she would suit in the new position, she had resigned her post with Lady Carrolton, packed her things, and boarded the Orwell coach for the journey to the Essex shore.

"As soon as we reach the manor, I must show you my laboratory," Gussie said beside her now, continuing the rather one-sided conversation she'd begun when they'd left the inn that morning, having spent the night after leaving London. "I'm itching to try the gypsum I purchased in town. It will be just the thing for scrofulous eruptions. I know it. I don't suppose you have any we might test the preparation on."

Patience hid her shudder from long practice. If she could humor her previous employer, who had been convinced she suffered from every illness imaginable, she could surely deal with the irrepressible Gussie. After all, were not the peacemakers called blessed?

"Unfortunately, no," she told her new employer. "But perhaps we can find some poor soul in need of help."

Across the coach, Miss Thorn cleared her throat. *She* had presence. That raven hair, those flashing lavender eyes. And she had an enviable wardrobe. Today it was a lavender redingote cut away so that the fine needlework on her sky blue wool gown showed to advantage. Nearly all Patience's clothes were grey or navy—Lady Carrolton had insisted on it—and none draped so neatly around her figure as the fashionable gowns Miss Thorn wore.

Then again, Gussie had insisted on having Patience fitted for new gowns and purchased accessories before they had left London. The dresses should arrive in a week or two, to be finished by the local seamstress, and the jaunty feathered hat, ostrich plume curling around Patience's ear, sat on her head now. The entire wardrobe had seemed an extravagance, but Patience had learned not to question the vagaries of the aristocracy.

"I believe we agreed that you would not experiment on Miss Ramsey," Miss Thorn said, looking down her long nose at Gussie.

Gussie waved a hand. "Of course, of course. It is merely my enthusiasm for the task speaking." She turned to Patience. "You must tell me, dear girl, when I overstep. I want ours to be a long and happy association."

How different from Lady Carrolton. Her constant complaints, her bitter spirit, had tried Patience in ways she had never imagined. She would be ever in the debt of her friend Jane Kimball, soon to be the Duchess of Wey, for suggesting that Patience might have the opportunity to change her circumstances.

She and Jane had sat together along the wall every week while Lady Carrolton took tea with her long-time friend, the Dowager Duchess of Wey, at the castle belonging to the duke's family. Jane had served as governess to the duchess's three granddaughters. Patience could only admire her dedication to the little girls. That and Jane's bravery. Patience had been taught that silence was a virtue, that one should never state one's opinions in company. Nothing stopped Jane from speaking her mind, not fear of losing her position, not concern that she might be deemed impertinent or a rudesby.

"If you ever want another position," Jane had said on one occasion when Lady Carrolton had been particularly difficult, "I may know someone who could help."

Even though something had leaped inside her at the thought, Patience hadn't accepted Jane's offer that day. Lady Carrolton had been kind to hire her when she had never worked before, had no reference other than the supportive words of the vicar. Surely she owed the lady loyalty, forbearance. Do unto others as you would have done unto you.

And then had come that terrible day when Lady Carrolton's daughter, Lilith, had lashed out.

"How dare you presume to advise my mother on her medications?" she had spat, pale blue eyes drilling into Patience. "You have no education, no family of merit, absolutely nothing to recommend you. If you dare to contravene my suggestions again, I will see you up on charges. How well will you fare sitting in jail with no one to plead your case?"

It had been all Patience could do to hold back her tears until she had left the withdrawing room. All her selfless service, all her care, and this was her thanks? She had a gentlewoman's education, little different from Lady Lilith's. Her father and mother had been good, kind people who hadn't deserved their deaths of the influenza. She had only been trying to help her ladyship over the illnesses that plagued her. It seemed none of that mattered in the Carrolton household.

There had to be some place she might earn respect, some work where she could find purpose and honor. A position under an employer with integrity, an ounce of human kindness, and an unwillingness to berate those around her.

Miss Thorn had been all understanding. Patience had thought it might take some time to find a new situation, especially as, once again, she had no reference. But she hadn't been in Miss Thorn's company more than a quarter hour before the woman had whisked Patience off for an interview with Miss Orwell. And Gussie had only asked a few questions before declaring Patience perfect for the role as her assistant.

Now, here she sat, leaving her former life behind, riding into a new bright future.

She hoped.

"Such a lovely creature," Gussie said, eyeing Fortune, Miss Thorn's cat, as she cuddled against Patience's chest. "I don't suppose she has any scrofulous eruptions."

Miss Thorn put her nose in the air. "Certainly not. And you may not experiment on her either. Surely you remember our agreement."

Miss Thorn had been very precise in her terms. Patience was to receive her own room, generous compensation, and a half day off every week in her role assisting Gussie in developing salves and lotions to improve the skin. The work could be no messier than tending to the ailments of a quarrelsome lady and with so much more purpose! Miss Thorn had even insisted on traveling out to the Orwell estate to make sure everything was as Gussie had portrayed it. She had been determined that the matter be settled quickly and precisely, and Patience was rather glad of it.

If everything happened quickly, she had no time for regrets or second thoughts.

"Of course I remember our agreement," Gussie said with a sniff. "I remember everything. You might take note of that Miss…Thorn."

Patience's benefactress turned toward the window, but not before Patience saw her cheeks brighten with pink. Embarrassment? Impossible. Surely nothing could discompose the indomitable Miss Thorn.

As if she thought otherwise, Fortune roused herself and leaped across the space to rub her cheek against her mistress' arm. Miss Thorn glanced down at her gratefully.

Gussie nudged Patience. "Look there, up that hill. That's your new home."

Patience turned to the opposite window. Though the sun was nearly at the western horizon, the air felt suddenly warmer, the day brighter. The fields had given way to fens and marshes, their grasses undulating in the breeze from the water. Close at hand rose a promontory studded with trees and topped by a sturdy, square manor house. The red brick glowed in the spring sunlight; the multipaned windows gleamed. She drew in a breath and caught the scent of the sea.

The proximity to the waves was even more obvious as they rolled across the causeway that led toward the promontory. To her right lay miles of tide flats, brown and muddy; to her left, the twisting maze of creeks and channels that made up the marshes.

"It floods on occasion," Gussie said with a nod to the track. "I can remember springs when we didn't see another person until after Easter."

Patience's stomach dipped, but she managed a polite smile. Since her parents had died, she had always been alone. The isolation of the house would make no difference.

They followed the drive to stop in front of the stone steps leading to the front door. A manservant in a navy coat and breeches came out to open the carriage door and then went to help the coachman with the horses. Patience followed Gussie and Miss Thorn up the steps, through tall white columns and the wide, red-lacquered front door into a spacious, dark-wood-floored entry hall. More white fluted columns held up the sweeping stairs leading to the second story, and opened doors in all directions invited her to explore the house further. But the portraits hanging from the high ceiling against the creamy stuccoed wall, life-sized and rich in their gilded frames, stopped her movement. Miss Thorn paused to eye them as well. In her arms, Fortune twitched her tail as if finding the portraits equally compelling.

"My grandfather," Gussie said as if she'd noticed them staring at the swarthy fellow standing with his hand on a globe as if he owned the world. "He earned the baronetcy through some effort that pleased the Crown. A merchant, they say, making his fortune on the high seas. A pirate, if you ask me."

Patience blinked. So did Fortune.

"That is my father," Gussie continued with a nod to the next gentleman, who was seated beside a green baize table. "Nearly gambled away our entire fortune before his untimely death. My brother attempted to take up the challenge. He was killed in a duel over the accusation he had cheated at cards before we ever had the opportunity to have him painted."

Patience swallowed. Fortune turned her face away.

Gussie's censorious look eased into something warmer as she motioned to the final portrait of a man standing gazing out a window that looked very much like the ones on either side of the front door. "And then there's Harry. I raised him as my own. They say heredity will out."

Patience frowned. This fellow boasted a shock of mahogany hair, curling against his brow; blue eyes that gave no quarter; a solid chin that brooked no disobedience; and shoulders broad enough to take on any challenge. It seemed Sir Harold Orwell had inherited his forefathers' chiseled good looks. How sad if he had inherited their less attractive attributes as well.

Through one of the many doors came a small fellow in the navy livery that must belong to the house. White hair, short cut, sat like a wreath about his head, leaving his dome bare. His round face was as wizened as a winter-nipped apple, and nearly as red. He hurried up to Gussie. "Your ladyship. I regret that you have guests."

Miss Thorn turned from their perusal of the portraits. "Invited guests, sir." Fortune drew back as if just as insulted by the comment.

He inclined his head in their general direction. "My apologies, madam, but I was referring to the other guests. The ones who arrived earlier this afternoon."

Gussie frowned as she removed her hat and offered it to him. "Other guests? What other guests?" Suddenly, her eyes widened, and Patience would only have called the look horrified. "Cuddlestone, no! Please tell me it isn't so."

He sighed, so gustily that his chest deflated. "I wish I could, your ladyship. They claim to have been invited to stay for Easter. Sir Harry had already left. I could not in good conscience send them away before consulting with you."

"You could, and you should," Gussie insisted. She rubbed her forehead. "I will not allow this."

Miss Thorn took a step forward, holding Fortune protectively close. "Is something wrong, Miss Orwell?"

As if in answer, there was a cry from above. Patience looked up to find a lady about her age on the landing. She rushed down before Patience could register more than pale blond hair and big eyes.

"Gussie!" She enfolded the lady in a hug. "You've returned! How marvelous. And with company." She pulled back and aimed a happy smile all around. Every bit of her trembled with obvious joy, from the ringlets beside her creamy oval face to the pink satin bow under her bosom, to the double flounces at the bottom of her white muslin skirts.

Gussie drew in a breath as if overwhelmed to find someone even more effusive than she was. "Yes. Miss Thorn, may I present Miss Villers. I imagine her brother is about somewhere."

"Taking a walk in the garden," Miss Villers confessed. She inclined her head to Miss Thorn, who returned the gesture, and beamed at Fortune. Then she turned expectantly to Patience, who smiled dutifully. Would Gussie even think to introduce her? In the Carrolton household, she had become used to being overlooked. Good companions, as Lady Lilith had enjoyed saying, should be invisible.

"And you must meet Miss Ramsey," Gussie said. "She's going to marry my Harry."

On the Essex shore below the manor that night, Sir Harry Orwell crouched on the sand, hooded lantern in hand and sea breeze fingering through his hair. Out on the waves, something flashed once, twice, so quickly anyone not looking for it might have missed it. He stood, returned the signal, and waited.

Around him, the grasses sighed. He nearly sighed as well. Responsibility bent a fellow, yet he would not wish it otherwise. To flee responsibility made him no better than his great-grandfather, his grandfather, his father. Yet he thought he shared at least one trait besides the family chin.

To risk was to live. His great-grandfather had chosen the saying for their family crest. Harry had grown up reading and believing it. He just chose different risks, risks he hoped would restore the family honor, once and for all.

A long dark shape grated against the sand. Harry moved forward to meet the smugglers.

Thomas Undene gripped his arm as the others climbed out of the boat and began unloading their cargo. No voice was raised to call out. Sound carried, and one could never be sure who might be waiting, even on English soil.

"What news?" Harry whispered.

Undene's grip was hard. The village blacksmith, he had hands as strong as his vises. "No news. She never sent word, never met us herself. You've lost your informant, Sir Harry."

Cold settled in his gut. Yvette, unmasked? It didn't bear thinking about. The daughter of a deceased French count, she had been his eyes and ears in France, sending messages across that he saw safely to the War Office in London.

"You're sure?" he pressed.

"Nothing's sure over there," Undene said. "She could have been imprisoned, she could have given up. She could have sold us out to old Boney."

Never. Not his brave Yvette.

Something sparked on the fens, and he heard the bark of a pistol a moment later. The bullet slashed his arm, burning. The rush of warmth told him he was bleeding before the pain lanced through him.

"Down." Undene tugged, and Harry flattened himself to the sand. Flashes and roars on all sides showed his companions fighting back. He only caught glimpses of them. Undene's teeth barred in a snarl, Lacy's arm extended with his pistol. Then they gathered what they could and ran.

He knew the routine. If the revenue men showed up, scatter in all directions, into the braided paths of the marsh, where no one could follow them. But if this attack came from the Revenue Service, why weren't the agents calling out in the name of the King? Why weren't other shadows dashing down onto the beach to confiscate the remaining cargo?

No time to find answers. Fingers pressed to his wound, closed lantern swinging, he stumbled into the reeds. All he could hear was his own ragged breath.

He forced himself to calm, to slow, to reach out with his senses. The moon hadn't risen yet. He could just make out the tops of the grasses. No sound of pursuit. No whisper of friends or enemies around him.

But if he stayed here, they'd track him by the blood.

He removed his hand from the wound long enough to set down the lantern and pull off his cravat. His man Cuddlestone always urged him to try a more elegant fold. Harry's method of folding was easier off; he quickly accomplished it and managed to wrap the cravat around his arm one-handed. Retrieving the lantern once more, he edged through the marsh toward higher ground, which led to the manor.

Lights from the withdrawing room warned him Gussie was home and entertaining the Villers. He hadn't been completely surprised when the pair had shown up. It seemed they believed the door to the manor perpetually open. Gussie's enthusiasm had that effect on people.

Fortunately, he had been able to slip away from the house without greeting them. He'd planned to head straight to London with any news Yvette sent, avoiding the house entirely. Only there was no news, and he needed somewhere to tend to his wound.

No use trying the front door and meeting cries of alarm. Likewise, the kitchen was out of reach. The fewer staff who suspected the true nature of his nighttime activities the better. He would have to slip in his bedroom window and pretend he had come in too late to be noticed. It wouldn't be the first time.

The trellis was sturdily built—Gussie had made sure of it.

"Sooner or later you'll climb down or up it," she'd told him before he headed to Eton as a lad. "Might as well be prepared."

Now he hid the lantern among the shrubs at the base of the manor and positioned his feet carefully, relying on one hand for balance. His arm was throbbing, demanding that he see to it. He'd have to prevent Gussie from trying one of her concoctions on him. He was never sure what was in them.

He heaved himself up to the chamber story and onto the balcony, then fumbled with the latch. The glass-paned door opened silently. He drew in a breath as he slipped into the room. But once past the thick curtains, he realized he must have been expected. A lamp glowed beside the bed, and a fire warmed the hearth. Count on Gussie to think of everything.

Even a welcoming committee.

The young lady stood beside the hearth. Hair flowed like honey about her slender shoulders. The loose nightgown whispered of curves beneath the creamy flannel. She'd picked up the empty coal shuttle and held it ready. Despite her willowy frame, he thought she was fully capable of swinging the thing at his head.

He spread his hands. "Forgive the intrusion. But may I point out that you are in *my* room?"

CHAPTER TWO

Patience gripped the shuttle. She couldn't doubt the
intruder's words. Even in the dim light, she could make
out the features of Sir Harold Orwell. His hair was even
more mussed than in the portrait, and that square chin was
more solid. He wore no cravat and seemed to be holding
one arm slightly behind him. Still, to blunder in through
the window? Surely even in this unusual household that
should be considered odd.

Perhaps it was the lateness of the hour or the ruse she
had agreed to perpetrate against her better judgment, but
she had no trouble stating her opinion this time.

"Your aunt assigned me to this room," she informed her
visitor. "Had you consulted her first, you might have saved
yourself the trouble of climbing in the window."

"Ah, but I chose to climb through the window to
prevent having that discussion with my aunt." He had the
audacity to wink at her. "A gentleman never kisses and
tells, you know."

So, that was it. He'd been out cavorting and didn't want
Gussie to learn the truth. Disappointment bit sharply.

"Be that as it may," she told him, "I'm certain since you
were raised in this house you could find another suitable
bedchamber far sooner than I could. See yourself out, sir."

"Happy to oblige, madam," he said with a lopsided bow
that likely spoke of the state of his sobriety. "Once I locate

a change of clothes."

He started for the wardrobe on the far wall, and Patience took a step closer, shuttle up against her shoulder.

"You'll find no suitable clothes in here," she informed him. "Mr. Cuddlestone moved your things elsewhere."

He jerked to a stop, and she clutched the shuttle tighter. How was she to know whether he was the sort to accost the servants, or a lady he probably thought was one of his aunt's guests? She had never met anyone who took liberties while inebriated, but her friend Jane had been discharged from her previous post because of a master who had lost his head.

But as he stopped and turned to face her, the arm he had tried so hard to hide came into view, wrapped in a cloth stained red.

With blood.

Patience gasped, and the shuttle slipped from her fingers to clang against the floor. "Your arm. You've been injured."

He glanced down at the makeshift bandage as if surprised to find it affixed to him. "Yes, it appears so. Hence the need for a change of clothes."

Patience shook her head. "That requires tending. It will turn septic if you don't take a care."

He eyed her a moment. "Who are you, exactly?"

She bobbed a curtsey, feeling her cheeks heat. "Patience Ramsey, your aunt's new assistant."

He reared back. "I will not allow Gussie's preparations on my person."

Patience raised her brows. "Are they so horrid?"

"You'll have to ask the previous assistant. I believe she finally regained the use of her fingers, but I expect that rash will last for some time."

Patience swallowed, then noticed the gleam in those blue eyes. "You're making fun of me."

"Never, madam," he assured her. "But I can tend to my own wounds."

"One-handed? Or have you a manservant you can enlist?"

That seemed to stop him. She could almost see the thoughts flying behind his eyes. If he didn't want his aunt to know of his midnight prowl, perhaps he didn't want the servants to know either. But, of course, someone would notice the ruined coat. Just like the master not to think of that.

"Very well," he allowed, going to perch on the chair near the fire. "I would appreciate your assistance, Miss Ramsey. Thank you."

So meek. She didn't trust him for an instant. But she'd never been able to turn away someone hurting, whether illness, injury, or heartache. She went to the tall dresser, where she'd arranged the rosewater and ointment her mother had taught her to make. Funny how setting them in place had made the room feel more like home, for all she'd never had such a lovely space before. The room's pale green walls, deep green carpet, and warm wood furnishings made her feel as if she wandered into a forest on a summer's day.

She nearly hadn't reached the beauty and solitude of the room. When Gussie had uttered that ridiculous statement about Patience being Sir Harold's betrothed, Patience had been tempted to run back to the coach then and there. What sort of place was this where guests appeared without invitation? Where the mistress betrothed people without so much as an introduction? Had her eagerness to sever ties with Lady Carrolton's stern household led her to something far worse?

But Miss Villers had stared at her dumbstruck, and Miss Thorn had demanded a moment of Gussie's time. Before she knew it, Patience was sitting in a pretty withdrawing room done in shades of blue while Gussie paced about the thick carpet wringing her long-fingered hands.

"It's all my fault. I had hopes of Harry settling down, so

I took to inviting young ladies to visit. He never showed the least interest, but Miss Villers and her brother simply do not know when to call for the coach. I don't remember inviting them for Easter, but either Harry or I must have done so because here they are." She had stopped to gaze imploringly at Patience. "You understand, don't you, Miss Ramsey?"

Not in the slightest, but that was nothing new. She'd never figured out why something would set off Lady Carrolton, resulting in a whooping cough, explosive sneezes, or worse. She had done her best to smile encouragement to her new employer. "I could see why you might feel uncomfortable evicting them, your ladyship, but why introduce me as your nephew's bride-to-be?"

Gussie had grown positively teary-eyed. "For Harry's sake. He's trying so hard to be the gentleman his father and grandfather could never be. He is determined to earn a spotless reputation. Miss Villers is equally determined to have him, no matter his reputation. If you pretend to be his betrothed, surely she'll give it up and go. Harry should be away for several days. He won't even know of our little deception."

So much for that plan. Not only would Sir Harold hear of it, but he was clearly not the gentleman his aunt thought him to be.

Pulling a wool shawl off the bed, she carried the rosewater and ointment to his side. She'd never particularly liked the shawl, a hand-me-down from Lady Lilith, but it had been warm those days when the fire in Lady Carrolton's hearth didn't quite reach the dressing room cot, where Patience was supposed to be forever on duty even at night. It would keep away the chill now.

Or perhaps Sir Harold's look would do that.

He did have the loveliest blue eyes, wide and guileless, and a dimple had popped into view at the side of his mouth as she approached.

She held up the ointment. "My own preparation, made from my mother's recipe. It has rosewater, lavender, and glycerin in it."

His mouth quirked. "So, I'll smell like a garden, but I won't expire."

She fought her own smile. "Exactly."

He untied the makeshift bandage, which she realized was his cravat. "Help me with this coat."

She set the rosewater and ointment on the table beside his chair and eased the sleeve off his shoulder. As the coat came free, she saw the swath of red spreading across the muslin of his shirt. Peering closer, she spotted the tear and the angry line of the wound.

"What happened?" she asked, plucking the fabric away from the cut.

"Caught myself on a briar on the way home," he said, watching her.

"I would commend you on your ability to lie," Patience said, "but it's not a convincing lie. No briar, sir, cuts through a sturdy wool coat and muslin shirt. I cannot tend to the wound unless I can see all of it. Remove your shirt, please."

It was likely the urgency that made her speak so boldly. It was likely his injury that made him obey. She went to fetch the washbasin and cloth that had been left for her. Turning toward him, she tried not to stare at the bands of muscle, the sprinkling of dark hair. Clearly, he did something other than gamble and drink the days away.

"If you must know," he said, "I was shot at. One of the pitfalls of chasing a married lady."

Oh, but he was wicked. "You are fortunate the husband was such a poor shot." She wet the washcloth with the rosewater and dabbed at the wound. The blood was congealing now, oozing slowly from the gash.

"I only wish I'd run faster," he replied. "Ouch!"

Patience glanced up with her sweetest smile. "Forgive me. It will be tender for some time. Unlike your feelings for the lady, I suspect." She busied herself opening the jar and dipping up a fingerful of the ointment.

He flinched back. "You're certain it's safe?"

Patience raised her brow. "I'm hardly going to poison you, Sir Harold."

"Why not? Gussie tries on a regular basis."

"And why would your own aunt want to poison a gentleman of your standing?"

That grin popped into view, bringing out the dimple again. "As you can see, she has countless reasons. Very well, do your worst. I'll endeavor to bear it like a man."

Patience bit back a response but spread the ointment over the wound. "And when I'm finished, you must retire to another room."

He inspected her handiwork, then refolded the cravat to tie it over the wound. "But you've made me so comfortable here."

Patience handed him his shirt. "I've done all I can. If you refuse to leave, I'll simply have to ask your aunt for other accommodations. Even if Miss Thorn, Miss Villers, and her brother are in residence, there must be somewhere I can sleep undisturbed."

In the act of pulling on the shirt, he stiffened. "You can't ask Gussie. Not in front of the Villers."

Why did he look even paler than a moment ago? Well, she was about to make it worse yet again. He could not rise in the morning innocent to his aunt's machinations.

"I must," Patience told him. She drew herself up. "And you may as well know all. Your aunt asked me to pose as your betrothed. If you don't leave this room immediately, you may have no other choice than to follow through and marry me."

Harry shook his head. He was a bit weak from lack of blood, but he could not have heard her correctly. "Gussie asked you to pose as my bride-to-be?"

"Yes." Color was climbing in her cheeks, so she must know how that sounded. "She explained that Miss Villers is determined to marry you, so she felt announcing a betrothal might cause the young lady to lose interest."

It might at that. It might also allow him another way to hide his activities with Undene and the French. If he went missing for a time, his supposed beloved could make his excuses, especially since she was in Gussie's pay. His aunt ever had his best interests at heart, even if she sometimes had odd notions of how to show it. Still, a false engagement?

"We'll sort this out in the morning," he promised, shrugging into his coat and trying not to wince. "I'll go to Gussie's chambers and wait for her. I assume she's entertaining the Villers."

She nodded. "And Miss Thorn, who accompanied me here. I retired early so I wouldn't have to think of answers to their questions."

Rising, Harry frowned at her. "Questions? What sort of questions?"

She was turning pink again, the exact shade of the tulips his aunt had planted at the back of the garden. "About our engagement—how we met, when we plan to wed."

And she did not like having to lie to them. Trust Gussie to pick a woman of integrity for her assistant. Yet if she was so intent on truth, why agree to the ruse?

His arm was starting to throb again, despite her excellent nursing. He needed somewhere to hole up. He moved toward the door but couldn't help glancing back at her. "Thank you, Patience."

She put her hands on her hips, pressing the flannel closer to her figure. He forced his gaze to her face, which had a decidedly determined cast. "I see no need for you to use my first name, sir."

She was right. He'd indulged himself. Yet, after her help in such an intimate setting, it seemed impolite to call her

Ramsey as if she was no different than any other member of the staff.

"We must be on a first-name basis with the engagement," he pointed out. "But have no fear. I'm leaving."

He cracked open the door, made sure no servants were about, then slipped down the corridor to Gussie's rooms. As he started to open Gussie's door, he glanced back to find Patience watching him. He winked at her. She snapped the door shut.

Interesting female. He could hardly wait to ask Gussie about her.

Unfortunately, he had to wait another hour before he heard his aunt approaching. Gussie was always moving and generally talking, as if the sound of her voice fueled her steps or vice versa. He pressed himself against the wall as she opened the door, heard her bid someone goodnight. As she shut the door, her gaze hit him, and her eyes brightened.

Harry put a finger to his lips and jerked his head toward the dressing room door, where, any moment, her maid Emma would appear. Gussie nodded and hurried in that direction.

"Go to bed, Emma," she called through the dressing room door. "I'll see to myself tonight."

Emma was obviously so used to her mistress' singularities that she did not argue.

"You'll pay for that," Harry predicted as Gussied hurried back to his side. "Don't ask me to help you out of your corset."

"I'll just cut the string," Gussie said. "It's worked before. Oh, Harry!" She threw her arms around him, and despite his best efforts, he grunted at the pain.

She drew back, eyes wide. "What happened?"

"I wasn't the only one meeting the boat," he explained, motioning her to the two wingback chairs that faced the hearth. How many times had they sat here, sharing hopes, failures, dreams of something better? He didn't remember his mother, refused to remember his father, but Gussie had been everything any boy could have wanted—half playmate, half provider, and all supporter.

"Revenue agents?" she asked as she took her accustomed spot.

"I don't think so," Harry said, taking the other chair. "I didn't hear anyone claim to be under the King's authority. I'm just glad the night was dark, and their aim was poor." He turned to show her his torn and bloody sleeve.

"Oh, Harry!" She popped to her feet. "We must send for the physician at once."

He held up his hand. "Peace. I don't want the episode publicized. My informant in France has gone missing, and I'm not entirely sure of the bullet's intended target."

Gussie shivered. "I'm sorry to hear about Miss de Maupassant. But you must have treatment." She perked up. "I have it! My newest preparation…"

"Will stay safely in your laboratory until we are certain it works," Harry informed her. "And I already had treatment of a sort. From the woman who is to be my bride."

He thought she might look guilty at the reminder, but she merely offered him a delighted grin. "Oh, good. You met Patience. Isn't she a treasure?"

"Unusually levelheaded, given the circumstances," he agreed. "Where did you find her, and what possessed you to ask her to pose as my bride-to-be?"

Gussie gripped the arms of the chair. "I was looking for an assistant in my work, and she had all the right skills. It wasn't until I learned that Lydia Villers and her odious brother had invited themselves for Easter that I conceived of you and Patience being engaged." She edged forward on the chair, firelight bronzing her high cheekbones. "It truly is the perfect solution, Harry. Patience can work with me as I had intended, but her presence will frighten off other young ladies like Miss Villers and leave you free to pursue more important matters."

Her thoughts matched his own, but, as usual, she had failed to consider the consequences. "And when, after some months pass, we never wed, what of Miss Ramsey's reputation? Having been introduced as my bride-to-be, what else is she to do?"

"Move to Bath," Gussie answered readily. "We have friends there. Surely, we can convince one of them to take her in, establish her in the town."

Harry frowned. "Has she no income of her own?"

"Not at all. I take it she was an orphan who found a place with the Carroltons, where she served as the countess' companion for several years."

Small wonder she wasn't easily upset. Lady Carrolton's incessant illnesses and nagging needs were legendary.

"Then how is she to support herself in Bath?" he asked.

Gussie fidgeted. "Perhaps we could offer her a fee."

Now his head was starting to throb with his arm. "You would bribe a put-upon orphan to pretend a false engagement, bartering her only possession, her reputation?"

Gussie refused to meet his gaze. "That sounds unkind and manipulative. I know how you feel about reputations, Harry, but we have a greater need at the moment."

Harry leaned back. "Not that I can see. I wonder that Miss Ramsey agreed."

"It required some persuasion," Gussie admitted. "But when Miss Thorn took my side, Miss Ramsey gave quarter."

Patience had mentioned the name as well. "Miss Thorn. Another charity case?"

Gussie finally looked up, smile once more in place. "No, indeed. She has a Fortune." She giggled, and he wasn't sure why the fact that Miss Thorn was an heiress amused her so. "Besides, I knew her mother—delightful woman. Miss Thorn apparently doesn't remember me, but I certainly remember her. She now runs an employment agency. She found Patience for me. I invited her to stay for Easter."

He must be wearier than he'd thought, for he could not follow his aunt's logic. An heiress who ran an employment agency, making herself at home at the manor? That made as little sense as Gussie's mad idea to have Miss Ramsey pose as his bride.

"We'll straighten this out in the morning," Harry said. "I understand my things were moved. Where?"

She made a face. "Sorry. We're all full at the moment. It had to be the master suite."

The master suite. His father's rooms. Something inside him recoiled. By the look on Gussie's face, she commiserated.

"It's all right," he said, rising. "At the rate I'm fading, I won't even notice whose bed I'm in." At least, he hoped so, for if he spent too long thinking about his father, he would be in no mood to make a decision regarding Patience Ramsey and their so-called engagement.

CHAPTER THREE

"I just think it's wonderful that Harry is betrothed," Miss Villers gushed as she and Meredith Thorn headed for their bedchambers, having left Gussie at her door. "Miss Ramsey seems like such a dear. How are you related again?"

Meredith managed a smile, arms secure around Fortune. Miss Villers had been trying to learn more about Patience since the moment Gussie had announced the betrothal. Instead of decamping as Gussie had hoped, the brother and sister had merely declared they must stay a while longer to help celebrate. By the hints she had been dropping all evening, Gussie was still trying to convince them to leave in the next day or so.

"Miss Ramsey is my client," Meredith replied, stroking Fortune's fur with one finger. "I own the Fortune Employment Agency."

She waited for the younger lady to protest, at least draw herself up in disdain. Patience had agreed to further the ruse Gussie had started, but Meredith saw no need to hide her own status. Many in the aristocracy and gentry would have found it appalling a woman in trade would be allowed to mix with them as an equal.

But Miss Villers was more focused on Fortune, gaze soft and wistful. "How commendable that you named the endeavor after your cat." Her voice turned into a coo. "Sweet kitty, pretty kitty."

The sugary comments, also of a repetition Meredith found tiring, had not endeared the girl to Fortune. Her cat turned her face away now, tail twitching.

Her own face falling, Miss Villers stopped by the paneled door to her room. "Have I offended her?"

About to pass for her own room, Meredith hesitated. She generally relied on Fortune's opinion of people's character to guide her. Meredith's opinion had certainly proved faulty over the years, particularly with those who should have loved and protected her. Look at what had happened with Julian Mayes, the man she had been set to marry. He'd abandoned her when she'd needed him most. Just the thought of how he'd try to insinuate himself back into her life recently sent a shudder through her. She'd made it her goal to ensure any gentlewoman fallen on hard times had greater opportunity.

She had attempted to introduce Fortune to both Miss Villers and her brother at various points that evening, but Fortune had been strangely reticent to make their acquaintance. It wasn't the unusual surroundings; Fortune traveled everywhere with her and never evinced the least concern. She had begun to think the feline's behavior indicative of the Villers themselves. She had not been impressed with Miss Villers' brother Beauford, a dark-haired fellow with a perpetual curl to his lip and too many platitudes on his tongue. And she hadn't much liked the way he'd excused himself early, as if the company of three woman and a cat could never be sufficiently entertaining.

Now she glanced down into Fortune's copper-colored eyes. "What do you think? Are you willing to befriend Miss Villers?"

Miss Villers pasted on a bright smile and leaned forward. The very fact that she did not question Meredith's conversation with the cat boded well for the young lady's character, but then again, perhaps the young lady was the sort to speak to inanimate objects like dolls as well.

Fortune swiveled in Meredith's arms to regard Miss Villers. The cat's little ears moved forward, back, as if she was listening for the young lady's thoughts. The blonde drew in a breath, hope vibrating through her very being.

Fortune arched her neck, giving Miss Villers access to her pearly throat.

The young lady reached out and touched the fur. "I am honored. I promise to be the very best friend you could want, Fortune."

Excessive even in this, it seemed. Meredith could only be glad the young lady wasn't one of those who thought a cat required rigorous rubbing instead of a gentle touch.

"I expect you and your brother will be leaving shortly," Meredith said, watching Fortune turn her head from side to side to allow Miss Villers to stroke behind her ears as well. "But you are welcome to pet her again before you go."

Miss Villers glanced up, eyes wide. "Oh, Beau says we aren't leaving until after Easter. But thank you." She pulled back and wiggled her fingers at the cat. "Good night, dear Fortune." Still beaming, she slipped into her room.

Meredith frowned as the door closed. If Miss Villers was only here to ensnare Sir Harold, why insist on staying when she thought him engaged? Or had she and her brother another reason for visiting the manor?

It was some time before Patience fell asleep that night. She'd made sure Sir Harold had found his way down the corridor to Gussie's rooms, then closed the door. As she'd started back for the bed, her bare feet had stepped in a damp patch on the deep carpet. For a moment, she'd recoiled, thinking it blood. But how could there be blood by the door when she'd bandaged him by the fire? Peering closer at the carpet, she could trace the dark spots back to the window. Had he tracked in water?

How? It hadn't rained today, and the dew wouldn't rise until morning. Had his escape from the jealous husband taken him through a stream?

Just the idea of his midnight antics made her shoulders bunch. Her father had been a faithful man, loving her mother until the day they'd both died, lying beside each other on their bed. But not all words of love were true. She knew from experience that some men were very good at saying one thing and doing another.

She crawled into the great bed and lay staring at the pleated satin that made up the inside of the canopy. She hadn't thought of Robert in years. They'd grown up together, children of neighboring families. She'd been certain he was meant to be her husband. Her parents and his had encouraged the match. He'd told her often enough he longed to call her his. But he'd gone off to war and come home with a Spanish bride whose dark eyes only looked at Patience with pity. Better than what she saw in Robert's eyes—regrets that he'd ever spoken so lovingly to her.

She sighed as she rolled over on the soft pillow. She had more than enough reasons for melancholy and as many reasons for contentment. Yes, she was alone, yet Gussie had made her feel welcomed. Mr. Cuddlestone had inspected the room and insisted that everything be to her liking. Emma, the lady's maid who had helped her undress tonight, had unpacked the rest of her trunk with loving care. She suspected their support stemmed largely from the story Gussie had concocted. They wanted to embrace the woman who was marrying the master. How would they feel when Sir Harold revealed the truth tomorrow?

She wiggled deeper under the covers, feeling as if the fine linens weighed her down. She had no reason to feel so guilty. She hadn't meant any harm. Sir Harold was supposed to be away. Miss Villers and her brother were apparently scheming opportunists, though Lydia had been nothing but happy for her. Gussie and Miss Thorn had encouraged Patience to go along with the ruse. Surely, they had her best interests at heart. And the matter had been so important to Gussie. Patience had always believed in supporting her employer's goals, even at the expense of her own at times.

She must have fallen asleep, for she woke to the sound of movement. She sat up, reaching for the shawl. "So sorry, your ladyship. Do you need the eye drops or the vinaigrette?"

In the act of taking out Patience's corset from the dresser drawer, the diminutive, dark-haired maid blinked. "Miss Ramsey?"

Patience's face heated. She was no longer sleeping in the dressing room next to Lady Carrolton's bedchamber. She was a lady of the manor, Sir Harold Orwell's betrothed.

At least for a few more moments.

"Good morning, Emma," she said, sliding off the big bed onto the soft carpet.

"What would you have to wear today, miss?" Emma asked politely, laying the corset on the bed and heading for the wardrobe.

"The grey poplin with the diamond pattern along the hem," Patience advised. Might as well look her best for whatever would happen this morning. She might have to tender her resignation. Surely Miss Thorn would help her find another position. She could only hope Miss Villers and her brother did not move in exalted circles, for their testimony of her perfidy could prevent her from landing with another aristocratic family.

"It's very nice to have a young lady to do for," Emma chatted as she helped Patience dress. "Miss Villers is very sweet, of course, but she's not part of the family."

Neither was Patience, nor would she ever be. "Have you worked at the manor long?" she asked, hoping to nudge the subject away from her.

Emma was happy to answer. "My mother was Miss Gussie's nursemaid and became her lady's maid. I took her place when her hands started to shake. Miss Gussie didn't care, mind you, but Mum did. Would you like me to do your hair?"

Patience had managed her own hair since she was a girl. But Emma looked so eager, Patience didn't have the heart to say no. Or perhaps she was merely delaying the moment she had to face Sir Harold and the others again.

"Yes, thank you," she said, seating herself on the bed.

"It's good you're to marry the master," Emma continued, deft strokes making Patience relax a little. "Such a sweet boy he was. Used to bring us wildflowers from the marshes for the kitchen table. And fish! Oh, but he was a wonder at catching the things. Why, some days, he'd bring back enough for the whole house. He can't do that now, of course, not with…" She stepped back, face florid. "There now, I shouldn't be talking so, but it's that nice to have a lady who listens. You look marvelous. I best check on Miss Villers. She tends to lay abed until the morning's half past." She bobbed a curtsey and hurried out.

So, even little Emma knew of Sir Harold's nighttime activities. Patience wasn't sure why that made her sad. It wasn't as if she'd met the little boy who'd thought enough of his staff to bring them flowers and fish. Perhaps it was the way Emma felt comfortable confiding in her. At the Carrolton household, she'd been considered above the other servants and considerably below the family. Any talk in the servants' hall had quickly ceased the moment they caught sight of her approaching.

The same manservant who had met them the day before led her to the dining room, where the others had assembled for breakfast. Mr. Cuddlestone smiled at her as she entered. She hated to think of that smile being replaced with dismay. She made herself look at the walls instead. Very likely they were terracotta colored, but it was hard to tell because every inch of space was filled with massive paintings.

The first Orwell to rise to the title had apparently liked to see himself, for she recognized his handsome features in at least three of the paintings, on horseback, sword raised; hunting with a pack of hounds; and standing at the helm of a sailing ship. Other paintings might depict places he had visited—the countryside of Spain, the pyramids of Egypt, and the shore of some exotic island. The long table, which could easily seat twenty in the elaborately scrolled, high-backed chairs, seemed almost small beside all that grandeur.

Sir Harold was seated at the head, dressed today in a bottle green coat and green-and-gold striped waistcoat. By the way he held his cup, his arm was giving him no trouble. Gussie, on his right, wore a handsome blue gown that fastened under her bosom with a gold clasp. Miss Thorn beside her looked her usual polished self in lavender stripes. Fortune, who was exploring the carpet as if determined to find something of interest, sported a matching purple bow on her collar. Miss Villers was in white again, all frills and furbelows. The saturnine fellow beside her with the long nose and thin lips must be her brother. Odd that they looked so little alike.

Patience forced a smile. "Good morning."

Everyone looked up, but Sir Harold rose and came down the table toward her. Perhaps he'd already exposed her. Very likely he'd tell her the coach was waiting to return her to London. Surely, they'd allow her that dignity.

He smiled as he took her hand, blue eyes twinkling. "Good morning, Patience, darling. Come join us for breakfast. Nothing but the best for my bride."

The lovely Miss Ramsey stared at him, and Harry could only hope she was quick enough to realize he wanted her to continue the role she'd agreed with his aunt. It had taken no more than awakening in his father's room to make him realize the necessity of the deception. Though Sally the housemaid still dusted, the space was largely the same as when his father had been alive, down to the pack of playing cards sitting on the dressing table. Marked. Harry had looked at them once to confirm it. His father had been a fraud, a trickster, a man with no honor. How ironic that the only way to convince Society of Harry's honor was to play the rogue.

"Shouldn't be too hard for you, my boy," Lord Hastings had told him when he'd approached Harry with the possibility of being an intermediary between British supporters in France and the War Office. "Your family has had dealings with the French in the past. The smugglers should be glad to have use of your cove without fearing interference from you."

Harry had pushed deeper into the armchair at White's, the exclusive gentleman's club in London. His father had been banned from the premises. It had taken thirty years of right living and no less than eight gentlemen willing to stand as references to allow Harry entrance. Now this dapper gentleman, rumored to be the head of an elite force of aristocratic intelligence agents, wanted Harry to throw all that away by pretending to be no better than his forefathers?

"Yet you ask me to lie, to risk my family name," Harry had pointed out. "To what purpose?"

"The safety of every man, woman, and child in England," Hastings had said solemnly, brown walrus mustache quivering. "We cannot lose this war. We cannot allow Napoleon to prevail." He'd laid a hand on Harry's arm. "I know you want to regain your family reputation, lad, but a true gentleman does what must be done, regardless of the cost to him."

And there lay the rub. To be the man he dreamed of being, he had to pretend to be less for a time. Which meant, unfortunately, that Miss Ramsey would also have to pretend.

But once again her soft features hardened with obvious determination. "I am not—" she started.

"Hungry," Harry finished. "Understandable given all the excitement. Perhaps a stroll. I'm sure the others will excuse us."

Her lips tightened, as if she fought harsh words.

"I cannot excuse you, Harry, old boy," another male voice cut in, low and drawling. "First you tarry in London instead of entertaining us at your own house party, then you go and get yourself engaged. The least you could do is make me known to your charming bride."

Harry gritted his teeth. Now, there was a man who thought only of himself. Dark-haired and sloe-eyed, Beau Villers had spent a lifetime cozying up to any fortune or title that would have him. Now he positively oozed charm as he came up to Patience.

Harry pasted on a smile, turning even as he slipped an arm around Patience's waist and fit her against his side. "Forgive me, Villers. I understood you met last night."

"Beau was out for a stroll when Miss Ramsey arrived," Lydia put in helpfully. "She didn't feel well and retired before he returned." She smiled prettily at Patience. "I do hope you're feeling better this morning."

The lady in question eyed Harry. "That remains to be seen."

"In any regard," Harry said breezily, "Miss Patience Ramsey, may I present Beauford Villers."

"Delighted," Villers said, smile as shiny as the silver buttons on his paisley waistcoat. "But now that I see your lovely face, I'm certain we've met before. Were you at Lady Baminger's musicale last week?"

"Alas, I hadn't the pleasure," she said with a smile that wasn't nearly as bright. "Though I understand Genevieve Munroe acquitted herself well."

"If you enjoy that sort of thing," he acknowledged. His dark gaze roamed over her figure, today more evident even in the plain grey gown. If Harry had been engaged to the lady, he would have been highly tempted to plant Villers a facer.

"But you, Miss Ramsey," the fellow all but purred, "you must have exceptional talents to convince Harry to give up his bachelor state."

He had made it sound as if Miss Ramsey was some sort of seductress. Did the miscreant truly think Harry would allow such a slur?

"I like to think any gentleman might welcome marriage to the right lady," she said. Then she turned to Harry. "Didn't you mention a stroll, Sir Harold?"

"Indeed. One should never keep a lady waiting. Excuse us." He hustled her from the room.

"You can release me," she said as they reached the entry hall. "There's no one about."

Indeed, there wasn't. Wilkins their manservant was likely helping in the kitchen, while Cuddlestone did duty in the dining room. Sally was no doubt scrambling to clean six bedchambers instead of the usual two. Still, the nice thing about the manor was its compact arrangement. One never needed to walk more than a few steps before returning to the entry hall.

Yet even though none of his guests or staff was here to see his so-called devotion, letting go of Patience Ramsey proved surprisingly difficult. Harry settled on holding her hand. "Will you be warm enough if we go to the garden? We're less likely to be interrupted there."

"I can manage for a time," she said, and he led her out the back of the house.

His great-grandfather had insisted on planting a formal garden behind the house, shrubs hacked into unnatural symmetrical shapes, flowers regimented into precise lines in separate boxes. His grandfather and father had left things to run naturally, mostly because not having to pay a gardening staff meant more money for things they found more interesting than a garden. Now tulips had invaded the daffodil beds, bright reds vying with yellow for supremacy, and Gussie's pink tulips huddled together for safety against the encroaching grass. The once cone-shaped shrubs resembled fattened sheep grazing among the color.

"You promised to settle matters this morning," she reminded him as they moved along the narrowing paths. "Yet we appear to remain betrothed."

Harry bent and plucked a weed from the gravel. "Gussie explained her reasons, and I concurred with them."

She stopped, and he pulled up short beside her.

"Are you certain?" she asked. "I will admit to having second thoughts that I agreed to this. I was easily swayed by her enthusiasm."

He chuckled, enjoying the sunlight on his face, the dew anointing flower and field. "Most people are. Gussie is a power unto herself. But her points were well taken. Miss Villers and her brother have been particularly attentive to me, with clear expectations of an offer that I have no interest in making. And being devoted to you should allow me to avoid other social obligations that have proven difficult."

"Too many husbands in attendance?" she asked.

Before he could respond, she covered her mouth with her hand and stared at him over it as if shocked by her own boldness. "Forgive me. It is none of my concern how you spend your time, Sir Harold."

"True," he allowed, kicking a rock back into place. "But you have every right to question your role in all this. Know that I will not abuse my so-called relationship with you, Patience. We are engaged in name only."

She lowered her hand. "Yet we will have to continue lying. It was one thing when we were protecting you from a cunning seductress, but I cannot see Miss Villers in such a role. And what of your loyal staff, your neighbors? People will think badly of you when you jilt me."

Harry clutched his chest. "Jilt you? Madam, how could I?"

She shook her head. "Then you expect me to play the jilt. I must consider my reputation."

Harry barked a laugh. "Too late. You were doomed the moment you linked your name with Orwell, a family considered black for three generations. My piddley indiscretions won't even tip the scale."

She frowned at him. "Do you really think so little of your family?"

"My father and his father? Certainly. They lived with no thought to anyone but themselves. Gussie would have been penniless if they both hadn't died mercifully young."

"And yet you seem determined to follow in their footsteps," she protested.

"Never," Harry spat. He realized his mistake even before her eyes widened. He made himself wink at her. "I gamble at love, not at cards."

"I fail to see the difference to your reputation," she said, raising her chin. "You are still living to please yourself."

"As to that, you will have to ask the ladies. I have never had any complaints."

She took a step back. "You have one now. Forgive me, Sir Harold, but I cannot continue with this lie."

Harry sighed. "Very well. I see only one way out of this." He went down on one knee and gazed up at her. "Patience Ramsey, will you do me the honor of marrying me?"

CHAPTER FOUR

Marriage? Was he mad? And Patience had thought Gussie mercurial!

"You do not mean that," she accused him.

Sir Harry climbed to his feet. "Not in the slightest. But I proposed. You can call yourself betrothed without lying."

Her mother and father had taught her to be respectful, particularly of those in a station above her own. Living with Lady Carrolton had taught her the value of obedience as well. Neither trait seemed appropriate in the face of his audacity.

"That paltry demonstration means nothing," she told him. "I have no intention of marrying you. I will not claim otherwise."

He took her hand, cradled it in both of his, and pressed it against the green and gold of his waistcoat, blue eyes tilted up beseechingly. "Please, Miss Ramsey. I need your help. Think of what would happen to poor Lydia, married to such a rogue."

Miss Villers seemed as vivacious as a puppy and as harmless. Patience could not see her in a happy marriage with Sir Harry.

He must have thought she was weakening, for he squeezed her hand. "Think of dear Gussie as well. She'll be mortified to be caught in her harmless charade."

Patience bit her lip. She had only known Gussie a short

time, but already she was eager to prolong the acquaintance. Gussie had only been trying to help her disreputable nephew.

"I know you must find my deeds unpalatable," he persisted as if he'd read her thoughts. "But I assure you I am trying to reform, for Gussie's sake as well as to repair my family name. Think how your good example could further that end."

She certainly believed in being a good example, living her principles. Could something good come from this pretense?

"I already promised to be the perfect gentleman," he murmured, pressing her hands against his firm chest, fingers massaging her own. "All you need do is smile and accept the congratulations or commiserations offered you."

His touch was hypnotic. She could not seem to think.

Patience pulled out of his grip. "It will not be so simple, sir. If you want to make people believe we are betrothed, you will have to play the part as well. Can you pretend yourself besotted?"

That grin, so engaging, so charming, emerged like the sun from the clouds. "Oh, my dear Patience, I assure you I can."

When he gazed at her that way, even *she* began to believe he had feelings for her. But that was silly! Everything he'd done so far indicated he had inherited every inch of his forefathers' self-centeredness. If Sir Harold Orwell loved anyone, it was himself.

"Well, I'm not certain I can look so delightfully in love," she said. "Every discussion, every question, will lead to more lies, and we will be too easily caught in them. Where did we meet? How did we court? When did you propose?"

He stuck out his lower lip as if impressed she'd thought things through. "I believe Gussie said you were companion to Lady Carrolton. We met on your day off."

"I never had a day off," she informed him. "I had a half

hour off every other week."

He frowned. "Truly?"

"Truly. Lady Carrolton considered me indispensable."

"She considered you a slave," he said with a shake of his head. "But I begin to see the problem. Very well. Try this for a story. I saw you when you attended Lady Carrolton at the opera in London and made it a point to learn everything about you. We engineered stolen moments in secret, becoming ever more attached. I encouraged Gussie to invite you to the estate, where I proposed in the garden on bended knee."

"Plausible," Patience said, trying not to sound complimentary of his ingenuity. Surely it was wrong to admire someone's ability to lie. "But you will have to find a reason why you would settle for a penniless nobody."

"Anyone with eyes could see the reason," he said, and heat rushed to her cheeks.

"Regardless, there are other women with more money and better connections," she insisted. "What of Lydia Villers?"

He shrugged. "Little money and questionable connections. Her brother is hunting a title. Because of my family history, he assumes mine must be for sale cheap."

She felt for Miss Villers, and, oddly, for Sir Harry. How frustrating it must be for everyone to always think the worst of you. "Still, she is lovely."

"Not nearly as lovely as you."

Once again, the warmth in his voice made her pause. The blue of his eyes seemed to deepen, drawing her closer. If she tipped up her chin, their lips might meet.

As if he knew it as well, he released her and stepped back. "And that is what I will tell anyone who asks. So, what will it be, Patience? Will you pretend to be engaged to me for a time, after which I will show you my undying gratitude?"

Patience narrowed her eyes. "Undying gratitude? What do you mean by that?"

"Gussie and I discussed it. When the time comes for us to end our association, we will send you to friends in Bath, where you can start a new life with a small income of your own."

Yearning pressed against her chest, until she thought her heart would stop. An income of her own? No one to tell her when to rise, what to do, where to go? For the first time in her life, she could be her own person, make her own decisions. The enormity of it nearly knocked her off her feet.

She must have swayed, for he put a hand to her arm. "Patience? Miss Ramsey? Are you all right?"

No, she was surely mad to consider such a thing. Yet would it be so wrong? Was there truly anyone harmed? She might help Gussie and Sir Harry too. And when it was all over, she would finally be beholden to no one.

"Very well," she said. "I'll pretend to be engaged to you."

His look eased into a smile. And she was glad he did not question her sudden capitulation, for she could not fully account for it, even to herself.

Gussie, Miss Villers, and her brother had left the dining room when Patience and Sir Harry reentered, and Mr. Cuddlestone was not in evidence, so at least no one had no opportunity to comment on her cheeks, which felt suspiciously warm. The food had been cleared away, the table tidied of all save a rose-patterned tea service and matching cups.

As if she had been waiting for them, Miss Thorn sat sipping tea, one hand stroking Fortune in her lap.

"A pity you returned sooner than expected, Sir Harry," she remarked. "Most inconvenient."

Sir Harry raised his brows, even as Patience bit back a smile.

"I believe you two met this morning before I came

down to breakfast," Patience said, going to sit beside her benefactress and still feeling a little wobbly after her conversation with Sir Harry. "Miss Thorn introduced me to your aunt."

"Then I must be forever in her debt," Sir Harry said, moving to return to his seat at the head of the table and pour himself a fresh cup of tea.

"My aunt mentioned you operate an employment agency," he said to Miss Thorn as he dropped three lumps of sugar into the brew. "What made you think of my dear Patience for Foulness Manor?"

Foulness Manor? Up until now, she hadn't thought to ask the name of the place, assuming the manor Gussie and Miss Thorn kept mentioning was called after the Orwell family. Now she fought not to wrinkle her nose at the unkind appellation. Why hadn't Sir Harry changed it? Or did he take pride in the fact that even his home heralded his family's disgrace?

Miss Thorn smiled fondly at Patience. "I chose her because she is perfectly suited to assist your aunt in her studies, having learned stillroom craft from her mother. She developed a number of her own treatments for her previous employer, Lady Carrolton. But as her devoted groom-to-be, I'm sure you were aware of that."

He couldn't have been, but Sir Harry merely smiled. "I am constantly amazed by what I learn of her."

Very likely.

Miss Thorn set down her cup. "And I am never amazed by the stories I hear of you, Sir Harry."

His smile slipped just the slightest. "Then I must redouble my efforts to earn your good opinion, madam."

"My good opinion is immaterial." Miss Thorn nodded to Fortune, who climbed from her lap to balance on the white damask. A cat on the table? No, no. Patience reached for her, but Miss Thorn raised a hand to stop her from taking Fortune down.

Fortune stood a moment, licking the fur on her shoulder as if she had nothing whatsoever to concern her. Glancing up, she seemed to notice Sir Harry for the first time. She aimed her great copper eyes at him.

Sir Harry stared back.

Fortune strolled down the table, turned in front of him, eyed him from the right, then turned again to walk past and eye him on the left. Then she returned to her owner.

"Inconclusive?" Miss Thorn asked.

Patience frowned. Was this a test of some sort? Fortune had risen to greet her when she'd first met Miss Thorn, in a coffee shop no less, but she had reached out to offer the cat her hand to sniff. Sir Harry had made no such overture.

As if in response to her mistress' question, Fortune looked over her shoulder to regard him again. This time when she walked toward him and reached his side, she bent her head and rubbed it against his hand on the table. Sir Harry raised his other hand and stroked the fur.

Even as Patience let out a breath she hadn't known she was holding, Miss Thorn sat back.

"Well." She smiled at Patience. "It seems the situation is nicely suited to you, just as I'd hoped. Perhaps I'll continue on my way."

She was going? Though Patience had only known Miss Thorn and Fortune a short time, the thought of them leaving her behind made her breath catch anew.

She seized the lady's hand. "So soon? I was sure Gussie said you would stay through Easter. Or is there someone waiting for you?"

Something flickered in those lavender-blue eyes. "No. No one I care to associate with. Very well, since you are concerned, I'll stay for a time. After all, you might need help entertaining."

As Patience released her, Harry chuckled into his tea. "That is an understatement. Gussie prefers to stay up late and wake up later, and I'd wager you'll find her in her laboratory about now and for the better part of the day."

Patience frowned. "But her guests."

"Will be left to their own devices, if I know my aunt." Harry drained the cup and rose. "I must be off. Correspondence waits for no man." With a bow to them both, he strode from the room.

"Surely he's mistaken," Patience said to Miss Thorn.

She merely smiled. "Correspondence could very likely wait. But I think you'll find he's correct about Gussie."

Quite right, Patience quickly saw as they left the dining room for the entry hall where Mr. Cuddlestone was directing a maid to her work. When they looked at him askance, the butler was happy to inform them of the disposition of the other inhabitants of Foulness Manor.

"Sir Harry has gone to his study," he reported, balding head shining as he inclined it toward the door beside the massive marble fireplace that took up much of the farthest wall in the entry hall. "The mistress is in her laboratory and expecting you shortly, Miss Ramsey. Mr. Villers expressed interest in going out for a ride. I believe he is changing into his riding clothes. And Miss Villers is enjoying a scientific treatise in the withdrawing room."

He turned to look at Miss Thorn, his head on a level with Patience's. He was, most likely, one of the shortest butlers in England.

"Might I suggest a stroll about the gardens, Miss Thorn, in this lovely sunshine?" He smiled helpfully.

Miss Thorn's gaze met Patience's frown. "Miss Villers first, I think, and then Gussie. Thank you, Cuddlestone."

"My pleasure, madam," he said with a courtly bow.

"Does she intend to ignore them into leaving?" Patience whispered as she and Miss Thorn crossed the entry hall for the withdrawing room, their heels clicking against the hard wood floor.

"Rude behavior has been known to have that effect," Miss Thorn said, hand on the door latch. "But not, I think, with the Villers."

She opened the door, and they peered inside.

"Oh, there you are," Miss Villers proclaimed. She abandoned the book she had been reading before Patience could confirm whether it was a scientific treatise or the latest gothic novel and hurried toward them. "Is Harry with you?"

Her big eyes, a misty green, gazed at them so trustingly. If she hadn't asked about Harry, Patience could easily have believed her the innocent she seemed to be.

"He is detained on estate business," Patience told her as they entered the room. At least, she hoped it was on estate business. She didn't like the idea of him sitting in his study writing love letters to some lady.

He'd said he was reforming. She should believe him until he proved otherwise.

Miss Villers blew out a breath. "Oh. Well. I suppose we might find something useful to do."

"Gussie has no plans for the day?" Miss Thorn asked, wandering toward the sofa. As Patience shut the door, Miss Thorn released Fortune to allow the cat to scamper about the room.

Miss Villers shook her head. "Gussie never has plans. Beau and I generally have to suggest possibilities every time we visit."

Which sounded quite frequent. "The manor must be a challenge to you," Patience said, moving toward the window, where Fortune had jumped up onto the sill to peer out. "The countryside can be very quiet."

The view confirmed it. Greening fields swept away on every side, dotted with copses of trees. Birds darted about the branches, keeping Fortune's attention. Through the thickening leaves, Patience spotted the dark grey waters of the Channel.

And someone moving among the shadows. It seemed that bottle green coat had had a purpose this morning, for it made Sir Harry almost invisible as he hurried away. Where was he going? Why did her chest hurt to think of it?

"Very quiet," Miss Villers said, joining her.

Patience purposely put her back to the window, blocking the view. "You are lately come from London, I understand. You must miss the excitement."

"A bit," she admitted. "But Beau says it's important to spend sacred holidays with friends and family."

She could like him for that. "I quite agree. My mother loved preparing for Easter. She'd clean the house from top to bottom, decorate with flowers, boil and dye eggs, and bake all kinds of treats."

Miss Villers clapped her hands, pretty mouth turning up once more, even as Fortune started. "Just the thing! You must ask Harry to do that here. Not the cleaning, of course. But searching for flowers and coloring eggs might be entertaining, and you could suggest menus to the cook."

Patience dropped her gaze to the blue and white pattern of the carpet. "Oh, I couldn't presume."

Miss Villers dipped her chin to see up under Patience's gaze. "Why not? You're engaged to be married. Surely he would expect you to have some say in family festivities."

Miss Thorn joined them. "I believe Miss Villers is correct. And I'm sure Gussie would be glad for the support."

Oh, right. Helping Gussie was Patience's job, not following Sir Harry with her eyes like a love-struck schoolgirl. "Then perhaps we should discuss the matter with her."

Miss Villers was no longer attending, gaze latching onto Fortune, who had peered around Patience's waist at her mistress's arrival.

"And how is my precious girl?" Miss Villers said in a sing-song voice. She rubbed Fortune's head.

The cat's ears flattened, and she ducked away.

As Miss Villers made cooing noises no doubt intended

to put Fortune in a more receptive mood, Patience leaned closer to Miss Thorn. "Inconclusive?" she murmured.

The lady's mouth quirked. "Oddly enough, Fortune is quite fond of Miss Villers." She raised her voice. "Perhaps a subtler touch, my dear. Enthusiasm can only carry one so far."

Correspondence, Harry had claimed, as if anything ever arrived at the manor besides bills and instructions from Lord Hastings. As it was, Harry had no idea what to say to his superior. *I lost your best informant* hardly seemed the report his lordship expected. And it certainly did nothing to aid the war effort.

So, Harry moved from tree to tree across the estate, on the lookout for trespassers. The landing cove Undene and his men used was on the edge of his property, and he'd given them leave to embark and land from it so long as they agreed to carry information, and occasionally him, along with the goods they smuggled to and from France. The fact that no revenue agent had come knocking on his door, demanding to know why he abetted criminals, confirmed his suspicions that the shot last night had not come from the Crown. Someone else had met the boat. Who? Why?

He found no indication of trespass. Daffodils raised sunny heads from the grass, making a golden carpet that would have showed any sign of disturbance. The air smelled fresh, clean, with no scent of smoke from a careless camper's fire. If only his conscience felt as clean.

I am watched more closely, Yvette had written in her last note. *It may be time for a change.*

He had thought she'd meant to disappear in France. Now he wondered whether she'd been hoping he'd bring her to England. She'd been a child at the start of the Revolution when her family had been taken from her. Since turning eighteen ten years ago, she'd risked her life to secretly work with the British, hoping to pull Napoleon from power. That she might be willing to leave those efforts behind told him how dire her straits must be.

Had someone else expected her to come with Undene last night? Had the shot been meant for her?

Or him?

He couldn't have been so careless as to reveal himself. In the area, only Undene, his men, and Gussie knew he sent and received news from France. His family reputation provided sufficient diversion that no one thought to ask what else Sir Harry might be doing at night. Yet someone knew something. He had to learn more.

He cut across the woods for the village beyond. When his great-grandfather had built the manor, he'd wanted to distance himself from his prior profession of privateer. He'd ordered a grand house that showed pride in his elevation to the title, paintings by every itinerant artist in the area to commemorate his success. He'd dug a fine cellar for his wines, and the goods that arrived in the dead of night. Harry's grandfather and father had encouraged a trade that brought them illicit luxuries few could boast.

It was, oddly enough, because of his forefathers that the villagers trusted him now. They thought he was happy to continue turning a blind eye to their trade, so long as it netted him a profit. Most had no idea that profit wasn't in wine or silk but the information that was vital to England's defense.

Now he intended to discover whether anyone else knew the identity of the shooter from last night. It was early in the day for Undene and his men to frequent the common room at the inn, but the innkeeper could answer his two most urgent questions: the safety of the smugglers and the presence of a stranger in their midst. He was relieved to hear that Undene and the crew from last night had all been seen going about their work, hale and hearty. It seemed he had been the only one shot. Curiouser and curiouser.

The innkeeper also reported that no one had seen any revenue agents in the area recently.

"And the only strangers are your friend Mr. Villers and his new manservant," the burly fellow confided, pausing as he swept the common room floor. "But then, as often as Mr. Villers visits, folks have generally become accustomed to seeing him wandering about."

Perhaps too accustomed?

Harry couldn't help wondering as he made his way back to the manor. No one in the village would have shot at the smugglers—too many depended on the income from the trade. If there were no revenue agents or other strangers about, that left only Beau Villers. Harry had originally assumed the fellow had spent the evening with Gussie and the other guests. But Lydia had mentioned he'd been out until after Patience had retired for the evening. Had he been on the grounds? At the shore? Why? And why shoot at Harry?

Or was it merely his habit to escape the company of the ladies? He had made a point of spending time with Harry on previous visits, but as he had spent much of that time praising his sister's merits, Harry had been fairly certain why Villers had singled him out for attention. Or had he another reason for visiting the manor beside trying to throw his sister at Harry's head?

He couldn't very well ask without giving away the game, but he resolved to keep a closer eye on Lydia's brother.

Now, if he could just convince himself he shouldn't keep an equally close eye on Patience Ramsey, for entirely different reasons.

CHAPTER FIVE

Gussie was more than glad to conscript Miss Thorn into Easter planning.

"I'm not terribly good at entertaining," she said, straightening from the tulips she had been beheading in the garden, where Patience and her benefactress had finally located her. "I generally put everyone in a room and hope something happens."

Patience could imagine any number of things happening among Lydia Villers, her brother, and Sir Harry, and few were good. She and Miss Thorn had barely managed to escape the withdrawing room without Miss Villers dogging their steps. In the end, she had agreed to stay and take care of Fortune, who looked only slightly mollified at being left with the young lady and a shiny blue ribbon.

"Nevertheless," Patience told Gussie now, "you hired me to assist you in your laboratory. I feel some concern in abandoning you for entertaining."

"I would far prefer you at my side," Gussie assured her, "but I know from experience that, left to their own devices, the Villers tend to get into trouble. Mr. Villers nearly lit the house on fire by adding entirely too many candles to the kissing bough at Christmas, and his sister insisted on baking implements into the Twelfth Night cake. I nearly choked on the bean."

Miss Thorn shot Patience a look.

Gussie paused to frown at the already-wilting pink flowers in her hand. "What do you think, Patience? Tulip petals to provide that silky feeling against the skin?"

She had heard of people who conflated visual or sensual properties for healing abilities. It seemed Gussie was one of them. All the more reason for Patience to be in the stillroom with her employer instead of the withdrawing room with Lydia Villers.

"I'm not sure that would be efficacious," Patience said gently. "I believe I read in my mother's stillroom notebook that the bulbs can be poisonous if ingested. Rubbing them on the skin, particularly open wounds, might prove equally harmful."

"Oh." Gussie dropped the dead flowers back into the bed and dusted off her hands. "Ah, well. It was a thought."

"And I've had another," Miss Thorn put in. "Perhaps you two could discuss activities, and I'll consult with the cook about current plans for Easter. We can reconvene shortly."

"Excellent." Gussie waved her free hand, and Miss Thorn headed for the back door of the house.

Clutching her sheers close, Gussie peered in both directions, as if expecting someone to come darting out from behind one of the prickly shrubs.

"Come with me," she murmured to Patience, grabbing her arm with one hand.

"But Easter plans," Patience protested, trying not to dig in her heels on the gravel.

"Yes, yes, we'll discuss those shortly." She towed Patience across the garden and drew up before another door at the back of the house. Releasing Patience, she threw the door open, and the combined scents that escaped nearly knocked Patience backward.

"My laboratory," Gussie said with an expressive wiggle of her brows. "Watch where you put your fingers, and don't eat or drink anything." She sailed through the door, tossing the shears onto a shelf with a clatter.

Patience followed her more slowly into the long, low room. The white plastered walls and the carved door leading back into the house gave testament that the space had served as a more formal room once. Now neat blue cabinets with high shelves and low drawers lined two walls. Books and strange substances in glass bottles crowded the shelves. Steel bowls, copper kettles, delicate spirit lamps, and more sturdy braziers littered the stained marble top of the walnut worktable in the center of the room. Herbs hung drying from the beam in the ceiling, and a mist fogged the windows overlooking the garden. All Patience could think was that, in another age, Augusta Orwell might have been branded a witch.

She was all business now, moving down the room with brisk efficiency. She stirred that pot, sprinkled powder into another.

"My goal," she announced to Patience as she peered into a marble mortar, "is to create cosmetics and healing balms for various afflictions of the skin without the aid of deleterious substances." She whirled and thrust a finger at Patience. "Did you know many face powders contain lead or arsenic?"

"No," Patience admitted. Her mother had never allowed her to use cosmetics. She'd thought it because of an old-fashioned notion as to the character of the women who employed such artifice, but perhaps her mother had known the physical dangers as well. She had been talented in the stillroom, bottling tonics for indigestion, ointments for chafed hands, and aromatic sachets for a happy spirit.

"Most of them," Gussie declared. "I contend that Nature herself has provided a better pattern in the plants around us—lavender, witch-hazel, gum Arabic."

"Roses," Patience added. "My mother was convinced they had healing properties."

"Roses." Gussie rubbed her chin, leaving a streak of green. "No, too plebian. But we will persevere. Let's get to work."

Patience glanced down at her dress, which was one of her best. Still, she could hardly protest, given that Gussie's gown was made from far finer wool and more fashionably cut. Instead, she searched around and managed to locate an apron already well speckled with Gussie's work. At least, she hoped the reddish-brown stains were plant-based.

Gussie set Patience to grinding some dried thyme into a powder in a mortar and pestle.

"Fresh would be better," Gussie fussed, peering over Patience's shoulder. "Lord Carrolton has a greenhouse, does he not? Perhaps he has thyme."

Patience twisted the pestle against the marble. "Lord Carrolton may not be willing to do us a favor, considering that I left with little notice."

Gussie waved a hard. "He's known Harry for ages. They attended school together. I'm sure he won't mind."

Perhaps not. Lord Carrolton was by far the kindest person in that household, his easy-going nature at odds both with his magnificent physique and his mother's and sister's constant complaining. He had made no effort to detain her. Had the eligible earl even noticed her departure? It was rather lowering to think that, though Lady Carrolton had called her indispensable, no one had protested her resignation. The butler had actively assisted her in leaving, as if he couldn't be rid of her fast enough. But then, it couldn't be easy serving as head of staff in that household, particularly with Lady Lilith's frequent tantrums. The earl's sister had gone through four lady's maids in the last year alone.

Knowing she'd left all that behind fueled Patience's work. She had a chance for more now, first helping Gussie, and then, wonder of wonders, leaving to start a new life. Gussie kept hopping about behind her, so Patience finally handed her the mortar and pestle and began tidying things around them instead. They had just added the powdered thyme to

Gussie's most promising formulation, when the door to the laboratory opened and Mr. Villers poked his nose in.

The guests. Easter. Oh, dear.

"Ah, there you are," he declared. He opened the door wider to admit himself and his sister. Miss Villers stared around the room, eyes even wider than usual. Apparently Gussie didn't share her laboratory with everyone.

"What are you doing?" Miss Villers asked.

Patience waited for Gussie to explain, but her new employer merely put a lid on the formulation and turned her back to it. "Nothing of any interest, I'm sure."

Miss Villers craned her neck as if to see beyond her host. "I'm quite interested. Miss Thorn came to fetch Fortune, so I am entirely at your disposal. Is it something edible, something for Easter, perhaps?"

"No," Patience hurried to assure her. "Gussie is perfecting a formulation to improve the skin."

Miss Villers brightened. "Oh, you must let me try it."

Patience eyed her creamy complexion, which hardly appeared to need improvement. But perhaps Miss Villers' perfection came from a bottle.

Her brother didn't seem to think so. "Nonsense," he said with a scowl her direction. "You have no reason to be interested in such preparations."

His sister looked at him, eyes wide. "Gussie is interested in them. Miss Ramsey is interested in them."

His scowl deepened, but he wisely decided not to comment.

"Our fascination need not be yours, Miss Villers," Patience said. "It can be tedious work, even for those who enjoy this sort of thing."

"Painstaking," Gussie added. "Exacting. I'm not sure you have the temperament, Miss Villers."

Another woman might have taken umbrage, but Miss Villers stepped forward with a flounce of her dainty white gown. "I promise you, I find this sort of thing fascinating.

Science in the service of mankind and all that. What have you tried so far?"

Her eager curiosity won over Gussie, who drew her closer and began going over all the details as to the ingredients and ways of preparing them, Miss Villers nodding encouragement.

Her brother put his hand on Patience's arm and drew her aside. "Thank you for humoring her. She bores so easily. Sometimes I run out of ways to entertain her."

Watching Miss Villers stir more of the thyme into the formulation, gaze rapt, Patience found it hard to believe her so vapid.

"Perhaps you should try a different approach," she suggested. "Instead of insisting she pursue the expected, allow her to find what interests her."

He spread his hands, smile engaging. "But Miss Ramsey, everything interests my sister. Just not for long. Not every lady has your perseverance or refinement of spirit."

She wasn't sure she had either some days, and he certainly had no basis on which to claim such, having met her only this morning. As she gazed up at him, his grip on her arm tightened. He leaned closer until she could smell the bay rum cologne he wore even over the myriad of other scents in the laboratory.

"Sir Harry is a very fortunate fellow," he murmured, dark gaze holding hers. "If you have any doubts as to his affections for you, please know you will find a ready ear in me. And, rest assured, there is at least one other gentleman who would be glad to pay you court."

Was he talking about himself? Surely no fellow with any sense could form such an attachment on so short an acquaintance. He was trying to turn her up sweet. Why?

Her gaze darted to the preparations bubbling so merrily around her. Could Mr. Villers be even more interested than his sister?

A noise made her glance toward the door to the house.

Sir Harry was standing there, eyes narrowed to slits of blue lightning. Jealous? Impossible. Had every gentleman in the area gone mad? Or was even the scent of Gussie's preparations more potent than she knew?

Harry took one look at Beau Villers standing ridiculously close to Patience, hand possessively on her arm, and something tightened inside him. He wanted only to stalk across the space, pull them apart, and tell Villers never to touch what was his again.

Jealous? Impossible! He might have convinced Patience to pretend an engagement, but he had no real claim on her affections. Until the war was over, and he reclaimed his reputation as a gentleman, he had no business thinking of marriage, with anyone.

But he could play the concerned lover.

He moved into the room, smile ready. "Have a care, Villers, or I might think you were trying to steal my beloved."

Villers immediately raised his hands and voice in protest, but color brightened Patience's cheeks, and she stepped back from him. Had the fellow truly been imposing himself on her? Harry had to put his hands behind him to keep from accosting the impudent pup.

As Villers sputtered to a stop, something else splattered and sizzled.

"Entirely too many people in my laboratory," Gussie complained. "Miss Villers and Miss Ramsey may stay. You two kindly take yourselves off."

Villers' dark brows rose.

"Actually," Harry said, linking his arm with Patience's, "I have need of my sweetheart. Wedding preparations, you know. Perhaps a game of billiards later, Villers?"

As his aunt's guest inclined his head, Patience removed the well-used apron, and Harry drew her out the door into the garden.

She pulled her arm from his as soon as the door closed behind them. "As there is no wedding requiring preparations, perhaps you could tell me why you wanted to talk with me. Or was it merely an excuse to get out of the laboratory?"

"Both," Harry assured her, striding away from the house. She fell into step beside him, grey skirts swaying. She didn't seem to realize that a green glob of Gussie's preparation had affixed itself to her cheek.

He stopped behind one of the bushy shrubs, glad for the cover from a day that was turning cloudier by the moment. "Was Beau Villers bothering you?"

She made a face, and he nearly crowed in triumph.

"A bit," she admitted. "But I wonder whether his actions stem from boredom rather than any attachment to me. Still, even boredom cannot fully account for his behavior."

Had Villers tipped his hand? Patience could not know Harry's suspicions, yet she had seen through the fellow's superficial manner.

"What's troubling you?" Harry asked.

Her gaze was on the trees edging the garden, where branches bobbed in the rising breeze. "I know Gussie hoped they would leave when they learned you were engaged, but they show no sign of decamping. In fact, Miss Villers doesn't seem the least affected by the loss. She appears genuinely happy for us. I imagine they could find a more congenial place closer to London to spend the Easter holiday. Why remain at Foulness Manor?"

Harry rubbed his chin. "You have a point." He eyed her. "Why do you think they remain?"

She glanced either way, as if making sure no one was close enough to overhear, then took a step closer, and he steeled himself to learn that Villers had mentioned something to do with the smuggling.

"Is it possible," she whispered, "that Mr. Villers and his sister are out to steal your aunt's formulation?"

Harry reared back. "What?"

She rubbed her fingers, where now he saw more of the green globs had congregated. "Oh, forgive me. I must be as mad as the others to suggest it. It's just that your aunt seemed to think Miss Villers dim, and her brother went out of his way to confirm it. Yet I have found her bright and inquisitive. And she seemed inordinately interested in the balm."

Harry shook his head. "So why not come up with her own? Why steal Gussie's?"

"Such recipes are kept within families," she told him.

He rubbed his arm. "Like the one you used on me. Your mother's recipe, you said. It worked wonders."

"And Gussie's might do more. Ladies will pay a pretty penny. Physicians as well. You said Mr. Villers and his sister had few funds. Why not find a way to augment them without marrying her off?"

She was so intent, gazing up at him, that he could almost believe Villers had nothing more serious on his mind than women's cosmetics. Harry took his thumb and wiped the green from her cheek. Her skin certainly needed no improvement, not that silk. Something in him urged him to bend closer, see if her lips were as soft.

Voices echoed across the garden, and Harry's head jerked up. What had he been thinking? He might play the rake, but he would never take advantage of a lady. Patience was his to protect, nothing more.

Her gaze darted to where Gussie, Lydia, and Villers spilled into the yard.

"I must apologize for my sister," Villers was saying to Gussie. "I told her it was none of her affair."

Lydia spread her muslin skirt, where a bright green stain spread across the white. "It's nothing, Beau. I can soak this out. I'm sorry I knocked over your pot, Gussie."

Patience sent Harry an arch look, then led him back toward the group. "Let me help, Miss Villers," she offered.

"I have some experience removing noxious stains."

Having spent three years with Lady Carrolton, Harry could imagine she did.

Lydia gave her a grateful smile, and the two headed for the house.

Villers rubbed his hands together. "What about that game of billiards, Harry, my lad?"

"Go ahead," Harry said with a nod toward the house. "I'd just like a word with my aunt."

Villers nodded and strode for the door.

Harry closed the distance between him and Gussie. "What happened?"

Gussie shook her head. "A minor mistake, a common occurrence, I assure you. Though I am sorry to have ruined Lydia's dress. She can scarce afford to replace it."

"Your concern does you credit," Harry said, "But I begin to wonder whether money doesn't play a part in these incessant visits."

Gussie sighed. "You don't have to marry her."

"I have no intention of marrying her. But there are other ways to profit from the association."

"Such as?" Gussie asked with a frown.

Harry watched the door close behind Villers. "Patience thinks they are after your balm."

Gussie's eyes widened. "Oh, the villains. I'll throw them out immediately."

Harry caught her arm as she started past. "Easy. There's another more likely reason. Villers may be here to discover what I've been up to."

That stopped her more surely than his hand. "You think he knows about your dealings with France?"

"Someone shot at me," Harry reminded her, "and he and his valet are the only strangers spotted in the area."

"All the more reason to send them packing," Gussie insisted.

"I'd rather keep Villers close," Harry said. "Watch what

he does, where he goes. I'll need a day or two before I'm ready to cross the Channel in any event."

She paled. "You intend to go over?"

"I must. Yvette de Maupassant may be in danger. She has served England too well to be discarded."

She nodded. "You care about her."

"She is a stalwart ally," Harry replied. "One I cherish. Now, if you'll excuse me, I should engage Villers in conversation."

Before he confessed that there was another lady who occupied his thoughts as much.

CHAPTER SIX

Alas, nothing Patience or the estate laundress tried removed the stain from the white muslin. Miss Villers was surprisingly good about it.

"It's all right," she told Patience as they returned from the laundry outbuilding. "I'll simply have to put another piece over the spot, perhaps dye the gown. I look good in green."

Patience could only admire her practical nature. Still, the fact that she sought to repair rather than replace the gown suggested the rumors of their financial situation were true. Were Patience's suspicions of their reason for remaining at Foulness Manor equally true?

Harry had not been convinced. She'd seen the skepticism on his face. But the more she thought about it, the more she became convinced that Beau Villers had a deeper reason for visiting Gussie than trying to further a marriage between his sister and Harry.

She mentioned the matter to Miss Thorn when they regrouped later. Harry and Mr. Villers were off in the gaming room behind the withdrawing room. Gussie had felt badly enough about Miss Villers' dress that she'd offered to take her shopping in the village. So, Patience and her benefactress found themselves alone in the withdrawing room, Fortune prowling about the room.

"I would need to consult my sources to be certain," Miss

Thorn told Patience as they sat together on the elegant sofa. "But I believe Sir Harry is correct about their constrained circumstances and Mr. Villers' avid desire to see his sister marry well. We haven't heard the last of them, I fear."

She clucked her tongue to warn Fortune away from the upholstered chair, which the cat had shown every intention of using to sharpen her claws. As if nothing were further from her mind, Fortune stalked past and leaped up into Patience's lap.

Patience stroked the soft fur. "Then our best option would be to keep them busy. So much for my afternoon off, I suppose. What did you learn from the cook?"

Miss Thorn shifted on the sofa, and Fortune perked up as if hoping they were leaving.

"Not a great deal," she confessed. "The cook has ordered a ham from the local farmer and planned a few special dishes to accompany it, but she would dearly love more inspiration."

The door opened just then, and Patience clung to Fortune to prevent her from dashing out. Mr. Cuddlestone came through with the tea cart, shutting the door carefully behind him.

"I thought perhaps you ladies might enjoy some refreshment," he said as he rolled the cart closer, china chiming.

She could not get over the willingness of Harry's staff to converse. Lady Carrolton had frowned on anyone speaking, except herself, of course.

"Thank you," Patience said. "That was very kind of you, Mr. Cuddlestone."

He beamed at her as he righted the pieces. "Not at all, Miss Ramsey. Only the best for Sir Harry's bride."

Guilt tugged at her.

"Perhaps you can assist us in another matter, Cuddlestone," Miss Thorn said.

He turned to her eagerly. "Of course, madam. What do

you need?"

"Information, for one," she said with a quick look to Patience. "What does one do for entertainment at Foulness Manor?"

He drew himself up, round face turning surprisingly hard. "This is a proper household, madam. We are not in the habit of entertaining."

"Clearly," Miss Thorn drawled.

Patience kept her smile inside. "I believe what Miss Thorn is asking, Mr. Cuddlestone, is whether there are any proper activities available—archery, lawn bowling, and the sort. Something that would keep Miss Orwell's guests happily occupied until Easter."

His stiffness eased. "Oh, indeed. Sir Harry was quite the busy lad. We have any number of games of that sort as well as fishing poles, kites, and rolling hoops."

She could imagine Harry running about the garden paths tugging on the string of a kite. "You knew Sir Harry when he was young, then."

His grey eyes warmed. "Oh, yes, miss. Such an active little fellow, always getting into mischief. Nothing serious, mind you," he hurried to add. "Sir Harry is not his father."

He sounded thankful and very certain. She hadn't the heart to suggest otherwise.

"Given that you know Sir Harry so well," Patience told the butler, "perhaps we could come up with a program. Would the estate have enough eggs for us to dye a few for Easter? I'm sure Gussie and I can come up with suitable dyes."

He drew himself up again, but the twinkle in his eyes belied the haughty look. "Of course, miss. Tell me what you want, and I'll see it done."

Patience released Fortune, who twined about the tea cart for a time until she realized no one was going to pour for her. Patience, Miss Thorn, and Mr. Cuddlestone spent the next little while laying out a plan for the next week and a half before Easter. The butler promised to work with the cook and the rest of the staff to accomplish everything. By the way he bustled from the room, Patience couldn't doubt him.

"You've given him a purpose," Miss Thorn said, rising to fetch Fortune from where she sat looking out the window, tail curling below the sill. "Now we need only make it through to Easter, and all will be well."

Patience thought so too. That is, until she refreshed herself before dinner and returned downstairs to the withdrawing room to find that Miss Villers had attached herself to Harry.

She was leaning on his arm as they stood by the hearth, white silk evening dress draped against his breeches and stockings, face turned up as if she craved each word that fell from his lips. Lashes fluttered to such an extent Patience wondered Harry did not take a chill. Then again, Miss Villers was standing so closely he was probably quite warm.

"Excuse me," she murmured to Miss Thorn, with whom she'd come down, and she moved to join Harry by the hearth.

Miss Villers did not look up at her approach, though Harry offered Patience a ready smile.

"Miss Villers," she said, "I'm so glad to see you took no lasting harm from this afternoon's contretemps. How did the shopping go?"

The girl turned as if surprised to find Patience at her side. "Oh, there you are. I'm fine, thank you. Shopping was delightful. We found the loveliest sky-blue wool. Gussie insisted on buying a length for you."

Patience stared at her. "For me? Why?"

"Because it will compliment your coloring," Miss Villers said as if anyone should realize that. "And you must call me Lydia. Harry does." She transferred her gaze once more to his.

Harry's smile was all charm, but he shifted ever so slightly and suddenly Patience found herself pressed against him while she could count the inches of blue-painted wall between Harry and Lydia.

"Very kind of you," Patience said, feeling oddly more charitable toward the young lady. "Then I must be Patience."

"Better that than what I call you in private, eh, dearest?" Harry lowered his head as if to whisper something intimate in her ear. But what she heard was "Thank you."

She still blushed.

Lydia beamed at them. "How utterly delightful. Beau was certain you were immune to marriage, Harry, yet there you stand, happy as a pair of larks."

He gave Patience a squeeze, and she felt warmer still. "All it takes is the right woman."

He was so attentive, so witty, through dinner that everyone perked up. By the time the strawberry trifle had been served, the ladies had all agreed to use first names with each other.

"You two are certainly smelling of April and May," Gussie remarked to Harry and Patience after they were all seated in the withdrawing room again.

"And why not?" Harry asked with a smile to Patience. "Was ever any man so fortunate?"

Villers crossed his legs at the ankles. "Seldom have I seen anyone so happy."

There was an edge to his tone, but Patience couldn't decide if he doubted their performance or was simply miffed he had lost Harry for Lydia.

Lydia sighed, gaze going to the fire. "If only everyone was as happy."

Was that a bid for attention? Patience simply could not be sure of the woman. But at least she could assure her things need not be bleak.

She sat taller in her chair next to Harry's near the fire.

"Meredith and I have been discussing Easter preparations and the remaining days of the house party."

As Patience had hoped, Lydia brightened, and her brother cocked his head as if willing to listen.

"If the weather continues to hold fair," Patience told them, "we hope to conduct activities outdoors. Archery, lawn bowling, and the like."

"Visits to the local antiquities?" Lydia suggested.

Harry chuckled. "Sorry, but this part of Essex boasts nothing worth seeing."

"There's a reason it's called Foulness Manor," her brother joked.

Gussie scowled at him. "The name derives from a nest of waterfowl, sir, reference no doubt to the many nests in the hillside below the house."

He inclined in head, but his eyes glittered. "No doubt."

"Regardless," Meredith put in, "between the outdoor activities and the Easter preparations, you should have no cause for ennui, sir."

Harry took Patience's hand and brought it to his lips. "I am never bored in my Patience's company."

The most delicious sensation skipped up her arm at the touch of his lips. If Patience hadn't known better, she would have been convinced he loved her.

Dangerous game. It made her feel things, wondrous things, that had no basis. She had come to Foulness Manor to find a purpose and following Sir Harry Orwell about with puppy-like adoration hardly sufficed.

Particularly when he cheerfully bid them all goodnight early, leaving his guests with little excuse but to retire to their rooms as well.

"I cannot decide whether I even admire him," Patience told Meredith and Fortune the next morning as they took a turn in the garden while they awaited the rest of the guests to awaken. The wind was quickening, and clouds rose high and dark to the southwest. Patience and Meredith had taken advantage of the moment before the rain to exercise Fortune. Her benefactress had affixed a jeweled collar and leash on her pet to allow the cat some freedom. Fortune scampered about until she felt the tug, then rolled onto her back and wiggled as if to rid herself of the encumbrance.

"Fortune approved of him," Meredith pointed out, flicking the leash to try to encourage her pet to rise again. Fortune ignored her.

"Yes, but how would she know if he was a scoundrel at heart?" Patience asked. "His forefathers certainly failed in their obligations. And when I first encountered him, he admitted to returning from an assignation with a married woman."

Meredith stopped, and Fortune righted herself and set off stalking the first robin of spring. "I will tell you something, Patience, and you must promise not to reveal it to a soul."

Patience stared at her. "Of course, Meredith. You've done so much for me, believed in me when few others did. What is it?"

Her gaze went off toward the trees at the edge of the garden, but Patience thought she wasn't seeing the bright green leaves. "I loved once, thought he was everything. But when I needed him, when I had nowhere else to turn, he abandoned me. He never offered explanation or apology. One of the reasons I wanted to leave London is that he appears to wish to renew the acquaintance now years later."

Her gaze returned to Patience, the lavender surprisingly sharp. "What I learned from the whole distressing incident is that scoundrels can wear a pleasant face. They can say all the right words, walk as uprightly as the next fellow, until they don't. Be very, very sure of the man before you commit your heart."

Patience nodded. "I will. Thank you for confiding in me. I'm truly sorry your love proved unworthy. Will he follow you here?"

She shook her head. "I know of nothing that would

cause Julian Mayes to abandon his beloved London for long. Very likely his desire to see me again was no more than a passing fancy. By the time I return, he will no doubt have forgotten all about me."

How sad. The story could only remind her of Robert. He too had murmured words of love before departing for Spain, only to return with a different bride on his arm. Was there no honest and true gentleman left in England?

Which begged the question: just how much of a scoundrel was Sir Harry Orwell?

It was a good thing Harry wasn't the scoundrel he pretended to be. Another fellow embroiled in a false engagement might have emboldened himself to take liberties. As it was, every time he and Patience were in a room together, he found himself drawn to her side before consciously remembering that was where he was supposed to be. She had a kind word, a reasoned response, to everyone.

Everyone but him.

The look in her eyes when she was reminded of his supposed past, the way her pink lips tightened, the few sharp words he'd heard from her all told him she had little use for rakes and rascals. He had played the role too well, it seemed, and he dared not trust her with the truth. Her life, his life, even Yvette's could hang on the wrong people not realizing the true motivations of Sir Harry Orwell. So, against every wish, he must continue to play the scoundrel a while longer.

After sending his guests to bed, he had slipped away the previous evening to talk to Undene in the shadows at the back of the smithy. None of the smugglers had been able to determine who had been waiting for the boat. When they'd returned under cover of darkness, they'd found the craft still mired in the sand because of a lower tide, the remaining cargo intact. No rival smuggling gang then, nor the revenue agents. Either would have confiscated the goods. But the shot had left them all wary nonetheless.

"There's a storm coming," Lacy had said, tapping his knee as if he felt it in his bones. The cobbler had hitched himself higher on the bench where he sat. "We'll not be putting out to sea until it's passed beyond the Channel."

Which meant it would be some days before they would be willing to cross to France again. Harry had offered encouragement, even silver. All they would promise was that they would alert him when they intended to go.

Leaving Harry with no answer as to Yvette's safety or the identity of his enemy.

Though he'd kept a close eye on Villers, the fellow had proven to be something of a tame lion. To be on the safe side, Harry had enlisted Cuddlestone to watch the valet. His man had proven singularly delighted at the prospect.

"He's entirely too quiet," the butler confided as he helped Harry dress that morning. Since his father's valet had been turned off years ago, Harry had never hired one for himself. Cuddlestone had seemed too comfortable in the role.

"May I inquire what you suspect him of?" the butler asked now, stepping back as if to admire the cravat he'd just tied at Harry's throat.

Harry adjusted the fold to his liking. "Some of the villagers mentioned him prowling about. It may be nothing, but I thought it wise to take precautions."

"Assuredly, sir," Cuddlestone agreed, reaching out to right the cravat. "I will endeavor to learn more. And might I suggest a silk handkerchief for your pocket?"

Harry readjusted the cravat, wrinkling it. "You can suggest, but we both know I'd lose it at the first opportunity."

Cuddlestone sighed. "Yes, Sir Harry. Of course."

Harry shook his head as he headed downstairs. His pretend bride-to-be thought him a dastard, his butler a lost

cause when it came to fashion. Only Lydia seemed happy
with him, no matter the circumstances. Whenever Patience
was out of the room or engaged in conversation with his
aunt or Meredith, she'd sidle up to him, blinking her big
green eyes. He did his best not to look too interested.

"Have I bored you?" she asked that morning while they
were eating in the dining room. The smuggler's prediction
might prove correct, for a heavy rain was drenching the
grounds. "Beau says I must do better about being amusing."

Harry glanced to where her brother was sitting farther
down, raptly listening to Gussie. Much as he loved his aunt,
he found it hard to believe her story was so fascinating. Was
Villers still encouraging Lydia to pursue Harry despite the
engagement? Or was he attempting to extract information
from Gussie?

"Why must you be amusing?" Harry asked Lydia.

She blinked innocently. "Why, to interest a gentleman,
of course. No man wants a boring bride. Beau says it's bad
enough that I'm helping your aunt. Some might think me
a bluestocking."

He could imagine worse fates. "But every man has
different things that interest him. Some prefer a winsome
voice, a comely face, or a willowy or ample figure. Others
demand intellect, talents of various sorts, the ability to
economize."

She gazed up at him. "What do you prefer, Harry?"

A movement at the door caught his eye—Patience
entering. Though her navy gown was in no way as
fashionable as Lydia's white muslin, it became her. Or
perhaps it was the light reflecting in her hair, the soft pink
that illuminated her cheeks, the curve of her smile as she
glanced Meredith's way. It was no work at all to seem
admiring.

"I prefer my bride," he told Lydia.

She smiled in approval. "Good for you. I hear reformed
rakes make the best husbands."

"And I am well on my way to being reformed, I assure you. Excuse me." He rose and headed for Patience.

"Good morning, dearest," he greeted. "Meredith."

Her companion inclined her dark head, but Patience was looking down the table.

"Miss Villers seems attentive," she murmured.

Was she jealous? Why was he grinning? He took her hand and bowed over it. "Alas, her beauty pales before yours, like the moon in the brilliant rays of the sun."

She turned her gaze to his, the brown surprisingly cool, though she smiled as if for the others' benefit. "Very prettily said, sir. I might think you besotted."

"You carry my heart in your pocket," Harry assured her, tucking her hand in his arm.

Meredith shifted, and he realized she held her pet. Singular woman. He had never known one more devoted.

"Mr. Villers has yet to be properly introduced," she said as if she'd spotted surprise on Harry's face.

"This should be interesting," Patience murmured as her friend moved toward the table.

"You expect the cat to react?" Harry asked.

"Fortune is like a sundial," she explained. "I didn't realize it when I first met her, but she is an astute judge of character. If she approves of you, you may be certain you are worthwhile."

Harry eyed her. "I feel like preening. She approved of me."

"After some consideration," Patience pointed out. "And there is always the exception."

He chuckled, turning to watch the tableau.

Meredith moved resolutely to the Villers's side, and Lydia rose and scurried around the table, smiling at the cat. Fortune, however, had her eyes on Villers, as if she'd spotted a plump mouse.

"Mr. Villers," Meredith said, "may I present my Fortune."

The fellow blinked, then recovered himself. "Honored,

madam. I had thought her a charming creature, much like her owner."

"I think she's beautiful," Lydia said, reaching out a hand.

Fortune crouched deeper in her mistress's arms, ears flattening and eyes narrowing. A hiss flew past her teeth.

Lydia dropped her hand, face crumbling.

But was it Lydia or her brother who had met with the cat's disapproval?

CHAPTER SEVEN

Patience and her friend had been chased from the garden by the advancing storm. So much for her plans for outdoor activities today. She'd come inside to find that Lydia was apparently set on amusing herself at Harry's expense. And she was not entirely sure who Fortune had rebuked, Lydia or her brother.

The cat remained out of sorts as Harry led Patience to her seat next to his at the table and Meredith took her own seat. The cat refused to settle down after her introduction to Mr. Villers, squirming and protesting in Meredith's arms until her owner was forced to leave the room with apologies all around.

"No one likes being penned," Mr. Villers muttered into his tea.

Lydia fluttered her lashes at Harry. "It's so difficult to be restive. I'm sure you could find us something to do today, Harry."

Not if Patience could help it.

Her brother eyed Gussie. "Were you not in the middle of an experiment, madam?"

And that avenue of inquiry needed to be headed off as well. Oh, this house party would be the death of her!

Gussie shoved back her chair before Mr. Cuddlestone could come hold it for her. "I was indeed. I want to try the gypsum I purchased in London. The effect against the thyme should be interesting. Patience, join me." She started for the door.

As if he thought otherwise, Mr. Cuddlestone was gesticulating wildly in Patience's direction, lips moving silently. She wasn't entirely sure of the message he was trying to send, but she rose. "Gussie, wait."

Her employer turned, brows raised in obvious surprise. Lydia and her brother looked equally surprised. As if afraid he had been caught and would be censored, Mr. Cuddlestone froze. Only Harry offered Patience a smile of encouragement, though he could have no idea of her purpose. She squared her shoulders.

"We agreed to spend the day with our guests," she reminded Gussie. "The weather may have foreclosed outdoor activities, but surely we can find something indoors."

Mr. Cuddlestone offered her a thumbs up.

"Like what?" Lydia asked eagerly.

"Charades," Patience said, and the butler beamed at her.

"Perhaps a hand of cards," Mr. Villers added with a look to Harry.

Gussie ventured closer to the table. "Or word games. I'm rather good at those."

Harry leaned back in his chair. "Excellent suggestions. That should take us through the morning. This afternoon, we can each think of some talent or skill to amuse the others. Performances will be after dinner."

They all exclaimed their approval of the plan, but Patience couldn't help glancing at Harry. His smile could only be called satisfied as he gazed into his teacup. He must know what he'd proposed left all his guests to their own devices this afternoon. Very likely Gussie would scramble for her laboratory. Patience would have to make sure Lydia's brother didn't follow. Would that leave Harry to Lydia's devices, or had he some other reason to avoid the rest of them for a while?

He was the perfect host that morning, taking his turn at charades. There was something endearing about the way he so earnestly acted out his riddle, his chagrin when the answer Lydia called proved wrong, his grin when Mr. Cuddlestone blurted out "Patience is a virtue," which made everyone laugh and Patience blush. True to her word, Gussie proved more adept at the word games that followed, making up rhymes with great abandon.

"I would never have thought to match orange with porridge," Lydia marveled.

"Nor meander with lavender," Meredith commented, stroking Fortune in her lap. The cat had been subdued since returning to their midst, watching them with her copper eyes as if she couldn't determine the reason for their animation. It was only when Harry, Gussie, Lydia, and her brother partnered for whist that things began to deteriorate.

Patience had seated herself on the sofa next to Meredith, and Fortune had climbed into her lap as if determined to find a new perspective. Lydia had attempted to partner Harry, but Gussie had taken the chair opposite him, forcing the girl to make a set with her brother. She wiggled on the chair at the card table Mr. Cuddlestone had erected, fiddled with her cards, and twisted a curl around one finger. Gussie was nearly as agitated.

"We can only hope for clearing by morning," Meredith murmured to Patience. "We won't survive another day of this."

"Interesting move," Mr. Villers commented as Harry took a trick, sweeping the cards toward him. "It's almost as if you had that card at the ready."

Gussie stiffened, but Harry merely smiled. "It's all in knowing which card to play and which to hold in reserve." He lay down a card. "Your turn, Lydia."

She studied her cards, teeth worrying her lower lip. "Maybe…this one." She set it down with a flourish.

Gussie pounced on it. With a roll of his eyes at his sister, Mr. Villers played, and Harry raked in the trick.

"You're as lucky as your father," Mr. Villers said.

Harry lay his cards face down on the table and pushed back his chair. Mr. Villers tensed. So did Patience. Harry turned her way, smile pleasant. "Meredith, surely you'd like an opportunity to play. Come finish my hand while I keep my beloved company."

Lydia's brother collapsed against the back of his chair, then straightened in a manly show of nonchalance as Meredith rose to take Harry's seat.

"That was badly done of him," Patience murmured as Harry sat beside her.

He reached out and rubbed Fortune's head. "I've heard it many times before."

But never liked it. Though his smile remained, she felt the tension in him. Was Lydia's brother so bored he felt it necessary to provoke his host?

Perhaps he realized his folly, for he was first to declare himself ready to practice for the evening's entertainment. Gussie readily agreed to part company, no doubt dreaming of her laboratory. To Patience's surprise, Harry offered to accompany his aunt.

"What's your talent, Harry?" Lydia asked, watching him head for the door.

Harry looked back to wink at her. "You'll find out tonight."

Lydia giggled.

Meredith gathered Fortune from Patience. "Do you sing, Lydia?"

She nodded, but she didn't look pleased by the fact.

"Then come with me," Meredith said, holding out her free hand. "Perhaps the two of us could make a duet."

Lydia brightened and jumped to her feet to join her. "And perhaps I can make up with Fortune. I can't imagine why she would take me in dislike."

"Cause for reflection," Meredith agreed as they headed out the door.

Patience found herself alone in the drawing room with Mr. Cuddlestone. He offered her a smile. "Do you play an instrument, Miss Ramsey?"

Patience shook her head. "I never learned. But I have been told I have a pleasant singing voice."

"I can well imagine. If you have no further need of me, I shall inquire whether the others have any needs I should address."

That he had asked her first made her smile. "I'm fine, thank you." She hesitated as he started for the door. "But Mr. Cuddlestone…"

He turned eagerly. "Yes, miss?"

"If you should see Mr. Villers by the laboratory, will you let me know?"

His grey eyes lit, and he tiptoed closer, lowering his voice. "Do you suspect him as well?"

Patience blinked. "You suspect him too?"

He drew himself up. "I manage this household, miss. Nothing much escapes me. I have my eye on Mr. Villers and his valet Teacake."

Patience pressed her fingers to her lips. "His name is Teacake?"

"Teacake, Tecay, something of that sort," the butler said with a wrinkle of his nose. "I certainly wouldn't allow him on staff here—he's never at his post when needed, and he ties a rather common fold."

Patience had never noticed anything untoward about Beau Villers's cravat, but then she'd never had to tie one so perhaps she was missing the nuances. "And have you noticed anything more nefarious about his master?"

Mr. Cuddlestone sighed. "No, worse luck."

Patience rose and patted his shoulder. "Well, I appreciate your determination. Someone has to look out for this family."

"Exactly." With a smile, he excused himself and left her.

Patience wandered to the window. The rain had slowed, and a patch of blue sky showed to the west. Perhaps they wouldn't have to hide away until Easter.

It seemed, however, that Lydia's brother wanted to escape now. He didn't even attempt to hide himself as he strode across the grounds, heading toward the hillside that overlooked the sea. And somehow it didn't surprise her when Harry darted away from the house after him.

Where was Villers going? Harry moved from bush to tree, keeping the fellow in sight even while Harry kept out of sight. Villers had gone out of his way to antagonize him that morning. Showing his hand, perhaps? Or throwing down the glove?

His unwanted guest cut across the grounds, turning up his collar against the drizzle that persisted. The waters of the Channel were shrouded in mist, as if the world ended just beyond the hill. Harry thought Villers might drop down to the shore, but he followed the path along the edge of the estate, moving away from the village. What did he hope to find?

Who did he intend to meet?

He reached the curve at the back of the gardens, where the ground dropped away to the causeway, and stood there, hands clasped behind his back and greatcoat swaying about his boots. Harry hung back, waiting, moist air brushing his cheeks. Aside from a gull, disappearing into the mist with a mournful cry, nothing moved.

Villers raised a hand as if bidding the gull farewell, then turned and started back toward the house.

Harry stepped into his path. "What do you think you're doing?"

His quarry drew up short. "Harry! You could scare the life out of a man." He peered around him, then met his gaze. "Are you alone?"

Not that he'd admit. "Cuddlestone and the grooms are likely about somewhere. Why did you leave the house?"

He shrugged. "I felt the need to stretch my legs. I'm not the sort to rusticate, you know."

Since when? The fellow begged invitations so he could spend most of the winter and summer at someone's country estate, doing as little as possible.

"What a hardy fellow, venturing out in the rain to admire the scenery," Harry drawled.

He shook water off his greatcoat, face turning petulant. "If you must know, I wanted a look at the causeway. Gussie claims it floods in the spring. With the rain, I wanted to make sure Lydia and I could leave if needed."

"Ah," Harry said, watching him. "Feeling the need to escape, are we?"

"Well, it's painfully obvious you're no longer on the market, old fellow." He cocked his head. "I must say, I never thought you'd truly settle down, Harry."

"And here I thought you intended me to settle for your sister."

Red fired his cheeks. "My sister is a lady, and you would have been fortunate to wed her, which is more than I can say for Miss Ramsey."

Harry's hand fisted. "Have a care, Villers, when you speak of my betrothed."

"Of course, of course," he said, but he stepped back out of reach. "Still, you could do so much better, Harry. I grant you she's easy on the eyes, but a man wants a wife who will do him credit in all areas of his life. She is docile, dare I say servile. I struggle to see her fitting in at Almack's."

As if the famed ladies' club in London would ever have let Harry darken its door. "Perhaps I see more in her than you do."

"I have no doubt," Villers said, voice once more resembling Fortune's purr, with none of its charm. "But can't you see,

Harry, how she's insinuated herself into your life? You're so besotted you allowed this employment agency owner to address us as if she were an equal, let her cat dine with us, because the woman is Miss Ramsey's acquaintance. And what of your household staff? Already they dance to her call. I fear Patience Ramsey is an opportunist."

He would know, being cut from the same cloth.

Harry shook off the feeling. "You're wrong, Villers. Patience Ramsey is everything a man could want in a wife."

He snorted, smile patronizing. "So sayeth the man in love. Watch her, Harry. You'll soon see through the veil. And when you've come to your senses, you'll realize Lydia is the right bride for you." He reached out and clapped Harry on the shoulder. "This should be an interesting house party. Come, I'll walk you back to the house."

Bemused, Harry allowed the gesture. Talking to Villers was like whistling in the wind. But the fellow was dead wrong. Harry would never marry Lydia. And, unless he settled this business with Yvette and his mysterious assailant, he very much feared he'd never earn a reputation worthy of a woman like Patience Ramsey.

CHAPTER EIGHT

By the time they regrouped in the withdrawing room before dinner that night, Patience felt as if she were tied in a knot. Gussie had spent the afternoon in her laboratory, coming out only once to question why Patience hadn't joined her. Patience could hardly tell her she'd stayed by the window until she'd seen Harry return to the house. At least Mr. Cuddlestone reported to her that Lydia's brother had never ventured close to Gussie. He had also suggested that she might sing a sentimental ballad, claiming Harry was quite partial to them. That she found a little hard to credit. Harry somehow seemed the sort more given to rousing sea chanties or boisterous tavern songs. As she knew none, she'd practiced a more appropriate tune or two.

After all, what she sang didn't really matter. She had no need to posture. Harry's guests thought she and Harry were betrothed. He would have to look pleased even if she croaked the words out of tune.

Everyone else seemed eager for the evening's entertainment. Mr. Cuddlestone and Wilkins had brought in a spinet from somewhere else in the house and positioned it by the windows, the drapes framing the dark instrument in blue silk.

"I'll go first," Gussie announced, rising to fetch a basket from the side of the sofa. "I never liked playing, and I'm not much of a singer. I could declaim, but I do that on a regular basis. So, I made you samples."

She moved about the room, handing out little jars. "It's hand cream, just the thing to ward off chafing in this damp weather."

Lydia thanked her, her brother smiled and set the jar aside, and Harry waved her off. In Meredith's arms, Fortune sniffed at the jar, then sneezed twice. Patience allowed herself a smile.

"Well, go on," Gussie urged, looking around at them. "Try it."

"Perhaps later," Patience suggested. "Softened skin might make playing difficult."

Gussie seemed to accept that and returned to her seat. Meredith handed Fortune to Patience and rose. "Lydia and I next, I think." She went to seat herself at the spinet. Lydia hurried to join her.

The pair sang together, Meredith's alto blending nicely with Lydia's soprano. Mr. Villers shot Harry a look, all triumph. Was he finally proud of his sister?

Patience had wondered if Harry played, but he set his back to the instrument when he stood to take his turn.

"I intend to amaze you with a prodigious feat of prestidigitation," he declared. He held up a guinea. "Behold, a simple coin. Would you attest to its solidarity, Mr. Villers?"

Lydia's brother reached out and fingered the gold coin. "Quite solid, sir, though some might not make the same claim about your character."

Patience frowned, but Harry laughed. "Only too true." He held the guinea higher and flicked it with his fingers, which were suddenly empty.

"Why, where could it have gone?" Harry cried, glancing around. His gaze lit on Patience, the blue of his eyes dancing with merriment. "Ah, I see it." He reached out and caressed her cheek, his touch warm. As he drew back, the coin was shining in his hand.

"Patience had it," Lydia said, beaming.

"Nothing gleams more gold than true love," Harry murmured, his gaze on Patience's. Her cheeks heated once more.

After that, her song and Mr. Villers's surprising pleasant baritone solo could not compare.

Harry insisted on walking her to her room when they retired, in considerably better spirits than when they'd woken. Patience could feel Lydia's gaze on her as Harry paused before Patience's door, but the girl merely offered them a smile before going into her own room.

"She's gone, so you can stop posturing," Patience told Harry, who had been leaning closer as if to steal a kiss. Just the thought set her pulse to racing.

Harry showed no sign of straightening. "You smell like roses."

"So do you," she pointed out. "It's my mother's ointment."

He chuckled. "Will nothing shake your composure?"

"I am hired staff, sir," she reminded him. "I am paid to remain composed. Hysterics are the privilege of wealth."

He shook his head, straightening at last, and the air felt cooler. "You promised to play a role. If you are not at least a little friendly toward me, the others will suspect our ruse."

Patience put her hand on his arm, fluttering her lashes as she peered up at him. "Why, Sir Harry, how could any lady fail to be friendly toward a manly fellow like you?"

He threw back his head and laughed.

"Hush," Patience said, cuffing his arm as she drew back. "They'll suspect we're mad. But you can see my point. I have no experience with flirting. If I attempted the role, it would come off false."

He peered closer. "How could a lovely lady like you have no experience flirting?"

He made her sound an oddity. "There weren't many young gentlemen near me growing up, and I thought myself engaged."

He sobered. "You have a suitor? Why hasn't he come forward to claim your hand? Better married than companion to Lady Carrolton."

She would not have this conversation with him. Even though it was nearly four years ago now, Robert's defection and the shame it had brought her felt suddenly fresh. "He decided we would not suit and married another."

"Idiot," Harry said. "You're well rid of him. Good night, Patience. I look forward to continuing our engagement tomorrow. At least you know I'm not about to wed another." With a bow, he left her.

Patience was still thinking about the exchange the next day. When Robert had married his Spanish bride, she'd felt as if she was somehow flawed, an outgrown coat left behind as Robert moved on with his life. What was it about her that he could so easily forget her, that Lady Carrolton felt justified treating her badly, that Lady Lilith could dismiss all the good she'd tried to do? But when Harry had called Robert an idiot, it was as if a weight had lifted, and she could truly draw breath for the first time in a long time.

The morning seemed to celebrate her feelings, for sunlight speared through the clouds, and everyone agreed to venture outdoors. Fortune alone remained inside for her safety, perched in the withdrawing room window and pawing at the glass as if determined to join them. Lydia offered to remain inside, likely hoping to further endear herself to the cat, but her brother insisted that she accompany them.

Mr. Cuddlestone had set up archery targets—placards on hay bales—on the front lawn, and they each took turns shooting. Lydia proved singularly adept. Her brother did not appear amused, but Harry applauded her.

"Quality will out," Mr. Villers said with a look to Patience, who had scored the lowest thus far.

Really, could the fellow be any more annoying?

Harry moved in next to her. "Allow me to assist you, my

love. We'll show them how it's done."

Patience eyed him. "I am capable of shooting, sir."

"Humor me," he murmured. He slipped his arms around her, his chest up against her back, his cheek close to hers. She could feel the length of him, the strength of him. She could not catch her breath.

"Now, raise the bow," Harry said, and her arms obeyed.

"Draw it back." His breath brushed her ear, and her fingers trembled for no fault of the difficulty of the bow.

"Harry," she warned.

"Loose!" he ordered.

She released, and the arrow arched up and into the nearest bush. She made a face at Harry, who laughed, holding up his hands and backing away.

The sound of a carriage approaching had everyone turning their heads. Patience's stomach clenched as she sighted the glossy black sides, the high-stepping pair.

Meredith must have recognized the coach as well, for she hurried to her side. "Never fear. She shan't have you."

Mr. Villers shaded his eyes with his hand. "I say, isn't that the Carrolton coach?"

Patience nodded, stomach churning. Why? Was she afraid? She wasn't a runaway slave. She hadn't stolen anything as she'd left Carrolton Park. She would always be grateful for the place she had been given, but she did not owe Lady Carrolton her last breath, or her dignity.

Harry strode back to her side and slipped his arm about her waist. "Don't worry, Patience. You're engaged to me, remember?"

But she wasn't. Not really. How could she lie to Lady Carrolton of all people?

As if he knew her thoughts, Harry gave her a squeeze. "Leave this to me." Pulling away, he strode to meet the coach as the driver reined in the horses in front of the house.

"I didn't realize Gussie had invited the Carroltons," Mr.

Villers said, paling as his hand fell to his side.

"Lady Lilith is a particular friend of his," Lydia said with a look to her brother.

Few could have contested the claim. Like her mother, Lady Lilith left the estate rarely, so no one in Society would know who she favored. Patience knew. Lady Lilith's sharp tongue and dark moods had estranged her from anyone who had ever attempted to befriend her. And Patience had never met Lydia or her brother at any Carrolton event. So why claim friendship?

"I doubt Lady Carrolton will stay long," Meredith said, watching as Wilkins opened the door to the carriage.

The pale face of Lady Carrolton peered out. Tall, impossibly elegant in the trim black gowns she favored, she squinted as if unaccustomed to the sunlight. She must have spied Harry standing there, for she shook her cane at him. "Jackanapes! What have you done with my Patience?"

"I never thought she had much patience," Lydia murmured. "I can't imagine why she'd think Harry would steal it."

"Are you related to the Carroltons, Miss Ramsey?" her brother asked with a frown.

"No," Patience said. "But I know the meaning of that scowl. Harry hardly deserves it. That was always my role." She started forward, and Meredith moved to block her way.

"You owe her nothing," she said.

"I owe her a great deal," Patience corrected her. "And I owe Gussie and Harry as much. I need to set things right."

Harry held the coach door open, but he did not offer the harridan inside his arm to descend. He knew Lady Carrolton. She was the mother of an old friend who had attended Eton with him. Gregory, Earl Carrolton, was a strapping fellow who had excelled at boxing, fencing, and riding. But one moment in his mother's company reduced the man to jelly.

Harry had no idea why the woman was determined to be so unpleasant. Unlike him, Lady Carrolton had reason to be proud of her family name, what her forefathers and mothers had accomplished. But he could not like how she treated her son nor the few things Patience had let slip about her time with the woman.

"Lady Carrolton," he said with a nod. "I regret you came all this way to be disappointed. Patience Ramsey will not be returning with you."

She glared at him. "That is not for you to say, boy. She was my companion, content in her post. You turned her head, led her astray. Just like an Orwell."

He refused to bridle at the jab. "If you had mentioned another lady, I might have pleaded guilty. But Patience came here of her own free will."

"Liar." She thumped the cane on the floor of the coach for emphasis. "

"I would never lie about my betrothed," Harry said, refusing to smile at the shock that crossed her lined face. "I hope you'll wish us happy. Patience is everything I ever dreamed of. I'm certain you agree to her worth."

Lady Carrolton recovered. "Not at all. She is far too good for the likes of you."

He merely smiled. "Then I am doubly fortunate she agreed to be my bride."

"She hasn't a penny to her name, you know," Lady Carrolton said, eyes narrowing as if she would see right through him. "When I die, I'll leave her nothing."

"Nor would I expect you to," Patience said, joining him. "Good afternoon, Lady Carrolton. How are the earl and Lady Lilith?"

Lady Carrolton hitched her shawl about her spare shoulders. "Saddened by your defection. As am I."

Patience inclined her head. "I was equally saddened, by

the way Lady Lilith slandered my good name."

What was this? He glanced between Patience's chin, which was up, and Lady Carrolton's gaze, which was down.

"She's just a silly girl," the older woman muttered. "You should pay her no heed."

"She is a grown woman, fully capable of forming and expressing her own opinion," Patience said. "She accused me of attempting to hurry your demise."

Interesting. He wouldn't have been surprised if a beleaguered companion attached to a dowager of Lady Carrolton's disposition didn't consider the matter, however fleetingly, but surely few would act on such thoughts, and never the upright Patience Ramsey. She had been named far too aptly.

Lady Carrolton waved her cane. "She was obviously distraught. She suffers from a nervous condition."

"Nothing that exercise outdoors and an examination of her conscience wouldn't cure," Patience informed her.

"It was all nonsense," Lady Carrolton insisted. "You've ignored her before."

So, the daughter made a habit of berating Patience? Small wonder she had been willing to take up with his aunt.

"This time she threatened to bring me up on charges," Patience reminded her. "I will not stand by and watch my reputation be ruined, madam, my freedom threatened. It was clear I was no longer welcome under your roof. You cannot blame me for seeking employment elsewhere."

Lady Carrolton gasped, cane clattering to the floor of the carriage as her hand clawed at her chest.

Harry started forward. "She's having an attack!"

Patience put herself in front of him. "One of many. Allow me."

She gathered her skirts and climbed up into the carriage to sit beside her former employer. Glancing around, she reached for a case that had been sitting on the forward seat. She pulled out a screened vinaigrette box and held it under Lady Carrolton's nose, all the while rubbing the lady's back with her free hand.

"Breathe," she encouraged her.

Lady Carrolton drew in a shaky breath and sagged against Patience. "Thank you, my dear. You are the only one who cares about me."

"Nonsense," Patience said, though her tone had softened. "The earl and your daughter care about you."

Lady Carrolton sniffed. "Gregory is entirely too busy, and Lilith has her own concerns. You were the only one who puts my needs before your own."

"Is that not something to which we all should aspire?" Patience asked her, returning the vinaigrette to the case. "Perhaps if you showed Lord Carrolton and Lady Lilith how much you love them, they might return the favor. At the very least, you might feel better about the matter."

Lady Carrolton's eyes were bright with unshed tears. "Doubtful, but I suppose it's worth a try. Could you not return with me, Patience? You are so good for my nerves, and you always know how to treat my complaints."

Patience rose from the seat. "You will find someone else to train. Just try to treat her kinder and stand up for her when Lady Lilith feels fractious."

Harry held out his hand to help Patience from the coach. "I can see why she wants you back. You are magnificent."

Her cheeks turned pink.

Lady Carrolton sighed. "Yes. Yes, she is. See that you appreciate her, Sir Harold."

Harry gazed down at Patience, her hand cradled in his. "I assure you I will, Lady Carrolton."

Patience turned to eye the lady. "How will you reach Carrolton Park tonight? We took two days to arrive at Foulness Manor from London, and the estate is a little way beyond that."

Oh, no. Harry wasn't about to allow the woman to spend the night. Who knew how many other fits she might attempt to convince Patience she was needed?

But Lady Carrolton shook her head. "Gregory accompanied me as far as Rainham. We have rooms at the inn. We'll travel home tomorrow." The grimace as she retrieved her cane was apparently her attempt at a smile. "Are you certain you won't join us, Patience? I could be persuaded to allow you two hours a week off, a better mattress on the dressing room cot."

Patience shook her head. "Thank you, but no. My place is here."

Once more Lady Carrolton pointed her cane at Harry. "I will be watching you, sir. You will treat my Patience well, or you will answer to me." She thumped her cane on the floor once more. "Coachman—return me to my son."

Harry closed the door and waved until the coach started down the drive. Then he shuddered.

"Horrible woman. I can see why even a false engagement to me might be preferable to continuing in her service."

Patience pulled away from him. "Lady Carrolton gave me a home when I had none."

"Which apparently consisted of a tick on her dressing room floor. And a half hour off every other week. You deserve more."

"Perhaps." She started to go, and he caught up her hands.

"You deserve more, Patience," he insisted. "Space to breathe, to dream. People who admire and respect you. Things that delight you. Someone who loves you."

She waited, as if expecting more. When he remained silent, she pulled out of his grip.

"You forget yourself, sir. We are not really engaged. You have no right to tell me what you think I need or deserve." She turned on her heel and left him standing on the drive.

CHAPTER NINE

Fool! For one moment, Patience had almost fallen prey to Harry's charms. That warm look, those sweet words, had called to her heart. If only they had come from his.

She couldn't rejoin the others, was ashamed to even glance their way. Surely, they would only question her about Lady Carrolton's visit and congratulate her again for escaping that prison for the freedom to marry Harry. She couldn't smile and pretend now, not with Harry's words ringing in her ears. She hurried around the back on the house instead, intent on losing herself in the garden.

As she came around the corner of Gussie's laboratory, however, she nearly collided with Lydia's brother.

He caught her arms to steady her. "Patience, forgive me."

She pulled away, arranged her skirts, hands shaking. "Think nothing of it. I'm sure you were hastening to your sister's side."

"Yes, of course." His words held no conviction as he peered around her toward the front of the house. "Will Lady Carrolton be making one of the party?"

If she hadn't known better, she might think he was hiding from the lady. "No. She had other plans."

He brightened, then composed his face to something like regret. "A shame. I would have been delighted to renew the acquaintance. I take it you are a particular friend as well?"

She forced a smile. "La, sir, you must have heard the story. I am well known to the Carroltons. I served as the countess' companion for several years."

"Ah, I thought you looked familiar." His smile was knowing. "But what an elevation—from paid companion to lady of the manor. How very generous of our Harry."

Anger poked at her. "You assume that a wife brings nothing to the marriage save money and position. Should I marry Sir Harry, I assure you he would receive a fair trade."

"Of that I have no doubt." His voice had turned silky.

Patience moved around him. "I will not detain you, sir." She started for the garden.

He hurried to pace her. "Forgive me. I allowed my admiration of you to overcome good manners."

It wasn't admiration, and he knew it. "Then pray exercise those manners now, and allow me some time to myself."

"In such a mood? I could not call myself your friend and leave you alone. What has Harry done to so incense you?"

He was like a burr on a slipper—once picked up, it was impossible to shake off. "You mistake me, sir. I have nothing bad to say about Harry."

"But much you wish to say," he insisted.

When she opened her mouth to argue, he held up a hand. "No, no. You need not speak. Rest assured that I am well aware of Harry's indiscretions. The opera dancer in London, the barrister's wife in Folkestone, and that barmaid in the village."

Each word felt like a stone dropped into the well of her heart. "I wish you would not belabor the issue."

He made a sad moue that did nothing to soften the lines of his face. "I only bring up the past to point out how he has changed. No woman keeps him busy now, I warrant, not having won such a prize. So, why does he stray from your side?"

Patience frowned at him. Those dark eyes were far too

bright. He reminded her of a hound who had caught the scent. "I was under the impression that any time Harry wasn't with me, he was with you. Or have you forgotten how he's beaten you at nearly every game?"

Something crossed his face. He didn't like looking second best, it seemed, even in something so trivial as a game. "I forget nothing. And there have been any number of occasions when Harry has disappeared for an hour or more while you were busy elsewhere."

Had he? Where was he going? He'd promised he was reforming. Was he still visiting his married lady? For some reason, she'd thought assignations carried out in the dead of night, not the during the middle of the morning. Of course, Harry might have gone out last night after she'd retired to bed. So long as he didn't attempt to climb back in via the balcony, she would never have known.

"Perhaps he enjoys a moment to himself as well," she said. "These house parties can be fatiguing for a host, always attending to the comfort of his guests. Now, if you'll excuse me, sir, I feel the need to return to the house, and I require no escort," she hurried to add as he offered her his arm.

This time he inclined his head, arm falling, and allowed her to pass. While she was glad to be free of him, she couldn't rid herself of his insinuations as easily.

Was Harry going out when no one was looking? Was he still embroiled in an affair? Did he spend his nights whispering words of love in another woman's ear? Why did she care? Their engagement was only a pretense. Even if he went back on his promise to reform she could not stop playing the role of his betrothed without hurting Gussie's reputation.

Yet she did care that he might love another. Despite knowing it was all a game, she enjoyed his attentiveness, his quick wit. She wanted that smile directed at her, his hand holding hers alone. He made her want those delicious feelings of courtship again.

The very idea left her trembling. Had she learned nothing from her experience with Robert? A one-sided attachment was built on air. She would not countenance another. She had thought she'd walled off her heart to prevent such a fate. She'd survived the last three years with Lady Carrolton by being quiet, respectful, diligent, and dutiful. Such traits had only made her more invisible to those around her, enough so that Lady Lilith had thought nothing of berating her for any imagined fault. A quiet companion with nowhere else to go could not have the luxury of feelings.

Now those feelings welled up inside her. Harry had said she deserved better. She was starting to believe that. She deserved a man who loved her, was faithful to her, who would work at her side, cherishing, supporting, and she would give as much as he gave. But could Harry be such a man?

The only way to know was to discover what he was up to.

What a bold thought! Yet the more she considered it, the more her determination grew. She had many things to prove Harry was a true gentleman—his care and concern for Gussie, his refusal to flirt with Lydia despite blatant encouragement, the way his staff adored him. All she had to indicate he was a scoundrel were rumors—some he had started, others from unreliable sources. She could ask him outright, but he'd likely evade an answer. Perhaps the only way to know the truth about Harry was to follow him on one of his midnight rambles and discover who he was meeting and why.

She was glad Gussie called for an early night, for Patience had barely managed to attend to the afternoon's activities, which had consisted of Harry and Mr. Villers playing billiards while the ladies determined how Patience could use the lovely wool Gussie had purchased by perusing copies of ladies' magazines Lydia had brought with her. Lydia had insisted on searching for patterns for a wedding gown as well, and Patience had done her best to look excited while her mind turned over possibilities to learn the truth about Harry.

As it was, as soon as she retired, she went straight to the wardrobe and pulled out her cloak. Grey, of course, a nice dove shade, far too light for blending in in the darkness.

Emma bustled in. "Let me help you, miss. I'll just…" She pulled up as Patience stared at her over the folds of wool. What a wretched spy she'd make! She couldn't think of a single reason why she'd need her cloak when she should be changing for bed.

Emma snapped a nod. "Right. You'll be following Sir Harry, then."

Patience blinked. "How did you know?"

"Only stands to reason," Emma said. "You're his lady and all. Why wouldn't he invite you? But that won't do. Wait here." She hurried back out again.

Patience glanced down at the cloak. Invite her? Did Emma think Patience would take part in Harry's affairs? Surely, she knew Patience wouldn't condone such activities. Or did the maid think Harry was up to something else? She couldn't very well ask without revealing her ignorance.

She had hung up the cloak again when Emma returned. "Here you go, miss. Dark as the night." She draped a black velvet evening cloak about Patience's shoulders and pulled the hood over her hair. "You'll blend in nicely, and you're already wearing half boots instead of fancy slippers."

"Where did you get it?" Patience asked, fingering the soft nap.

"'Tis the mistress', but she won't be needing it tonight. Will you climb down the trellis or sneak down the servant's stair?"

She sounded positively eager to abet her. "The servant's stair," Patience said.

"Right," the maid said with a nod. "This way."

Emma made a show of looking up and down the corridor before leading Patience to a hidden door in the wall, which opened to a narrow stair.

"Likely he'll be waiting in the garden for you," Emma said as they descended. "But if you're first, stop in the shadow of the big oak on the side of the drive. Sir Harry always passes that way."

"I'm surprised you know so much about his habits," Patience said.

"We take care of our own at Foulness Manor," Emma said. She stopped and cracked open the door at the bottom of the stairs. "All clear. Good luck to you, miss."

Patience crossed the kitchen and let herself out the back door. The moon was just rising, and clouds crowded what little light shone down. The glow was just enough to spot the figure moving toward the big tree on the drive. Patience hurried after.

Harry slipped across the garden, but his thoughts kept returning to the scene on the drive that afternoon. He still didn't understand why he'd spoken in such a manner to Patience. Something about her made him feel chivalrous, noble even. Any other woman would think him besotted. He could only be thankful Patience had more sense.

With his guests all safely abed, he'd hoped to head for the village to meet Undene. Though he had no reason to think the smugglers had taken a run since their last ill-fated one, they had likely been in contact with their brethren along the coast. News traveled swiftly among the free traders. If Yvette de Maupassant had been taken prisoner, someone might have heard of it.

He knew the path well enough that he didn't need to open the hood on the lantern immediately. But someone was less fluent with the territory. He heard the crack of a twig behind him, a muffled cry and scuffle as someone tripped. Had Villers followed him from the house? Or was this his unseen assailant, determined to finish the job? Ducking behind the oak, he set down the lantern and held his breath, listening.

The grounds had gone silent, as if waiting. Then footsteps approached, hesitant. His follower's breath sounded ragged. Was that because of worry? Fear? Excitement to see the deed done? He pressed his back against the tree until a dark shadow started past. Then he pounced, grabbing his follower by the shoulder, twisting to the side, and pressing the person up against the tree.

"Who are you? Why are you following me?"

The slight frame in velvet shuddered beneath his hands. A lad? No, a woman.

"Forgive me. I had to know."

He released her, stepping back. "Patience?"

She drew in a shaky breath. "Yes. Oh, I've made a mess of it."

He drew her close once more, holding her gently, heartbeat slowly returning to normal. "You startled me. That's all. I'm sorry I was rough with you. But it's not safe out like this. You could have met a poacher."

"Who are you meeting?" she asked.

So, that was it. He should laugh, claim a willing wench was waiting at the tavern. But lying to her was becoming increasingly unpalatable.

"I'm headed to the village," he told her, letting her go. "I have friends, acquaintances in the area. We meet to drink and swap lies. Very manly."

She must be recovering, for her voice sounded amused. "I see. And you could not have mentioned that?"

"In front of Beau Villers? Trust me, these are not his sort of people."

"Yet they are yours."

He shrugged. "The Orwells have always made friends

with the wrong sorts."

Her head moved, hair brushing his chin, as if she put her nose in the air. "There are many kinds of people in the world. Just because Mr. Villers doesn't find them suitable doesn't make them bad."

"I'm sure my friends would be delighted to hear it," Harry said, "if they cared what people like Villers thought."

"No one should care what people like Mr. Villers think," she said primly. "Your staff don't. They like you, Harry. I see it."

"And what of you, Patience?" he murmured. "Do you like me?"

He wasn't sure why he asked. He'd gone out of his way to make her think him a rascal. Yet once again, he held his breath.

"Yes, Harry," she murmured. "I like you. Far more than I should."

He let out his breath, allowed the cool night air to fill his lungs. It had never tasted sweeter. "Then go back to the house where I know you'll be safe. Can you find your way?"

She nodded. "I think so."

He bent and handed her the lantern. "Take this just in case. I won't be long. I promise."

She opened the lantern and lifted it, illuminating the glow of her skin, the depth of her brown eyes. She studied him by the light as if trying to see inside him, to the man he was. He willed himself not to flinch.

"I will hold you to that promise," she said. Then she turned, black velvet cloak swirling, and picked her way back along the path until the light from the lantern disappeared.

An opportunist, Villers had claimed. What nonsense. Harry would have wagered there were few truer than Patience Ramsey.

Feeling as if an invisible rope bound him to her, he started once more toward the village and managed to reach the tavern with only a few trips in the darkness. As he'd hoped, Undene and his men were cozied up in a corner of the public room, heads bent over tankards. Harry slipped onto the bench next to them. "Any news?"

"Nothing good," Undene said, face craggy in the lamplight. He glanced around the tavern as if expecting to see spies everywhere, then resorted to the code they often used in public. "Reports of much distress with our friends far afield. Rumor has it some have been demoted and are seeking vengeance against those who caused it."

Demoted? Yvette had once served the Empress Josephine but had been forced from the court when the Emperor divorced his wife. Yvette had maintained her connections at court, so she could continue sending information to England. Undene had to mean someone else.

"Surely not the ladies," Harry pressed.

Undene's large hands cradling his tankard. "A close relation. Some men think their ladyfolk must be kept close."

A close relation? Yvette's cousin must have discovered her secret. The creature had joined the Revolution to save his own neck, curried favor with Napoleon to line his own pockets. He'd have been happy to see Yvette cut down if it furthered his ambitions.

"How close?" Harry asked.

"In Calais under heavy guard, I hear," Undene murmured. "It might be wise to visit soon. That town can be dangerous."

Yvette could expect no help from her countrymen. Someone from England would have to extract her. He drew in a breath.

"Will you be travelling?" Harry asked.

"Soon," Undene said.

Harry nodded. "I'll send word to our friends in London. Just be advised you will need larger transport this time."

Undene frowned even as his men shifted, muttering.

"Larger? What cargo will we be carrying?"

"Something precious," Harry said. "A woman's life, and my own. Now, let's go somewhere we can talk further about our upcoming visit, and its potential consequences."

CHAPTER TEN

Patience managed to return to the house with no one being the wiser, except Mr. Cuddlestone. The butler let her in the kitchen door, then peered out into the darkness. "Did you see him, miss?"

Patience sighed. "Yes. He said he was on his way to the village to meet with friends."

Mr. Cuddlestone drew back to frown at her. "Friends? What sort of friends could a valet have in Foulness?"

Now Patience frowned. "Valet?"

Mr. Cuddlestone shut the door. "Mr. Teacake. The fellow made short shrift of his work with his master tonight, then disappeared on me. Emma said you were out with the master. I thought you might have seen the miscreant."

"No, sorry," Patience said, plucking at the cloak's clasp. "I seem to be singularly inept at this subterfuge."

"Now, then," the butler said in a commiserating tone. "You're a lady. Why would you do well with all this skulking about? You just leave the matter to Sir Harry. He knows what he's about."

Patience met his gaze, on a level with her own. "And what is he about, Mr. Cuddlestone?"

He blinked, paling. "Why, what he's usually about, of course."

"And that is?" Patience pressed.

The butler raised his head, making him an inch or so

taller though still no higher than her. "I'm sure I couldn't say, Miss Ramsey. Shall I see you to your room?"

"Not unless you can find it in your heart to be more forthcoming," Patience said.

He shifted on his feet, gaze dropping. "I regret that I cannot, miss. But pose your questions to Sir Harry. You're his betrothed. Surely he'll tell you the truth."

If only she was so sure.

She followed the servant's stair back up to the chamber story and slipped into her room, where she found Emma waiting. The maid swallowed a yawn as she helped Patience change.

"I'm sure Sir Harry was glad for your help," she said, bustling about with her usual efficiency. "It can't be easy being alone on the shore, waiting."

Patience turned to give her access to the back of the corset. "Alone on the shore?"

"Yes, miss."

She could feel the stays loosening, but Emma seemed to have run down like a clock in need of winding. As the maid pulled the corset free, Patience turned to meet her gaze.

"What is Harry doing on the shore?"

Emma tsked. "Now, then, I've said too much. Mr. Cuddlestone is always warning me to watch my tongue. *You will say something you oughtn't* he's claimed more than once, and see if he wasn't right." Sweat glistened under the rim of her ruffled cap. "Let's get you into bed, miss. Tomorrow will be a brighter day."

She didn't believe that either.

Still, the bed felt so soft, the covers so warm, she could feel her muscles relaxing. Subterfuge was certainly tiring. However did Harry manage it every day? As weary as she was, she ought to have been fallen asleep immediately. But she found herself lying awake, listening for a footfall in the corridor, a knock at the window. She got up twice to make sure Harry wasn't lying on the balcony, wounded. When she finally fell asleep, it was to frantic dreams in which she searched for something unknown.

The morning wasn't much better. Emma was decidedly tight-lipped as she helped Patience dress, then dashed off to help the other ladies. The maid knew something, Mr. Cuddlestone knew something. Surely, they wouldn't condone an affair or anything illegal. So, what was Harry doing at the shore in the middle of the night? Patience might not be Harry's betrothed, but she very much feared if she didn't learn the truth soon, she'd go mad. She hurried down to the dining room early, hoping for a moment with Harry and found only the butler.

"He returned before midnight," he murmured, pouring her a cup of tea. "Already up and shaving."

He seemed to think this very good news.

Gussie beat Harry to the table. She sailed into the room, waved off Mr. Cuddlestone's offer of toast, and plunked herself down next to Patience. "I have had an inspiration."

As if to prove as much, her eyes were shining, her skin glowing above her purple wool gown. Patience smiled at her. "Oh?"

"Eggs," Gussie said. "They contain all that is needed to nourish a chick. It stands to reason they would nourish skin as well."

Patience dropped her gaze to her tea. "But would any lady apply raw egg to her face?"

"She would if it improved her complexion," Gussie insisted. She rose. "Hurry and finish. I'll be in the laboratory. This might take all day."

"But your guests," Patience protested. "We promised to take them on a drive."

Gussie waved a hand. "Later. I'll ask Meredith to play hostess in our absence. I'm sure she can contrive."

And there went Patience's opportunity to question Harry. Though she tarried as long as she could over breakfast, he did not appear. She finally had to quit the room and go help Gussie.

But her day did not improve in the laboratory. She managed to break shells into Gussie's concoction twice, requiring that they toss it all out and start over. She had to beg more eggs from Cook, who complained about sabotaging the meal plans. And when they had finally successfully added all the ingredients and begun stirring, the noxious fumes made her gag.

"Are you certain this will work?" she asked Gussie. "I can only question the consistency and the appearance."

Gussie frowned as she peered into the pot, then wiped at her watering eyes. "We cannot give up so soon."

Patience dropped the spoon into the liquid. "And it stinks."

Gussie glanced up at her. "Why, Patience, it's not like you to criticize."

Patience sighed. "You're right. Forgive me. But look at it, Gussie. No lady would ever allow that in her house, much less on her face."

"Perhaps if we bring it to a boil," Gussie said, "burn off the more obvious elements." She turned up the flame on the spirit lamp.

Now Patience's eyes were watering. "Please, Gussie, just turn it off," she begged, backing away.

Just in time, too, for the potion gave a mighty burp and splattered itself all over Gussie's gown.

Gussie stuck a finger in the biggest glop and brought it to her nose for a sniff. "Hmm. Not enough gypsum. And I used up my store from town. I shall have to rethink the formulation. Clean that up, will you, Patience? We'll start fresh tomorrow." She hurried out.

Patience eyed the still-bubbling pot. She'd wanted a more purposeful occupation than tending to Lady Carrolton's imagined ills, but pretending an engagement, managing a house party, and cleaning up noxious messes didn't seem like much of an improvement. Still, it had to be done. She rolled up her sleeves and advanced on the pot.

Sometime later, she came out of the laboratory to find the house at sixes and sevens. Gussie, Harry, and all the others were gathered in the entry hall, while Mr. Cuddlestone and Wilkins hurried about with coats and hats.

"Ah, there you are," Gussie said as if she'd somehow misplaced Patience. "It's time for our drive."

Emma came down the stairs, arms full of cloaks and redingotes, and Wilkins began helping the ladies into them.

Harry moved to take the grey material of Patience's cloak from the manservant. "Allow me." He draped the cloak about her. His fingers brushed her neck, and she shivered.

"We won't all fit in our coach," he said, turning to look at the others as if oblivious to her reaction. "I'll take Patience up in the curricle; Gussie can lead the way with the rest of you in the coach."

Patience lifted her head. Her and Harry, alone in the carriage? What a perfect time to question him.

As if determined to thwart her, Lydia latched on to Harry's arm. "I'll come with you and Patience, Harry. I can play chaperone." She giggled.

Harry looked as if he would refuse, but Lydia's brother rubbed his hands together. "Perfect." He offered one arm to Gussie and the other to Meredith. "Shall we?"

Emma had been given charge of Fortune, who looked none too pleased about being left behind until Emma brandished a feather, so there was nothing for it but to venture out onto the drive where the carriages were waiting. It was tight squeeze fitting Lydia onto the bench of the curricle. Harry ended up in the middle with Patience on one side and Lydia on the other. He clucked to his horses, and they followed the larger coach up the drive for the road.

They drove first through the village, with its tiled-roof

cottages and half-timbered meeting hall. Many of the villagers stared as the carriages rolled past, but more than one man tipped his cap, and many of the ladies curtsied. Some of the younger ladies blushed and smiled at Harry, though he manfully ignored them. Patience was almost afraid to see some beauty lean out her window to wave while her husband scowled, but everyone was respectful.

As they came back through, rain began to fall. The hooded curricle kept most of the water at bay, but Patience could feel the cool mist on her cheeks.

"More rain," Lydia said with a sigh, cuddling closer to Harry. "Remember Christmas? The snow was so charming."

Harry turned to Patience. "If you look closely, darling, you can see the promise of spring."

He was right. Daffodils nodded among the greening grass, and she could imagine that grass higher, more golden, while birds darted through a blue sky. Harry's hand would hold hers as they walked through the light.

"Perhaps we should hold our wedding breakfast under the trees," he said as if he shared her vision.

Lydia released him to clap her hands. "Oh, a marvelous idea! When is the wedding, Harry? We asked Patience, but she was being coy." She smiled around him at Patience.

Patience pretended to watch the flowers bowing in the breeze.

"We're waiting on the weather to set a date," Harry said smoothly, taking the curricle around a curve. "But I imagine it will be after the Season starts."

"Oh, good," Lydia said, settling back in the seat. "Then Patience can come to London to visit us. I want to take her to Almack's. Maybe that will force you to attend, Harry."

Harry focused out over the team. "I am not admitted to Almack's, Lydia. Neither is Gussie. Still too close to piracy for the mighty patronesses who hold sway there."

His tone was glib, but she felt the sadness underneath.

Patience laid a hand on his arm. "No vouchers for me either. My family wasn't nearly important enough. We make quite a pair."

Harry met her gaze. "Yes, we do."

How easy to slip into the blue, float in the depths. How easy to let herself believe she was falling in love.

"Look, they're stopping." Lydia pointed ahead.

The road had curved around the top of the hill until they were west of the manor near the slope down to the causeway. Harry drew up alongside the larger coach, where Gussie, Mr. Villers, and Meredith stood staring, but he didn't ask the reason they had stopped. That was readily apparent.

Since the rains had started, the creeks that meandered through the fens had swelled. Now silvery water glinted everywhere. And where the causeway should be was nothing but a pond swirling as rushing streams met a rising tide.

They were trapped on the hill.

"Who's that?" Lydia asked.

On the last bit of dry land on the other side of the causeway, a lone rider sat on his horse. Looking up at the carriages and people on the hill, he seemed to make up his mind. He put heels to flanks and urged his horse forward.

Gussie was shifting on her feet as if she wanted to run down the hill herself. Her voice carried back to Patience. "What is he doing? He'll never make it through."

Before Patience knew what he was about, Harry had wrapped the reins to the brake and leaped down over Lydia, who giggled. Striding to the edge of the hill, he took off his top hat and waved to the rider. "Turn back! Danger!"

"How magnificent," Lydia said, and Patience wasn't sure if she meant Harry or the man below them.

The fellow certainly paid Harry no heed. Though the waves pushed his horse from one side, the creek from the other, he kept his reins high. Harry ran down the hill, looking very much as if he intended to dive in after the fellow. Patience gripped the wood of the curricle to keep from following.

In the end, Harry didn't have to rescue the rider. The horse swam, drifting sideways at times against the current, then broke free onto dry ground and trotted up the hill toward them, Harry jogging alongside. Meredith turned and clambered back into the coach.

As they reached the top, Harry grinned at his aunt. "See who it is, Gussie?"

She waved at the rider. "Julian Mayes! So good of you to join us."

Patience started, and Lydia frowned at her. "Do you know Mr. Mayes, the solicitor?"

Only what she'd heard from Meredith, and nothing good. Small wonder her friend had ducked into the coach.

Harry had no trouble with the newcomer. He clasped the hand the man offered from the saddle. "What brings you out this way, my friend?"

"Why, I heard you were having a house party," the other man said with a laugh.

"Indeed we are," Harry returned, "and I'll introduce you to everyone once we get out of this rain." He waved his aunt and guests back to the carriages.

But Patience couldn't believe Julian Maye's reason for arriving the way he had. He clearly hadn't been invited to the house party. And poor Meredith. Here he was, the man her friend was determined to avoid, and there would be no way for the two of them to escape each other until the waters receded.

Meredith huddled inside the coach, feeling numb. She hardly noticed when Lydia Villers joined them so that Julian might ride with Harry, horse tied behind. It seemed he and Harry were old friends.

And she could not imagine being friendly.

She was just glad Gussie and Lydia kept up an animated conversation on the drive back to the manor. Only Lydia's brother looked at her askance, as if noticing the difference in her, and she steadfastly turned her face to the window.

She excused herself as soon as they entered the manor, retrieving Fortune from where Emma and the cat had been chasing each other about the entry hall. The maid looked surprised by the abrupt movement, but Meredith climbed the stairs and nearly ran for her room. A mew of protest informed her she was holding Fortune far too tightly. Once inside and the door closed, she released her pet and flew to wardrobe. If she took only the essentials, she could send for her trunk later.

She had her nightgown and underthings stored in a bandbox when the door opened, and Patience slipped inside. Shutting the door, she stared at Meredith.

"It's him, your Julian Mayes, isn't it?"

No use denying it. Meredith nodded. "So, you see why I must leave."

"I see why *he* must leave," Patience said, venturing into the room as Fortune came to meet her. "I would not have considered him a gentleman from your description of him, but apparently he and Harry are well acquainted. I understand they went to school together."

"Half the gentlemen in London went to school together," Meredith informed her, tightening the straps on the box. "My bad luck he was in the right half. Where is he now? Can I avoid him on the way to the door?"

Patience bent and scooped up Fortune, then positioned herself between Meredith and the exit. "Since the day we met, you have never backed down from a confrontation, not with Harry, not with Gussie, and not even when we said farewell to Lord and Lady Carrolton. Jane Kimball says it was the same in her situation. Why would you run now?

You've done nothing wrong."

Her stomach knotted. "Not according to some people."

Patience frowned. "But you said he left you when you needed him most."

Meredith felt suddenly tired. Though everything in her urged flight, she sank onto the bed. Patience let Fortune loose, and the cat scampered to the bed and hopped up beside Meredith, where she watched her warily.

"What I told you about Julian Mayes is true, Patience," Meredith admitted. "But there is more to the story. He knew me under another name, when I was another person. Like your parents, mine both died when I was still young. The cousin who inherited the house ordered me gone. I was certain Julian would come for me. We had an understanding." Just remembering made her throat tighten.

"Though I sent him word," she made herself continue, "Julian never came for me. I was forced to accept the offer of an old friend of my father's to serve as companion to his sister. She belittled and berated me for years, made me feel small, miserable."

Patience's face fell, and she moved to sit beside Meredith on the bed. "That was my life with Lady Carrolton."

Meredith nodded. "So I had surmised. I am so very sorry, Patience. No one should have to endure what we did."

Patience lay a hand on hers. "But you survived. You escaped that cruel bondage. You built your own business."

Guilt was stronger than Patience's grip. "Because of her. She died of heart failure, you see, and I learned she had left me a small fortune."

Fortune mewed as if she recognized her name and pressed herself against Meredith's side. She stroked the silky fur as she had so often since those dark days. "I promised myself I would use the money to help others abandoned as I had been."

"And Jane and I are forever in your debt," Patience assured her. "But your story is admirable. Surely Mr. Mayes would agree."

"Not entirely," Meredith said. She swallowed. Might as well tell her all. With Julian here, it was only a matter of time before the story came out.

She met Patience's troubled gaze. "You see, my employer, Lady Winhaven, died in the middle of a tirade directed at me. There are those who say it was my fault, that I purposely drove her to it. That I killed my mistress, and I profited from her death."

CHAPTER ELEVEN

Harry wasn't sure why Patience had bolted for the house the moment he'd stopped the curricle on the drive. She'd been strangely quiet once he'd introduced her to Julian, even though his friend and colleague had kept the conversation light and general. As if he truly did delight in attending the house party. Harry could hardly wait to get Julian alone and find out the real reason for his arrival. Julian Mayes left London only for clients or in the service of the King.

As Gussie shepherded Lydia toward the house, Julian caught his arm. "Show me where to put my horse."

Wilkins would have been happy to take charge of the animal. Julian clearly wanted to talk alone as badly as Harry did.

"Certainly," Harry said agreeably. "We've added a new wing to the stable block since you were here last. I think you'll find the space suitable."

"Allow me to accompany you," Villers said, stepping away from his sister. "I'm always interested in where to house a prime bit of horseflesh."

Harry caught Gussie's eye, and she darted between them. "But my dear Beau, how would Lydia and I get on without a gentleman to escort us?"

Harry turned away to keep from showing his grin at the uncharacteristic statement, but not before he saw equal shock on Villers's face. Still the fellow was enough a slave to Society's rules that he could not gainsay her, and Harry and Julian were able to make their escape.

"Was it this situation with France that brought you out here?" Harry asked as they walked Julian's horse toward the stables. "How did you learn of it? I only spoke to Undene and his men last night and posted the note to Lord Hastings this morning. I can only hope it got through before the causeway closed."

Julian frowned. "What's happened that you must contact Lord Hastings?"

Harry pulled him up short under cover of the big oak. "Yvette de Maupassant has been imprisoned. I intend to rescue her."

Julian whistled. "You don't do it halfway, do you, my lad? You understand the risks."

Harry nodded. "But I can't leave her, Julian. Not after all she's done for England."

"Of course." Julian stood taller as if he'd made a decision. "I'll accompany you. Do you expect others? Trevithan? Laughton?"

"I'm hopeful," Harry admitted, "but they may not reach us in time, particularly with the causeway out. Undene and his men could leave at any time."

Julian started walking again, and Harry fell into step. "That doesn't give me much room to work, then."

Harry eyed him. "If you didn't come at Lord Hastings's request, what brings you to Essex?"

Julian looked sheepish. "I followed Miss Thorn from London, but the weather delayed me. Word was that the causeway was about to wash over. No coachman would chance it. I've been put up in Great Wakering for the last two days, but I decided to see for myself today. When I noticed you all on the other side, I had to try."

Harry shook his head. "You came all this way after Miss Thorn? I can't conceive you were that desperate to hire staff."

"I have no need to hire, I assure you," Julian said. He bowed his head as if studying the soggy ground. "You'll think me mad. At times, I think myself mad. But I believe I knew her years ago. I can't rest until I'm certain. She evaded me in town. When I learned she was heading your way, I had to follow."

They reached the stables and commended Julian's horse to the care of Harry's two grooms, who promised to bring Julian's saddle bags up to the house shortly. They would have their hands full seeing to the other horses and carriages as well.

"I've known you to pursue a winsome wench from time to time," Harry told him as they started back toward the house, "but Miss Thorn does not seem the sort to be interested in a liaison."

"Nor do I wish to offer her one," Julian assured him. "I told you it sounded mad." He lowered his voice as if even the rainy sky would judge him. "I was in love once—top over toes. I set out to make a fortune I could lay at her feet. She disappeared without a trace."

Harry stared at him. For all the years he'd known Julian, he'd never seen him like this. "And her family, her friends knew nothing?"

Julian's voice sounded bitter. "Her mother and father had passed. The cousin who inherited the estate claimed she had run off and good riddance. I asked around the area, but no one knew otherwise. I was not as well connected then, so I had no choice but to give up. And then I happened upon Miss Thorn, helping our old friend Wey with staffing. The duke had known my love and thought Miss Thorn looked familiar. The description, the age, and the similarity in names—my Mary Rose, her Meredith Thorn—was too coincidental. I have been pursuing her ever since."

Harry shook his head. "What we do for love, eh? You're welcome to stay as long as you like, though I can't promise you that Miss Thorn will be receptive."

Julian sighed as he strode across the grass, boots flashing. "What a web. Any other intrigues I should be aware of?"

Harry cast him a glance. "I suspect Beau Villers of spying for France."

Julian started chuckling. "Beauford Villers, the opportunist, forever pushing his pretty sister at men who wouldn't look twice?"

"The same. He's been skulking around the house, asking questions."

Julian's face hardened. "Then turn him in to the War Office. Hastings would love to question him."

"And I'd love to hear the answers. Unfortunately, I have no proof. All I know is that someone shot at me just as Undene and his men hit shore at the last run, and Villers has showed inordinate interest in Gussie's work."

"As an excuse to prolong his stay," Julian guessed.

Harry pulled him into the shelter of the side of the manor, unwilling to share his friend with the others just yet. "Possibly. Patience suspects he intends to steal Gussie's formulation."

This time Julian laughed outright. "Oh, Harry, what an interesting life you lead."

Harry laughed as well. "More than you know. Gussie decided I needed protecting from Lydia Villers, so she told her and her brother that Patience Ramsey and I are engaged."

Julian's brow shot up. "You sly dog. I wondered why the lady kept so close to you. I take it Miss Ramsey agreed to this charade."

Harry rubbed the back of his neck. "After a great deal of persuasion and the offer to relocate her to Bath with income to support herself."

Julian shook his head. "I should hire her. My staff must negotiate on behalf of our clients on a regular basis, and I daresay none of them would have won so much."

Harry grinned. "As I understand it, your Miss Thorn conducted the initial negotiations."

That sobered him. Harry still struggled to see his friend as the romantic, pining away for years for his lost love. Julian had always struck him as clever, determined, and rather cunning.

"So, you are pretending an engagement to track a spy," he said now, tone admiring, "all the while hosting an Easter house party, carrying on your usual activities for the Crown, and planning to travel behind enemy lines on a rescue mission. You're a rather busy fellow."

Harry chuckled again. "Far too busy some days, I promise you. At times, I feel as if I walk the causeway with water threatening on all sides."

"I can imagine. What will you tell them if you and I are gone for two days or more to rescue Lady de Maupassant?"

"Good question," Harry said.

Julian looked thoughtful. "We'll claim I came down this way because I was interested in purchasing property in the area. We went to look at some acreage before the Easter holiday."

A plausible story. "Gussie will play along. No one need suspect anything."

"Not even your Miss Ramsey?" Julian asked.

"Oh, she suspects I'm up to something," Harry said. "I've allowed her to think it was a married lady. So, she already believes the worst of me."

And he could not help the melancholy that stole over him at the thought.

Patience came down from Meredith's room determined to protect her friend. Mr. Mayes might be handsome with his red-gold hair so artfully mussed and those warm brown eyes, his build nearly as muscular as Harry's, but he had clearly let Meredith down. How horridly she'd been treated, and by people who should have cared about her. Small wonder she strived now to prevent other gentlewomen from falling prey to the same circumstances.

Still, Patience could not agree that flight was the answer today.

"Surely you are much changed from the girl he knew," she'd told her friend. "Even though he is a solicitor, he may not have heard about the case with Lady Winhaven."

Meredith shook her head, clutching Fortune closer. "His mentor led the opposition. I barely escaped without seeing jail. Just the thought of facing him unnerves me."

Patience gave her an encouraging smile. "You cannot leave, Meredith. You saw the state of the causeway. Mr. Mayes barely made it across. A carriage would be swept away. If you will not think of your own safety, think of Fortune."

Meredith glanced down at the little grey cat in her lap. Fortune gazed up at her, unblinking.

Meredith squared her shoulders. "Very well. I'll plead a headache tonight, but tomorrow I will go to the village to inquire about a boat."

Patience knew when to give up. "I'll make your excuses."

And do what she could to determine why Julian Mayes had arrived at Foulness Manor now of all times.

Harry and his friend were just entering the house as she came down the stairs. Mr. Cuddlestone appeared to take the newcomer's coat and hat, tsking at their wet state. He caught Patience's eye and jerked his head toward the wall. Perplexed, Patience went to join him.

"There's not another bedchamber available," he whispered. "What am I to do with him?"

She didn't question why he'd ask her. Gussie would have had no answer, and Harry's answer would likely have gotten someone in trouble.

"Move my things in with Miss Thorn," Patience advised him. "Mr. Mayes can have Sir Harry's old room."

He frowned. "But, miss, you're Sir Harry's lady. You should have the better room."

"If I am Sir Harry's lady, I can make decisions about the running of this household," Patience informed him.

With a nod, he went to do as she'd instructed.

Mr. Mayes evinced every desire to change out of his travel gear, but Harry insisted that he greet the other guests first. As they started for the withdrawing room, Patience made a point to walk beside the newcomer.

"It's an unexpected pleasure to have you with us," she told him. "Harry never mentioned you were coming."

"And isn't that just like Harry?" he returned fondly with a look to his friend.

Perhaps. "Are there others we should be expecting?" she asked, glancing at Harry as well. "I am helping Gussie plan for Easter celebrations, so we should know who might be at table."

Harry and Julian exchanged glances. So, they were up to something.

"You never know," Harry said genially. "But at least with Julian here we're almost even numbers at table. He can accompany Meredith."

Not while she lived. "And leave Lydia to be partnered by her brother? How very unkind." She linked arms with Mr. Mayes. "You must further your acquaintance with Miss Villers, sir. I think you'll appreciate her. She has a bright energy."

She felt a slight resistance, but he allowed himself to be dragged forward and introduced to everyone in the withdrawing room.

Gussie popped up and gave him a hug. Lydia giggled as he bowed over her hand, and her brother inclined his head in acknowledgement of his presence.

"And will Miss Thorn be joining us?" Mr. Mayes asked Patience with a winning smile.

"I fear she is unwell," she told the room at large, going

to take a seat near Gussie. "I suspect she'll eat dinner in her room."

"How sad," Lydia said, making a face. "Perhaps I should go keep her company."

"And I can make her a tisane," Gussie offered.

"No need," Patience hurriedly assured them both. "She has Fortune. I'm sure she'll be fine in no time."

"Fortune?" Mr. Mayes asked.

"Her cat," Mr. Villers drawled before Patience could answer. "She's more devoted to it than most engaged couples are to each other." He eyed Harry pointedly.

As if to prove his devotion, Harry started toward Patience, but Mr. Mayes took the chair next to hers. Lydia arranged her creamy skirts to make room for Harry on the sofa. He promptly went to stand beside Patience. Gussie returned to the sofa, and Lydia's face fell. Her brother took up residence beside the hearth.

"Quite the excitement this morning," he said. "Will our newest arrival affect your plans, Harry?"

Plans? Patience glanced his way, but Harry only smiled. "Not that I know of. But Patience is doing most of the planning."

Mr. Mayes aimed his smile her way. "Yes, Miss Ramsey, do tell us what you have planned the next few days. I hope Miss Thorn will be up to joining us. I understand you two came down together. Have you known her long?"

"Long enough to have formed a bond of admiration and loyalty," Patience said.

Lydia clasped her hands in front of her ruffled muslin gown. "How lovely. I must say, I feel as if we've all grown closer these last few days."

"At least some of us," her brother shot back with another look to Harry.

"And some of us never grow at all," Gussie said, scowling at Lydia's brother.

Lydia glanced among them. "Have I missed something?"

Harry stalked to the window. "Nothing important. It seems the rain has stopped for the moment. You'll excuse me while I take a turn in the garden. Lydia, would you care to join me?"

Lydia's eyes widened, but she popped to her feet and rushed to take Harry's arm. Her brother smirked as Harry led her from the room.

"Jackanapes," Gussie muttered. She motioned to Mr. Villers. "Well, don't just stand there, sir. Do your duty and converse politely with your elders."

"Elders, madam?" he said, spreading his coat tails to seat himself beside her. "Why, you could easily pass for Lydia's younger sister."

Mr. Mayes turned away, smile firmly in place. "I hope this illness of your friend's isn't indicative of deeper malady. She is generally well?"

Was that concern she heard? His face betrayed nothing, but then he would not have been a good solicitor if every emotion was written there. "Quite well," she told him.

He nodded. "Excellent. And did I understand she operates an employment agency?"

Was his curiosity indicative of snobbery? Patience raised her chin. "She does indeed, and her clients sing her praises. But what of you, sir? A noted solicitor, I believe?"

He inclined his head. "I have had some success."

"So, you earned your fortune and yet remain unmarried. Has no young lady caught your eye?"

He was silent a moment. Then he shifted, putting his back to the rest of the room and effectively shielding her from all other gazes. His eyes narrowed.

"The lady I loved disappeared with no word to me, and I have been trying to find her ever since. You might mention that to Miss Thorn next time you see her, good friend that you are."

CHAPTER TWELVE

Harry couldn't remember spending such an evening before. His aunt's quiet little house party had developed an undercurrent he could not like. Navigating it was like crossing the Channel the first time, constantly aware of the powerful currents beneath you, the waves around you, the challenges before you. Patience and Julian appeared to be at odds, Miss Thorn refused to come out of her room, Villers's gaze lingered on Harry as if watching for the least sign of weakness, and Lydia stuck to Gussie's side, gazing around at them all in obvious confusion. He was glad to bid everyone goodnight and retire.

He had suggested that Julian share his room, but Cuddlestone had informed him Patience had already seen to the arrangements. A shame. He wouldn't have minded the company. He still could not accustom himself to sleeping in his father's chambers. Cuddlestone had rearranged things on the dresser so that the playing cards were no longer visible, but Harry felt as if his father's presence still hung in the air like smoke, darkening everything it touched. He had lived beneath the cloud all his life. Only friends like Julian, Wey, Carrolton, Worth, and some others of their classmates had been willing to see him as his own person. Many of them were high enough in government circles that they understood what he was doing now. They realized the need and were willing to stand by him as rumors swirled.

But if he could bring Yvette de Maupassant safely to England, he would count the cost cheap indeed. He had never met a woman like her—fearless, determined, so skilled at playing the game of espionage that no one in the Emperor's circle had realized she gathered information for England. Napoleon thought she had thrown off her aristocratic background to embrace the Revolution. Someone must have betrayed her that she was in her cousin's custody now.

And yet, was Patience so very different? Like Yvette, she had been deprived of a family, forced to make her own way. She too had had to smile while people said poisonous things. And she was fiercely loyal to those she cared about. She might not have risked her life in the service of her country, but she had risked her reputation to protect Gussie.

What would it be like to be among the chosen few Patience Ramsey cared about? To have her smile at him, approve of him? To know he had earned her love?

To risk was to live. Somehow, he didn't think his great-grandfather had meant his heart.

With no midnight appointment to keep him up, Harry woke early the next morning. Perhaps that was why he met Patience coming out of Meredith's room. She'd left tendrils of her hair to curl about her cheeks. Sunlight had never looked as pretty.

"How is she?" he asked as she joined him in the corridor.

She glanced at the door. "Better. I may be able to convince her to come down later." Her look met his, troubled. "But Harry, we must talk."

He spread his hands. "Of course. How can I help?"

She opened her mouth, and Gussie trotted out of her room, tugging her gloves into place. "Oh, good," she said, gaze bouncing off Harry and Patience. "You're up. I've told Emma and Cuddlestone to fetch the others in time for services."

Services. It was Sunday. Palm Sunday to be exact. One

week left until Easter, and this house party ended.

He ought to be relieved. But when the house party ended, would Patience Ramsey feel any need to stay?

He shook off the thought as Gussie linked arms with Patience, dragging her toward the stairs, chatting about cockle shells and eucalyptus and other ingredients he found hard to imagine for skin balm. Patience glanced back at him once, and he shrugged. Gussie had ever been a force of nature. There wasn't much he could do until she latched onto something, or someone, else.

Unfortunately, that didn't happen until after services had concluded.

Harry had grown up worshipping in the little stone chapel in Foulness. His great-grandfather had purchased the stained-glass windows that flanked either side of the center aisle, the gilded cross over the altar, and the gold communion and offering plates. On one of his worst days, his father had asked the vicar to return the plates so he might sell them at auction. Harry would not have been surprised to learn the offering plates have been lighter after passing the man. Through investments Julian had suggested, Harry had begun rebuilding the family coffers, but it would be some time before he could do more than tithe.

His family had its own pew near the front. With Meredith remaining at the manor, Harry and his guests just filled the polished walnut bench. Behind them sat people he'd known all his life—Mr. Potter the merchant; the Abermarle family, all fishers; Lacy and Undene and others. The blacksmith caught his eye and shook his head. Not tonight then. Disappointment was sharp.

The vicar came to take Harry's hand at the end of service. A short, stout fellow with a heavy jowl, he beamed at Patience. "And this must be the young lady I've heard so much about. We must schedule those nuptials. Of course, you'll want to be married here at St. Mary's. When shall I start the banns?"

Patience looked to Harry.

"After Easter, I think," Harry said. "I'll send the particulars."

"Excellent." The vicar returned his gaze to Patience. "Sir Harold is such a busy fellow. I know you will want to continue the family tradition of supporting the church."

Patience's smile was all encouragement, but it quickly faded as the man moved on to greet other members of the congregation.

"Now I've lied to the vicar," she murmured as they started out of the church after the others.

"Technically, I lied," Harry pointed out. "Terrible habit. As my bride-to-be, I hope you can break me of it."

"So do I," she said darkly.

As they came out the door into the rain, Undene bumped into Harry.

"Tuesday," he muttered as he bowed.

Patience watched him hurry away. "Did he say Tuesday?"

"Did he?" Harry took her arm and steered her toward the waiting coach. "I thought he was apologizing."

And he only wanted to apologize to Patience, for lying to her once again.

Tuesday. The word kept echoing in Patience's mind as they drove back to the manor. The big fellow who had bumped into Harry had said the word as if it had a particular meaning. Perhaps he was one of Harry's unsuitable friends, setting up their next meeting. She should be relieved for this evidence of the truth of his tale, but she could not shake the feeling that more was involved.

At least the services had been pleasant. The church was warm, cozy. The members of the congregation had, on the whole, gazed at Harry and his friends with respect, admiration, and a little awe. Oh, the few times she'd glanced around during service she'd seen a frown or two aimed their way, always on the face of one matron or another, but most people had not been dismayed to find the scandalous Sir Harold Orwell in their midst. He was so easily accepted that she could believe he was a regular fixture. How did that jive with the wicked nature he claimed?

If only she could find an opportunity to question him. Harry's guests certainly required a great deal of his attention, especially when he might be expected to spend time alone with the woman he intended to marry. As it was, Lydia's brother carried him off to the game room on their return, and Patience barely escaped a stint in the laboratory by requesting time to check on Meredith. Lydia agreed to go to work in her stead, promising to wear an apron. With misgivings, Patience went to see her friend.

As she had expected, Meredith had had no trouble sharing the room. The bed had been plenty big enough for the two of them, though Fortune's purr had lulled them to sleep, and Patience had woken several times in the night as a furry body repositioned itself between them. Fortune scampered to greet her now, entwining herself around Patience's ankles. She bent and petted the cat a moment before going to where Meredith sat by the fire, book open in her lap.

"You aren't dressed for travel," Patience commented. "I take that as a good sign."

Meredith shut the book. "You were quite right. It was a momentary panic. I have nothing of which to be ashamed. I shall brazen it out."

"Good for you," Patience said with a smile.

Meredith set the book aside and rose. "At least until the causeway opens. Any news there?"

Patience shook her head. "The vicar asked for prayers for their deliverance. I take it they expect it to remain closed for several more days. You can go north to the River Roach, I gather, but even it's too swollen for the ferry."

Meredith sighed. "Then there's no hope for it. I shall simply have to ignore him."

Patience wasn't sure that was possible, but she decided not to argue. "Very well, then. Gather up Fortune. We will descend the stairs and beard the lion in his den."

One more game of billiards, and Harry thought he would begin shredding the green baize of the table. Yet Villers showed no sign of ceasing, perhaps because he had won the last two games, one each against Julian and Harry.

"What say we make this interesting?" he asked as he racked up the balls for another round. "A hundred pounds for the winner?"

"Gussie will throw you out in the rain," Harry informed him. "No gambling in this house."

Villers glanced up with a frown. "When did she institute that rule?"

Since his father had died, not that it was any of the man's business. Harry turned to Julian. "Is it still raining, by the way?"

"Afraid so," Julian said, leaning on his stick. "But that never stopped me from riding."

Villers's hands stilled. "Riding? I'll join you."

Julian glanced at Harry. "Delightful."

The other man abandoned the game. "Give me a moment to change. That lazy valet is never to be found when I need him, begging your pardon, Harry."

Harry shrugged. "It's no trouble. We'll meet in the stables at half past."

Villers headed for the stairs, but Julian moved more slowly, twisting to peer in the withdrawing room as they passed. What he saw made him stop so quickly Harry nearly ran into him. Following his gaze, Harry could see why the fellow was frozen in place.

Patience and Meredith were seated at the card table,

playing the two-handed game cassino by the look of things. He thought her friend might jump up and run at the light that flared in Julian's eyes as he approached them, but she kept her gaze on her cards, calming laying down an ace of spades to win the ace from the four cards face up in the center of the table. Cuddlestone did not look the least contrite to be found watching over them instead of his master.

"And what have you two been up to?" Patience asked, setting down a ten of diamonds to capture two more of the center cards.

"We thought to go riding," Harry said.

"In the rain?" She tsked.

"It's not bad," Julian said, far too eagerly. "You're welcome to join us."

Meredith said not a word, calmly playing her cards, though the cat in her lap peered at Harry around the pasteboard.

"Thank you, but no," Patience said, playing a card. "But perhaps you should ride down to the causeway and see how high the water has risen. That might tell you how soon you can leave, Mr. Mayes."

Harry flinched at the blunt statement. Meredith captured the last card on the table, and Patience dealt four more.

"I have no intention of leaving," Julian assured them both. "For the moment I am content to bask in your presence. Miss Thorn, I am delighted to make your acquaintance at last."

Still the woman refused to meet his gaze, studying her cards while her other hand rested on the cat in her lap. Fortune, however, had no trouble watching Julian, copper eyes inscrutable. Remembering what Patience had said about the cat, Harry waited to see whether Julian would meet with approval.

That he had not met with her mistress' approval was readily apparent by the chill in Meredith's voice. "Mr.

Mayes," she acknowledged at last. "Your play, Patience."

Patience lay a ten of hearts on the table and scooped up the four cards she had just dealt.

"Ah," Julian said. "You know what they say, Miss Thorn. Unlucky at cards…"

"Cease playing," she said, completely ignoring the usual ending of the saying: *lucky at love*. She smiled at Patience. "I admit myself defeated, my dear. If the rain truly is light, perhaps a constitutional?"

Patience gathered up the cards and rose. "Delighted. Give me a moment to speak to Harry first. Mr. Cuddlestone, would you be so kind as to find our things?"

"Assuredly, miss." The butler hurried out without so much as a glance in Harry's direction.

"Perhaps I might join you," Julian said to Miss Thorn, a bit like an eager pup.

"We wouldn't dream of troubling you," Miss Thorn said, rising and turning her back on him.

Pain darted across Julian's face, but he bowed as she strolled past him. As Patience moved to Harry's side, Fortune leaped from her mistress's arms to the carpet and advanced on Julian.

He smiled. "What a handsome animal." He started to bend.

Meredith whirled and scooped up her pet. "Don't!"

Julian straightened. "Forgive me. Is she easily frightened?"

"Never." Meredith held Fortune close. "She is merely terse with those she does not like. And she most certainly will not like you." Turning once more, she strode from the room.

Julian watched her for a moment. "If you'll excuse me." Without waiting for an answer, he took the door to the entry hall.

"That was interesting," Harry said with a shake of his head.

Patience sighed. "I fear hearts once wounded take time

to heal, particularly when neither is sure of the enemy."

"Unsure? It seems clear to me," Harry said. "He claims she disappeared with no word to him, despite an understanding between them."

"Does he indeed?" And he'd thought Meredith's tone cold. "Well, she claims he left her in her time of need, despite her requests for help."

Julian could be too focused on his own goals, but surely he would have come to her aid if he'd known she'd needed him. "Perhaps they should talk it out," Harry said, glancing after them.

She sighed. "I suspect even if we could convince them to talk, the tale is too complicated to resolve easily. Once trust is lost, it is impossible to regain."

Harry frowned. "Impossible? Surely if they still care for each other they can overcome."

"Perhaps," she said, and the word held a world of doubt. "But that isn't why I wished to speak to you in any event. I feel as if you're keeping something from me, Harry."

Once again, he should make some offhand remark about the lady waiting for him in the village. Only there was no lady. And he could not confide in Patience, not until he knew Yvette was safe.

He spread his hands. "A gentleman must keep his own council, alas."

"I see," she said. "May I remind you that we are supposed to be betrothed?"

He made himself shrug. "Well, perhaps if we really were betrothed…"

Her eyes narrowed. "There is no perhaps about it. When a gentleman asks a lady to marry him, he is offering to join their lives, all of their lives. I believe the vows include *in sickness and in health, for richer and for poorer.*"

Guilt tugged at him. "I agree that a marriage requires such a union to be successful. But we are only pretending."

"Yet I still require you to confide in me," she argued. "The

NEVER BORROW A BARONET   133

others have expectations. They imagine I know your plans, your mind, your heart. When I cannot respond adequately, their suspicions grow. Give me something, Harry."

He'd like to give her everything. "You ask a great deal."

Her gaze softened. "As do you. Because of this charade, I will have to change my entire life, move away from everyone and everything I've ever known. You asked me to undertake this ruse because of danger to you and Gussie. You appear to be salvaging your reputation. Lydia isn't a danger to you. I'm convinced something else is. At the very least, you owe me an explanation as to why you really wanted me to pose as your betrothed. In short, Sir Harry, I refuse to continue to lie for you unless I know the whole of it. What are you up to?"

CHAPTER THIRTEEN

There, Patience had said it. Jane and Meredith would be proud of her. By the light in Harry's eyes, he was both surprised and not a little impressed. Still, she half expected another charming lie to glide from his lips.

"Can you not believe me when I say that what I'm doing is important?" he asked.

Patience shook her head. "No. You have gone out of your way to play the wolf, sir. If you wish me to see you as a lamb instead, you will have to offer me the truth."

He chuckled. "I would never claim to be a lamb. A ram perhaps."

"Or a mule?" Patience suggested sweetly.

He chuckled again. "An apt comparison. Gussie would surely agree." He sighed. "Very well, Patience. You have earned the truth. I cannot tell you all—too many others and too much are at stake. But I will tell you this. I work with a band of smugglers to transmit information to and from friends in France. Gussie knows about it, as does Julian. He has been instrumental in finding funds and connections when needed."

Patience stared at him. "You're a spy?"

"Shh!" Harry took a step closer, gaze drilling down into hers. "I support the war effort like every good Englishman."

He was so fervent. Could she believe him? He must know how romantic the story sounded—the dark of night, secret messages, a world at risk. Who would she ask to confirm it? Julian Mayes was no more trustworthy, if Meredith's experience with him was any indication. Yet the tale made so many pieces of the puzzle fit together—his need to be out at night, his secrecy, Cuddlestone and Emma's cryptic remarks, his visits to the village. It even made sense of the burly fellow's comment after services.

"Tuesday," she said. "The smugglers are sailing or returning then."

He nodded. "They sail for France, and this time Julian and I are going with them."

Cold trickled down her back. "Why must you go? Surely it's dangerous for an English gentleman to be found on French soil."

He shrugged as if the matter did not concern him, and she wanted to shake him out of his complacency.

"A necessary evil," he said. "My key informant, a lady of the former aristocracy, has been imprisoned. Julian and I are going over to rescue her."

A lady needing succor, just like in the novels Lady Lilith had favored. A shame Patience had never had a gentleman ride to her rescue. Or sail, as the case would be. Still, it was such an easy story. For all she knew, it had been designed to keep her from asking difficult questions. She ought to denounce him for a liar, yet she would rather believe him in league with smugglers and spies than chasing after some married woman.

She gasped. "Your wound! There was no jealous husband, was there?"

As if she had reminded him of his injury, he rubbed his arm. "No. I was shot helping the smugglers come ashore."

She stared at him. "In England? But that makes no sense. Why would anyone on this side of the Channel want to shoot at you?"

"That," he said, gaze darkening, "is what I want to know."

Patience shook her head. "Beau Villers. It must have been.

I told you he was poking his nose where he shouldn't. I thought he was after Gussie's work, but it's clear your work is more important. We must stop him before he causes any damage."

She must have moved, for Harry caught her hands as if to keep her in place. "I suspect him as well, but you cannot accost him without proof."

She snapped a nod in agreement. "Then let's find proof."

Harry peered closer. "Fearless, are you? Good. Dealing with this mess will take a level of courage. But it's dangerous, Patience. I would not see you harmed."

She would not allow him to shield her. If he could work for England, so could she.

How extraordinary. All this time she had wished she could be as bold and brave as Jane. It seemed she'd merely needed a patriotic reason. Or perhaps the urging of her heart.

"I won't be harmed," she told him, "not if we continue playing our parts. I think I should be miffed at you."

Harry released her. "But I explained…"

"No, no, not *at* you." She could not stand still, not when so many thoughts crowded her mind. Was that why Gussie was always in motion? Regardless, she pulled from his grip and paced to the hearth and back. "I think I know how to catch Mr. Villers. He's already hinted he knows things about you. I should pretend to be miffed that you are not paying me sufficient attention. If it appears we are at odds, he may reach out to me. Then we will know him for a spy."

He shook his head. "That isn't proof, Patience. I need to catch him in the act."

In the act? Actually shooting at Harry? She didn't like that idea. There must be some other approach.

"Very well," she said. "Tell me what to say to him to trap him. If I dangle a carrot, and he attempts to take a bite, won't that give you enough to have him arrested?"

"At least detained." Now he paced to the window and

back, reminding her of his aunt at her finest. He was shaking his head again as he returned to her side. "No, it's too dangerous."

Patience put her hand on his arm. "Harry, for years I've dreamed of doing something more important than wiping noses and fetching smelling salts. I came here in the hopes of having a purpose. Let me do this, for you and for England."

How could he refuse? Patience's sweet face was turned up to his, every inch of her trembling with eagerness to help, and longing radiated out of her like sunlight.

He knew the feeling.

"Very well," he said, and her beaming smile tugged at his heart. "If Villers approaches you, tell him I've been going out at night, and you suspect I'll go again tonight. Say you've seen me from your window, heading for the shore. Julian and I will be waiting for him."

She nodded. "I'll do it. And thank you, Harry, for trusting me with your secret. I won't let you down."

How extraordinary. All his life, everyone but Gussie and his friends had expected the worst of him. If he received anything less than top marks in school, the dons would shake their heads and mutter, "Like father, like son." If he scored the best of all his classmates, a teacher would take him aside to demand to know how he'd cheated. That Patience believed in him now was a precious gift. She could not know how much he treasured it.

And her.

He shook his head as she hurried to the door. He must go carefully. His current situation prevented him from pursuing a lady in earnest. Rather ironic since the *ton* suspected he was pursuing any number of ladies. And what made him think, even if the war was over, a lady like Patience would ever want to align herself with a house so tarnished by scandal? She might have been forced into the role of companion, but her intelligence and beauty should attract a number of suitors once she reached Bath. She could do better than him.

He could only marvel at how well she played her part when their guests regrouped that afternoon. She and Meredith had taken a long walk down to the causeway and returned to report that the waters were still high. At least the rains had stopped for the moment. She'd asked Cuddlestone to set up lawn bowling, which made Lydia squeal with delight while Gussie kept glancing longingly back toward her laboratory. Meredith promptly declined, watching from the edge of the lawn, Fortune in her arms like a shield.

Villers, however, protested outright. "You cannot expect the gentlemen to agree to such prosaic pastimes," he told Patience, eyeing the little pins sticking up out of the damp grass. He turned to Julian and Harry, rubbing his hands together. "What about something more manly—displays of pugilistic prowess, feats of fencing?"

Lydia beamed at them all. "I learned to fence. I'd be delighted to try my hand."

Her brother rounded on her. "Your play bouts with Father hardly qualify. You would only do yourself a discredit."

Lydia's face fell, but Patience put an arm around her shoulders. "Your brother is right, I fear. We wouldn't want you to defeat the gentlemen, Lydia. It might wound their male consequence. We can't have that."

"Certainly not," Villers said, then he frowned as if realizing he'd been insulted.

Harry stepped closer. "I've practice foils in the house. Cuddlestone, if you'd be so kind?"

His butler toddled off.

"In the meantime," Julian said, starting to remove his jacket, "I'll take you up on that display of pugilism, Villers." He glanced back toward Meredith. "It couldn't hurt."

Lydia was gaping at his shirtsleeves. Patience tugged on her arm and drew her back from the two men. She and Lydia aligned themselves with Meredith. They all looked a bit miffed, and Harry was a little afraid it was not act, despite his conversation with Patience. Perhaps it would be better if he stayed with the gentlemen.

Gussie stepped between the two would-be opponents. "I want a fair fight, gentlemen. No hair pulling, eye gouging, or toe stomping. And if you spit, pray aim for the gravel instead of my daffodils."

Villers stared at her, but Julian saluted. "Aye, aye, Captain Gussie."

With a nod of satisfaction, she stepped back.

Villers pulled off his coat as well, handing it to Wilkins to hold, and he and Julian squared off.

"I'll go easy on you," he promised, circling the more muscular Julian, fists up and at the ready. "After all, the ladies are watching."

"Indeed they are," Julian said, and he laid the fellow out with a single punch to the chin.

"Oh, a mighty blow!" Gussie caroled as Harry fought a grin and Julian offered his hand to help the man up.

Villers sat with one arm braced behind him on the grass, rubbing his chin with the other hand. "Rather unsportsmanlike to strike a fellow before he's ready," he complained. "But if that's how you prefer it." He surged to his feet, wrapped his arms around Julian, and slung him to the ground.

Harry was moving before cries of alarm echoed from the ladies.

"Easy lads," he said, grabbing Villers's waistcoat to haul him off Julian. "This was supposed to be a friendly match, remember? What will the ladies think?"

"I am highly amused," Gussie assured him.

A glance toward the group at the edge of the lawn proved the others more concerned than amused. Meredith was white, Lydia had her hands clasped in front of her bosom, and Patience was glaring, but at the poor display or Harry, he wasn't sure.

Villers righted himself and straightened his mangled cravat, dark patches on his clothes attesting to his impact with the ground. "Yes, we must consider the ladies' tender sensibilities, eh, Mayes?"

Gussie snorted.

Julian gathered his composure and inclined his head, but Harry would not have liked such a look directed at him. "As you say."

Thankfully, Cuddlestone and Wilkins arrived just then with the practice swords. Each tip was baited with cork, the blades dulled. Neither of Harry's guests would be able to hurt another with them. As if Gussie knew it, she sighed and wandered up to join the other ladies.

Villers accepted one and sliced it through the air as if testing it. "What do you say, Harry? Care to have a go?"

Harry's gaze darted to Patience. Was she looking more interested now that he might take part? He offered her a smile, and she smiled back. Then she started as if remembering she was supposed to be at odds with him and put her nose in the air.

"Your servant, sir," Harry said. He pulled off his coat, handed it to Wilkins, selected one of the blades, and assumed the stance. Julian, Cuddlestone, and Wilkins drew back to give him and Villers room.

His opponent balanced on his feet, eyeing Harry. "I don't believe I've seen you at D'Angelo's."

For the very reason Harry knew he'd never be welcome at the famous fencing salon in London. "I had a private tutor."

"Ah, and did he teach you this?" Villers sprang at him, blade extended.

Harry parried. "Yes, actually. And this." He riposted, and steel rang on steel as his opponent blocked.

"Very nice." He circled to the right, and Harry followed him, keeping his sword up. Once more Villers lunged, and Harry positioned himself to block the blow.

It never came. Villers twisted and rammed the baited tip into Harry's upper arm.

Pain shot through him, and his blade tumbled to the ground. The heat through his sleeve told him the wound had reopened.

"Harry!" Patience's cry rang behind him even as Villers's eyes widened. His grin said he knew he'd scored in more ways than one.

But how had he known exactly where to strike to do the most damage, to Harry's arm and his reputation?

CHAPTER FOURTEEN

Patience ran down the lawn, skirts bunched in her fists. How dare that puffed up braggart strike Harry! Even from this distance she could see the red seeping through the muslin of his shirt. The blow had reopened the wound, and Harry had to be in pain. She had promised to tease out Beau Villers's secrets, which meant she ought to be sweet to him, but at the moment she wanted to order him from the estate.

Mr. Mayes was regarding the blade Harry had dropped. "I thought these were dulled." His eyes narrowed as he glanced up at Mr. Villers.

Their opponent held up his hands, blade still in one of them. "I only used the weapon I was given."

"Don't concern yourselves," Harry said with maddening calm. "It's an old wound. I should have realized exertion might open it."

"Indeed," Patience said primly, seething inside. "That is quite enough, gentlemen. I would have insisted you play cards this afternoon if I had had any inkling you were bent on bruising and bloodying each other."

Mr. Mayes and Mr. Villers had the good sense to look abashed. She was just glad Harry allowed her to lead him away, Mr. Cuddlestone scurrying after.

"There is a jar of ointment on the dresser in my room," Patience told the butler. "Will you fetch it, a basin of water, a wash cloth, and some sort of bandage?"

"A cravat will do," Harry put in. "And I could do with a fresh shirt as well."

Mr. Cuddlestone scowled at him before turning to Patience with a more diffident look. "Of course, Miss Ramsey. Might I suggest you perform the operation in the laboratory?"

She would rather have cleaned the wound in her bedchamber, as she had before, but even with their pretend engagement that wasn't wise. Reluctantly, she led Harry to the back of the house.

"And don't touch anything," she instructed, getting him settled on the tall stool Gussie favored. "Gussie and Lydia have been experimenting, and it wouldn't surprise me if the results didn't turn your skin green. Not that you don't deserve it."

"As Julian noted," he replied, removing his cravat with one hand, "the weapons were baited and dulled. They should not have been able to hurt anyone."

"So you say." She took the cravat from him and draped it over one arm to keep it away from the potions around them. "Open your shirt, if you please, so I can see the extent of the damage."

He grinned at her. "Haven't we done this before?"

"Why do I fear we will do it again?" Patience countered.

With a chuckle, he pulled the shirt down over one shoulder.

And her breath caught. Why did the sight of that smooth skin, the ripple of muscle beneath it, affect her more now than the night they'd met? She forced herself to study the wound.

"It's not bad," she told him. "It had already been scabbing over. The blow just broke it open."

The door opened to admit Mr. Cuddlestone, arms laden. "The items you requested, Miss Ramsey." He took in the state of Harry's undress and blushed for her. "Perhaps I should take things from here."

"Perhaps you should," Patience said. "Clean the wound, apply enough ointment to cover it, and wrap it tightly."

Nodding, the butler moved in next to Harry.

Harry caught her hand as she drew back. "Thank you."

Oh, but she could sink into that warm gaze, allow herself to be admired, loved.

No, not loved. He hadn't offered that, except as part of a play for the benefit of the enemy.

She pulled away. "You're welcome. Now, I must return to the others. I'd like a word with Mr. Villers."

As if he thought the fellow was in for a scold, Mr. Cuddlestone grinned, then schooled his face. Harry appeared to have taken her true meaning, but he didn't like it. His handsome face tightened, his eyes darkened. Still, he must know it was for the best that she follow through on their plan. He inclined his head, and she hurried from the room before she changed her mind.

She found the others in the withdrawing room. Mr. Mayes had apparently attempted to speak to Meredith, for she had linked arms with a startled Lydia and refused to be moved while Fortune prowled around her feet as if for protection. Gussie was nowhere in sight, and Patience could only hope she had not caught Harry in the laboratory and dosed him with something vile.

Lydia's brother was standing by the hearth, booted foot tapping against the stone as if he were already bored. Making sure none of her distaste showed on her face, she moved to join him.

"Come to berate me for abusing your intended?" he surmised, straightening away from the fire.

"No, indeed," Patience said. "He deserved exactly what he was given. You commented yourself how easily he defects from my side. I find myself much put out with him."

Her frustration must have made her convincing, for he

made a sad face. "I can only agree with you, my dear. You deserve better. But what, exactly, has Harry done to earn your wrath?"

Was he trying to commiserate or attempting to learn more about Harry's actions? Either way, this was her chance. She lowered her voice and leaned closer. "I fear he has made a liaison. He leaves the house at night. I've seen him from my window, heading for the shore. Who else would he be meeting except another woman?"

He put his hand on her arm. "Now, now. What lady could hold a candle to you? If you'd like, I could follow him, see what he's truly up to. That might allay your concerns."

She lay her hand over his. "Oh, Beau, would you?"

"Villers." Harry's voice cracked through the room. Lydia's brother straightened and stepped back from Patience. Harry strode to their sides. Though Cuddlestone must have retied his cravat, and Harry had pulled his coat back on, color lined his cheekbones, and his eyes were slits of sapphire.

"What do you think you're doing?" he demanded.

"Comforting a lady," Mr. Villers returned. "Which is, apparently, more than I can say for you. You, sir, are a poor groom."

Even though she knew this was part of the play, her cheeks felt hot as all other conversation ceased, and everyone looked their way.

"Am I?" Harry asked. "Well, perhaps I should rectify that."

Before Patience knew what he was about, he pulled her into his arms and kissed her.

Sensations exploded around her, inside her. Warmth, delight, pleasure, exhilaration. She was no longer sure where she was, what she had been doing. All she knew was that, in Harry's embrace, she felt truly alive.

And that was more dangerous than Beau Villers could ever be.

Despite his reputation, Harry hadn't kissed all that many ladies. Still, he had always enjoyed the act. Nothing like a quick kiss from a pretty lass to make a fellow feel spritely.

Only kissing Patience didn't make him feel more alert. He would have called his feelings tender, protective. He wanted to hold her close, whisper words of admiration against her lips. He wanted to cherish her, his treasure, his love.

He broke away and stared at her. His love? What was wrong with him? Had he been playing a part for so long he'd forgotten who he really was, what he was doing?

Her eyes had been closed, honey-colored lashes brushing her creamy skin. Now they opened, and she gazed at him with something akin to awe. His cheeks felt hot. Blushing? The scandalous Sir Harry Orwell?

She sucked in a breath, gathered her skirts, and fled.

Villers started after her. Harry stuck out an arm. "Don't," he said, meeting the upstart's gaze, "put yourself between me and Patience."

Brows raised, Villers stepped back, and Harry turned and went to find her.

He located her in the entry hall, facing the wall near the suit of armor his great-grandfather had purportedly claimed belonged to the family instead of being purchased from a wily antiquities dealer. She was standing quite still, as if absorbed in studying the contraption, which even now was rusting in the salty sea air. As Harry came up beside her, he heard her suck in a breath. Her cheeks were still pink, a color almost as deep as the shade of her lips, and he could not look at her without remembering how soft her lips had felt against his, how easily she'd responded.

"That was very good," she said, gaze on the armor.

For an insane moment, he thought she meant his kiss, and he nearly preened.

"You appeared quite the scoundrel," she continued, "seizing me in full view of the others." She turned at last, met his gaze. "That was your aim, was it not? To further the ruse?"

Ridiculous to tell her the truth, that he had not liked the way Villers had looked at her and had been determined to protect her. That his heart had overruled his head and still fought for supremacy.

"Of course," he said. "Did you have an opportunity to speak to him about the shore?"

She nodded. She seemed to be standing a little taller, as if as determined as he was to master the emotions the kiss had engendered. "Yes. I mentioned my concern about your disappearances, and he offered to follow you for me."

Harry smiled. "Perfect. Julian and I will be waiting. Thank you, Patience. You need not feel obliged to continue playing the aggrieved lover."

She frowned, brows gathering over her pert nose. "But we cannot retire from the field. We must make sure he sees I have a reason for my concerns. I think you should do something scandalous this evening."

Harry quirked a brow. "Strip to my small clothes and dance around the withdrawing room, perhaps? Or will drinking myself under the table suffice?"

By the way her lips tightened, she was fighting a smile. And there he went looking at her lips again!

"Neither, thank you," she said. "But you might flirt with Meredith and Lydia, just to prove you are not entirely devoted to me."

Who was she hoping to convince, the others or herself? He certainly needed a little convincing in that area. "Very well. I'll flirt with Lydia. I doubt she'll be in the least affected. And I fear neither Meredith nor Julian will approve of me approaching your friend. Fortune might even withdraw her approval should I trouble her mistress."

She pressed a hand to her chest. "Well, we can't have that.

Just be careful, Harry. This all sounds rather dangerous."
She shivered, but he had the impression it was more for
show. Excusing herself, she hurried up the stairs to freshen
up before dinner. Such a lithe form, light, graceful, like
sunlight dancing through the curtains on a cold winter's
day. He watched until she disappeared around the corner
of the landing.

Oh, but he had it bad, and to what effect? He was in
no position to offer a wife anything of worth. And, unlike
his forefathers, he refused to offer Patience something less
than marriage. She deserved the best. If only there was a
way to be that sort of man.

He turned to find Gussie watching him from the
doorway to her laboratory.

"What do you think you're doing?" she demanded,
striding to his side.

Harry affixed a smile to his face. "Why, nothing, Aunt."

She shook her head. "That tone never worked on me,
and you know it. I could hear the raised voices from my
laboratory. What happened?"

Harry shrugged. "Just a quick kiss. Nothing momentous."
Even though it felt rather earth-shaking.

Gussie put her hands on her hips. "Just a kiss, a private
conversation. From what I can see, you are disturbing my
assistant. I thought you and Patience had an understanding."

So did everyone else. "It is perhaps more complicated
than that," he said.

She narrowed her eyes at him. "Why is that the answer
to most questions about you?"

He shrugged.

Gussie lay a hand on his arm. "Be careful, Harry. Don't
lose yourself in the game. I raised you to be better than
our ancestors."

He stiffened, and her hand fell. "I assure you, madam, I
am not my father. Now, excuse me. I need to change for
dinner."

He was just glad she did not call him back.

He was positioned at the hearth, impeccable in his evening black, when Villers and his sister entered. He strode across the room as if drawn to her side.

"My dear Lydia, that color becomes you," he said, taking her hand and bringing it to his lips.

She blushed prettily, cheeks as pink as her evening gown, while her brother regarded him coolly.

"Allow me to steal you away a moment," Harry said.

Villers did not protest as Harry led her to the hearth.

"How can I help you, Harry?" she asked, looking up at him through her golden lashes.

Harry kept her hand tucked in his arm. "Must I need help to request a moment of your time?"

She fluttered her lashes. "You don't generally approach me voluntarily. I've noticed. I warn you, if you intend to ask me to intercede for you with Patience, I fear she won't believe me."

"And why would I need you to intercede for me with Patience?" he asked, bending closer. "I am all innocence, I assure you."

Her lips curved up. Funny how they held no appeal. "Beau would have it otherwise. He was encouraging me to accept you if you offered, to encourage you to offer even. But he seems to have changed his mind."

He knew her brother wasn't being thoughtful of the so-called engagement to Patience. "And why would he do that?" he murmured.

Her eyes widened. "Why, because you are besotted, of course. It's quite evident, sir. You love Patience Ramsey."

He could not allow her to be correct. "We have an agreement. Marriage would benefit us both."

She cocked her head, firelight setting the silver bobs at her ears to sparkling. "I see the advantages for her. It is the same as what Beau wanted for me. Marry you, and she becomes Lady Orwell. But she has even less fortune and family name than I have. What do you gain?"

Love. Companionship. Someone who believed in him, despite what others said. Someone who would help him become the man he wanted to be. But he could say none of that aloud. He was afraid how much he was coming to want it.

"I gain a biddable wife," he replied, "willing to overlook my peccadillos."

She giggled. "Oh, Harry, I doubt that's Patience. She coats her criticism with honey, but she's no milk-and-water miss. She'll argue with you."

Harry chuckled. "She might at that. Frequently."

Lydia smiled. "Not too frequently, I think. By the ways she looks at you, she loves you too."

Hope surged up. As if she saw it, Lydia laughed again as she patted his arm. "It's all right, Harry. Love can be very pleasant, I hear. You should enjoy it. Now, if you'll excuse me, I want to talk to Gussie about that latest preparation. I think we should add strawberries." Mouth wiggling as if she chewed on the idea, she wandered off.

Harry turned to find Patience standing in the doorway. The yearning on her face cut through him. She'd told him to flirt with Lydia. Did she regret it now?

Was Lydia right, and Patience felt something for him after all?

CHAPTER FIFTEEN

Why was it so painful to see Harry with Lydia? Even though the girl had joined Gussie on the other side of the room, the picture of her with Harry, heads together, Lydia's lashes fluttering, had seared itself into Patience's mind. She'd been the one to suggest the assignation. She should not have such regrets now. She made herself smile and went to engage Mr. Mayes in conversation. At least that was useful. It kept him away from Meredith, who had latched onto Lydia's brother, much to the fellow's consternation.

Somehow, Patience made it through dinner. Though she was seated to Harry's left as his betrothed, she spent most of the meal conversing with Julian Mayes on her other side. She was supposed to be angry with Harry, after all. She must play the aggrieved betrothed until Harry had caught Mr. Villers or proven his innocence. To her surprise, Mr. Mayes was pleasant, even witty. But then again, scoundrels should be good at that sort of thing.

After dinner, she partnered Meredith on a game of whist with Gussie and Lydia. The three men stood apart, eyeing each other. A shame her ruse prevented her from intervening. She accompanied Meredith to the bedchambers early as if just as loath to remain in their company.

Her friend looked weary, her steps slow as they approached the room they now shared. Even her fashionable purple skirts seemed to sag. Patience felt for her.

"Mr. Mayes shows no sign of giving up his pursuit," she ventured. "Perhaps if you spoke to him…"

"Never," Meredith vowed. She swept into the room and bent to see to Fortune as if dismissing Patience as well.

Patience sighed. So many hopes for romance, from Lydia, from her brother, from Julian Mayes, and from her, and none likely to come true.

After Emma helped her and Meredith change for bed, Patience turned down the lamp and sat by the window for a while, gazing out at the darkness. She'd claimed to have seen Harry from her window, but in truth she could see little with clouds covering the moon. Were Harry and his friend lying in wait for Lydia's brother? Had the fellow been caught? Had he confessed some dark secret for following Harry? She likely wouldn't know until morning, which was an inordinately long time coming.

She was the first one down to breakfast. Mr. Cuddlestone smiled at her as he poured her a cup of tea. He then offered toast and various pots of jam and honey before requesting to know what else he might bring her.

"Nothing," Patience assured him. Then she lowered her voice, mindful of Wilkins bringing in more toast. "Have you seen anything worth reporting?"

Mr. Cuddlestone sighed. "Precious little, miss. Yesterday was that valet's half day off. He didn't return to the house until late. I smelled alcohol about his person." He wrinkled his nose.

"And Harry returned safely?" she whispered.

"Hale and hearty. You needn't worry about him, miss. He can take care of himself."

She wished she believed that.

Gussie arrived just then, and Mr. Cuddlestone hurried off to relay her requests to the cook. "Have I missed the others?" she asked, taking her seat.

"No," Patience told her. "Everyone seems to have slept

late."

Meredith came in next, looking heavy-eyed and walking quickly, as if trying to outdistance Mr. Mayes, a few steps behind her. Even he looked as if he'd been up late, with shadows under his eyes and a yawn hidden behind his hand.

"Did you and Harry stay up playing cards?" Gussie asked.

He nodded as he sank onto a seat. "Though neither of us had much luck." He glanced to Patience.

No luck? Had Mr. Villers not followed them after all? She was certain she'd convinced him.

Harry arrived with Mr. Cuddlestone and most of the food. She thought many people would be fooled by the pleased smile Harry wore. She was more concerned that worry sat behind his eyes.

"Good morning," he said to the room at large. "I regret to inform you that Beau Villers is unwell. His valet let me know. Apparently, something he ate disagreed with him. He'll be staying in bed today."

"I will send up a tisane," Gussie offered. "And perhaps the newest formulation."

"I'd advise against that," Lydia said from the doorway. "At least on the formulation."

Harry turned and stumbled back from her. Patience pressed a hand to her lips. Lydia's usual creamy complexion was blotched red and speckled with large white bumps.

"I don't think strawberries were the missing ingredient after all," she said. "That may have been what sickened Beau. But I do think we should keep trying."

As Mr. Mayes stood with all propriety and Meredith held Fortune close, Patience hurried forward and took Lydia's hand. "Have you a fever? An upset stomach?"

"No," Lydia replied cheerfully. "It's just my face. No harm done."

Patience glanced at Gussie. "A great deal of harm done if we damage your complexion."

Gussie rose. "What is damaged can be repaired. Come,

Lydia. We'll try the ground chicken feathers next."

"Perhaps breakfast first," Patience suggested, surprised to feel the heat of temper rising inside. "Mr. Cuddlestone can make sure the room is ready for us." She glanced to the butler, who nodded his understanding.

"It will only take a few moments, madam," he assured Gussie before bowing himself out.

Gussie dropped back onto her chair. "Oh, very well. I could stand some tea." She raised her cup, and Wilkins hurried to fill it.

"Allow me, Lydia," Harry said, holding out a chair next to Patience's.

Lydia sat with a smile to them both. "Thank you."

Harry dropped his voice and bent closer as he pushed in the chair. "Allow me to apologize for my aunt. Her enthusiasm for her work is contagious, but we should not follow her against our better judgement."

"It's quite all right," Lydia assured him. "It wasn't as if I was having any luck attracting a husband."

Harry frowned.

"Nonsense," Patience said, laying her hand on Lydia's shoulder as she returned to her seat. "You are quick and good-natured. There is no reason you cannot make a match."

Harry nodded, straightening, and Patience could only be glad for his support. Mr. Mayes returned to his seat, and Meredith loosed Fortune, who scampered under the table.

"I'm a penniless girl from an upstart family one generation away from trade," Lydia said with no rancor in her tone as Wilkins approached hesitantly. "I'd much rather be useful than settle for a mess of porridge." She selected two pieces of toast from the footman's tray and requested a pot of chocolate.

Patience could hardly argue, as the sentiment matched her own. Fortune rubbed against her skirts, and she bent to lift the cat into her lap. Fortune regarded Lydia as if trying to determine whether she approved of the new look.

Mr. Mayes rose again. "Perhaps a stroll before breakfast, Harry?"

Harry glanced at Patience. Seeking permission? Not her borrowed baronet. He was surely playing his part.

"I'll just sit with Lydia for a time," she said.

His smile acknowledged her decision. He turned to join his friend, and the two headed out the door. Meredith's sigh of relief was audible.

Gussie popped back up. "I simply cannot be still. I'll help Cuddlestone. He may dispense with the wrong preparation."

And Gussie might prepare something worse. Patience smiled at her. "Mr. Cuddlestone has never harmed your experiments in the past. Besides, if you leave now, you won't hear my suggestions to Lydia."

"Suggestions?" Gussie tiptoed closer, as if unable to bear the suspense. Meredith covered her smile with her napkin.

Patience calmly sipped her tea before answering. "Yes. I have my doubts about chicken feathers."

"Indeed." Gussie perched on the other side of her, eyes wide and encouraging.

Patience nodded to Lydia to continue eating, then turned to Gussie. "The more I think about it, the more I dislike any association with fowl. Chickens, geese, pigeons—none of them have ever been associated with the improvement of the skin."

"More likely the plumping of pillows or comforters," Meredith pointed out.

Head resting against Patience's chest, Fortune purred her agreement.

Gussie pursed her lips as she took Harry's seat. "True. But perhaps they have more efficacious properties unknown because no other apothecary has dared."

Whereas Gussie dared far too cheerfully.

"Yet there are other things long associated with a clear

complexion," Patience persisted. "Cucumbers, lavender, roses."

"Cream," Meredith suggested. "Apricots."

Gussie wrinkled her nose. "Prosaic, the lot of them."

There had to be something she could do to keep her from putting something poisonous onto or into Lydia. Unfortunately, the girl had other ideas.

"Pearls!" she cried, shoving away the last of her toast. "Is that not why many a gentleman praises a lady? For her pearly skin."

Gussie pushed back her chair so quickly the footman had to catch it before it toppled over backward. "Of course! I have a strand in my room. We'll grind them to a powder and mix them into the formulation. Brilliant!" She rushed from the room.

Patience sighed. "I'm not sure ground pearls are any better for your skin then strawberries or eggs, Lydia, just costlier."

"Who knows?" Lydia said with a twinkle in her eyes. "That's the fun of experimenting." She started to rise, but Patience caught her arm.

"But at what price? Even if it works, what lady can afford to purchase skin ointment made from pearls?"

"Lady Carrolton, I imagine," Meredith put in, rising to come fetch Fortune. "The Duchess of Wey, the Duke of Emerson's daughters."

"Anyone with sufficient funds and interest," Lydia agreed. "Gussie could make a fortune."

Patience frowned at the dreamy tone. "Is that why you're helping her? With the hope she'll share the money?"

Lydia studied her nails. "The thought had crossed my mind."

"So, you would trade your beauty for income?" Meredith demanded.

Fortune raised her head, purr grinding to a halt.

Lydia raised her chin. "Many girls do. I'm certainly not

the sort men fall in love with. Beau's been dangling me like a worm on a hook for years, and the only fellow to show interest decided against me. Harry was our best hope. Not that I mind you winning him."

Patience peered closer. Even through the blotches on the girl's cheeks, there was no sign of a blush, no stiffening of her slender shoulders. Patience hadn't been so calm when Robert had defected.

"You really don't care that he chose another?" she asked.

Lydia smiled. "How could I when it's clear you love each other?"

Meredith frowned, holding Fortune closer as if she feared the emotion was contagious. But surely she knew there were no emotions involved. Even if Meredith could have forgotten their agreement, Patience and Harry hadn't done all that great a job of acting.

Still, she did not intend to lie to Lydia now.

"I care about Harry," she said, dropping her gaze to the pristine white tablecloth. "But I'm not sure he feels the same."

Lydia took her hand and gave it a squeeze. "He does. I see it in his eyes when he looks at you. All you need do is put yourself out a little, and you'll find him living in your pocket."

Meredith shook her head, as if altogether unsure of the wisdom of that advice. Yet something stirred inside Patience. Could Lydia be right? Could it be that easy? If Patience told Harry she was coming to care for him, would she find he felt the same?

And if he didn't, could she bear to learn he was truly a better actor than she'd thought?

Harry left the breakfast room feeling more comfortable than when he'd arrived. It had been a long night. Though he and Julian had waited near the cove for hours, Villers had never materialized. Returning to the house, they'd found him safely abed, snoring. Now he refused to come downstairs, pleading an illness. Had the fellow been too sick to carry out the surveillance he'd promised Patience? Had he recognized the trap and refused to enter? Or had they mistaken him after all?

And if their mysterious stalker wasn't Villers, who else could it be?

All in all, it was enough to put a fellow in a pucker. The only bright spot was Patience. She was levelheaded, practical, yet endlessly compassionate. Look at how she'd dealt with Lydia this morning.

Just to be certain she was safe from Gussie's blandishments, however, he checked the laboratory an hour later, after sending Julian to Undene to inquire about alternative landing spots given the trouble they'd encountered last time. Lydia was bent over a mortar, pestle cracking against whatever was inside. Patience stood over a pot resting on one of Gussie's spirit lamps.

"Tell me you won't eat that," he said, peering over her shoulder at the bubbling white substance.

"Never," Patience promised. "It's my mother's ointment. I've been going through my stock at an alarming rate. Gussie and Lydia were so busy I thought now might be a good time to make more. Gussie had all the ingredients, including dried roses for all she finds them boring."

"Finer," Gussie said to Lydia, gazing down into the bowl. "It should be as tiny as the grains of face powder."

Lydia wiped her brow on her sleeve. "I'll try, but the round shapes are hard to flatten."

Harry frowned. "What is she doing?"

"Don't ask," Patience advised. "And stay away for the next couple of hours or you might find it on you."

Heeding her warning wasn't as easy as it once might have been. Meredith had retired to her room again, Julian was still out, and Villers was moaning alone upstairs. Harry found himself strangely ill at ease in his own house. He'd never been one to take an active hand in running the estate—Gussie and Cuddlestone saw to that. Julian managed their holdings on the Exchange, so Harry had no investments to consider. His father and grandfather had spent nearly every extra penny, so there were no plantations on foreign shores to concern him. He refused to be so enamored of maintaining his wardrobe that he spent hours poring over waistcoats and the manner of tying his cravat, even if that would have delighted Cuddlestone. A shame he wasn't the man the *ton* thought him—he had no assignations to arrange, no card games awaiting the influx of his funds. He was merely glad Julian returned before the morning was spent so he had something to take his mind off Patience.

"The wisest move is to continue using the cove," Julian said, pacing about Harry's study. The space was more retreat than work area. The small desk was pushed under the windows, and two large leather-bound chairs faced the hearth. "With the water up all around, there isn't another stretch that open and dry for miles. The revenue agents may realize that, of course."

"As will our enemy," Harry pointed out. "Is your money still on Villers?"

"Absolutely," Julian said, navigating around the chairs. "First, he clung to you like a leech, then, just when he ought to think he has us backed into a corner, he stays abed, pleading a headache."

"He must have seen the trap," Harry said. "It's the only explanation if we discount his illness."

Julian humphed as he collapsed into the other leather-bound chair. "And what are we to do tonight? Give up our plan to rescue Lady de Maupassant?"

"Never," Harry vowed. "I've hated waiting this long. Every day puts her in more danger."

Julian eyed him. "I've been made privy to some of your reports. Rather colorful."

Harry shrugged. "You give me too much credit."

"Not at all." Julian crossed his booted feet. "You make a passionate case for believing the lady's reports. I had begun to wonder whether you intended to offer for her."

Harry grinned. "I did, last year, somewhat in jest. She answered in kind. She refuses to consider marriage until the tyrant has been put down. And I am not her sort. She prefers her gentlemen studious, dedicated, and French."

"Like her father, God rest his soul," Julian murmured.

Harry sobered. "Nasty business, that. I can't imagine the pain of watching those you love killed and having to pretend to applaud the savagery."

"Another lady skilled at subterfuge, it seems."

His friend's tone had turned darker. "Do you speak of Patience, or Meredith?" Harry asked.

Julian kicked at the hearth. "Both. Is it too much to ask that a lady share her true thoughts openly?"

"The ladies might ask the same of us," Harry reminded him. "And given the choice of a woman who says whatever comes to mind with no thought of the consequences, I far prefer Patience's diplomacy."

Julian smiled. "Yes, I noticed. You prefer a great many things about Miss Ramsey. Good thing she knows you're merely playing a part, or she might fall in love with you."

"And I with her."

Julian sat straighter. "What's this? The infamous Sir Harry Orwell, in love?"

Harry shook his head at the teasing. "More than you know. There are moments this is no longer a game, Julian. I'm coming to care about her, and it scares me. What hope would I have of winning her?"

"More than you think," Julian assured him. "Even the indebtedness of the manor would be better than an eternity of serving."

Harry sagged. "Yet I would not have her marry me to improve her standing, however little linking herself to me does that. I want her heart, to give her mine, tarnished though it is."

"I find myself wanting the same," Julian murmured. "Yet I begin to think my case more hopeless than yours."

He had never seen his friend so down. "A word of advice?" Harry offered.

Julian nodded. "Please, for I am at my wit's end."

"You want her to speak her mind. Perhaps you should start by speaking yours."

Julian threw up his hands. "She won't even talk to me!"

"Then talk to her," Harry said. "And soon, for I have a feeling she will not stay much longer."

And neither would Patience, once this house party was over.

CHAPTER SIXTEEN

Meredith caught herself peering both ways as she came out of her bedchamber and straightened her spine. Draping Fortune along one arm, she brushed off her lavender skirts with her free hand. Why did she keep running? She had no reason to act like someone caught with her fingers in the cookie jar. She wasn't that frightened adolescent who had been cruelly booted from her home. She had grown into someone stronger, wiser. She needn't fear Julian Mayes.

Even if dread gathered in her gut at the thought of speaking to him again.

"You understand," she murmured to Fortune, stroking the cat's head as she started for the stairs with the idea of convincing one of the other ladies to join her in the withdrawing room for cards. "There are predators and prey, and I dislike being the latter."

Fortune offered a supportive meow, then stiffened in Meredith's arms.

Julian was climbing the stairs.

Too late to retreat. Keeping her head high, she descended past him as if he were no more than a portrait on the wall.

"Mary," he chided, turning easily to follow her down.

Meredith reached the floor and stalked across the entry hall. Mr. Cuddlestone was inspecting the hearth as if determining whether the downstairs maid had done her job sufficiently.

"My first name is Meredith, sir," she told Julian, hurrying to the butler's side, "and I do not recall giving you leave to use it."

Julian's handsome face sagged. "Nor do you recall agreeing to marry me, it seems."

Mr. Cuddlestone glanced between the two of them. "May I be of assistance Miss Thorn, Mr. Mayes?"

"Yes," Meredith said, holding Fortune close. "Please inform Mr. Mayes that I have nothing to say to him."

Mr. Cuddlestone's mouth opened, but Julian spoke first. "And you may tell *Miss Thorn* that I have a great many things to say to *her*."

The butler looked from Meredith to Julian, then moved closer to her. "Miss Thorn, you have always struck me as a lady of excellent sense, if you don't mind my saying so. Might you be persuaded to speak to Mr. Mayes, who has always been welcome in this house?"

Meredith raised her chin. "No."

She could hear the butler's sigh as he turned to Julian. "Might I interest you in a nice cup of tea, sir?"

Julian's mouth was so tight the word barely slipped past. "No."

Mr. Cuddlestone stepped back, face bunching. "I regret that I am at a loss."

Meredith took pity on him. "It's all right, Cuddlestone. You may go."

He promptly scampered through one of the many doors that circled the entry hall.

She started for the door to the withdrawing room, but Julian darted in front of her. "Please, Meredith, let me explain."

If she could not flee, there was only one response left to her. Meredith rounded on Julian, Fortune positioned between them. "Why? You accuse me of forgetting our engagement. How easily the members of the Society you love forget things. Things like loyalty, constancy, keeping a promise."

He took a step closer, eyes narrowing as if he would see inside her. She refused to flinch.

"By the time I learned your cousin had thrown you out," he said, "you were gone. He disclaimed all knowledge of where."

Likely story. "The letters I wrote gave you no insight?" she asked sweetly. "I would have thought a solicitor better informed."

He frowned. "Letters? I received nothing from you, no word, no note. It was as if I'd fabricated you from whole cloth."

Meredith started. "That cannot be. I delivered them to the footman's hand to deliver to the post myself."

"Then perhaps," he said gently, "your quarrel is with the footman, not me."

Could it be? Could her vile cousin have arranged for the letters to perish before delivery to the post? She could well believe him that manipulative. Yet she could also believe the man before her now was equally devious. He was a solicitor after all. They excelled in honeyed words, pleasing tones.

Right before driving the knife home.

His mentor had been the same, claiming to want to help her settle the estate before denouncing her as a murderer.

"And you heard nothing from your mentor Mr. Prentice about my case?"

He frowned. "Your case? Were you forced to bring suit against your cousin?"

She peered closer. The confusion seemed to be genuine, his reddish brows drawn down over his nose. Had he truly heard nothing about the trouble with Lady Winhaven's estate?

Don't educate him.

The voice inside was insistent. She drew a breath and

focused on the larger issue.

"No," she answered. "I was in no position to contest my cousin's inheritance. That matter is settled. What concerns me now is this. You have distinguished yourself as a man able to solve problems. My employer even remarked on it, with great glee, when she learned you had once courted me. You will pardon me for thinking that you might have tried harder to find me."

He inclined his head. "You have every right. It is a matter I regret deeply. All I can say in my own defense is that I was younger then, less well versed in the ways of the world. By the time I had amassed the income and connections to conduct a thorough search, the scent had washed clean. It was only when Wey asked me to locate a Miss Thorn and described you to me that I began to wonder, to hope."

He moved closer still, gaze devouring hers. "Have I any reason for hope, Meredith?"

None! The word trembled on her lips yet refused to come out. What was wrong with her? He'd proven himself lacking in love, finding excuses for why he had failed her, never tried to find her. She should send him away just as surely. She would not allow her heart to be stolen again.

She must have been squeezing Fortune too hard, for her pet wiggled in her arms. She loosened her hold with an apologetic smile to the one being who had never disappointed her.

Fortune regarded her a moment with her copper eyes, then twisted and slid down to the polished wood floor of the entry hall. She righted herself and gazed up at Julian, who gazed back, unblinking. Oh, but he was in for it now. Would Fortune hiss? Sink her claws into his boots?

Fortune arched her back and rubbed herself against the black leather.

"Sweet kitty," Julian said with a surprisingly endearing tone and besotted smile she should not want so much to be directed her way instead. "Pretty kitty."

"That's quite enough," Meredith said, bending to scoop up her pet. Fortune's gaze leveled accusingly at her. Something constricted inside her.

"Well, at least your cat likes me," Julian said.

Unaccountable. Ridiculous. Betrayed too often, so many times she'd relied on Fortune's uncanny insights to tell friend from foe. What did it mean that her cat liked Julian? Had she mistaken him again?

By dinner time, Lydia's blotches had subsided to mere shadows. Gussie claimed it was the new treatment infused with pearls, but Patience thought it had more to do with her mother's ointment, which she'd slipped to the girl behind Gussie's back. She was also glad to see Meredith looking more like herself and joining in the conversation in the withdrawing room before dinner, even if Mr. Mayes watched her with obvious interest.

Lydia's brother remained out of sorts. He had stayed abed most of the day. His pallor and humility assured Patience he had indeed been ill. He pecked at the salmon and asparagus that served as the main course and made desultory conversation in the withdrawing room afterward.

"Julian and I intend to look at property near the river," Harry announced to all. "With the flooding, it's the perfect time to assess local stability. It should only take a few days. We'll be back in time for Easter."

Gussie frowned, Lydia sagged, and Meredith raised a brow at the defection.

"We had hoped you could accompany us, Villers," Mr. Mayes added. "But you clearly need your rest."

Patience waited for the fellow's reaction. If he was the spy they suspected, surely he'd brighten at the opportunity.

Instead, he merely sighed. "Yes, it's best I avoid travel for the time being. And, if you'll excuse me now, I think I will head back to bed."

"I'll send you up something," Gussie promised, at which he turned rather green and politely declined.

"Does this happen often?" Patience asked Lydia after he'd left.

"No, never," she replied with her ready smile. "Beau is generally the picture of health. But I'm sure whatever upset his stomach will pass shortly."

Patience wasn't nearly so sure, but at least with him safely in his bedchamber Harry and his friend were free to make their appointed run to France unnoticed.

As most of them settled back down following Mr. Villers's exit, Mr. Mayes rose.

"I understand you all shared talents with each other before I arrived," he said.

Lydia nodded, but Patience wondered who had informed him. She glanced at Mr. Cuddlestone to find him frowning.

"Perhaps you would allow me to do the same," Harry's friend continued. "As a solicitor, I have some gift for declaiming."

Gussie twisted to face him fully. "I appreciate a fellow who can speak well. Impress us, Mr. Mayes."

The others looked interested as well, but Meredith dropped her gaze to her hands in her lap as if wishing Fortune were filling them.

Her one-time swain struck a pose, head high, one foot forward, one hand behind his back.

"Had we but world enough and time,
This coyness, lady, were no crime.
We would sit down, and think which way
To walk, and pass our long love's day."

His voice was warm, beguiling as he quoted Andrew Marvell's famous words. Lydia sighed happily, Gussie beamed, and even Meredith raised her head as if willing to listen for once.

Harry's hand stole over Patience's, cradling it.

"Let us roll all our strength and all

Our sweetness up into one ball," Mr. Mayes continued, voice fervent.

"And tear our pleasure with rough strife
Through the iron gates of life:
Thus, though we cannot make our sun
Stand still, yet we will make him run."

Lydia burst into applause, and Gussie joined her. Patience sucked in a breath as Harry released her to follow suit.

Mr. Mayes sketched a bow. "And may I hope it pleased you as well, Miss Ramsey, Miss Thorn?"

He didn't fool Patience. The only approval he sought was Meredith's. Two spots of color stood out on her cheekbones, and her lavender eyes gleamed.

"An excellent rendition, Mr. Mayes," she allowed. "And something to consider."

He bowed again, but his smile remained on his face until they ended the evening.

Harry asked Patience to stay behind as the others started for bed.

Lydia hesitated. "Perhaps I should stay too, as chaperone."

Gussie caught Harry's eye. "No need. I'll remain with the pair. Check on your brother, Lydia."

With a nod, the girl left with Meredith.

"Am I invited to this conclave?" Mr. Mayes asked, turning from watching them go.

Harry slipped his hand over Patience's once more, but his words disappointed her. "Of course. Watch the door."

With a shake of his head, Mr. Mayes went to station himself by the portal, where he could spot anyone approaching.

Harry led Patience back to the sofa, but Gussie paced around the room, skirts rustling.

"What's happening, Harry?" she demanded. "And don't tell me you're going to look at property. I cannot conceive Julian wants to locate all the way out here."

Julian inclined his head in acknowledgement. "You

know me well, madam."

"We're going to France tomorrow," Harry told his aunt, though his gaze remained on Patience. "We intend to free Lady de Maupassant."

Gussie's eyes lit. "Excellent. I can hardly wait to meet her."

All enthusiasm, like her nephew. "But what will you do with the lady when you return?" Patience asked. "Surely people will wonder if a Frenchwoman suddenly shows up at the manor."

"We'll hide her in the village," Julian said with a glance their way. "Once the causeway opens, I can take her safely to London. Villers and his sister can leave as well. That rids us of any potential witnesses."

Gussie's nod set her greying curls to bobbing. "Perfect. Then you'll be off in the morning."

"That's the plan," Harry replied, though he did not sound as delighted as his aunt.

Julian straightened. "Well, if we're done here, I should sleep. See you in the morning, Harry."

Harry nodded, and Julian saw himself out. Gussie came around the sofa to face him and Patience.

"I won't tell you to be careful, Harry. You won't be. Just come home." She bent and kissed his cheek. Straightening, she eyed Patience.

"I am impressed with your mother's ointment. Perhaps we could improve upon it. It will be our next experiment."

Patience could only stare as she sailed from the room.

"You've made a conquest," Harry teased, rising and pulling her up.

"Until she decides to try something more interesting, like turnips." Sobering, she gazed up at him. "Are you truly prepared for this?"

He smiled. "Believe it or not, I am. Julian spoke with Undene today. He's the fellow who bumped into me at services. He's learned where my contact is being held.

Our men are loyal and skilled. We'll be to France and back before you know it."

Not likely. Already she felt each moment pass too slowly. "I cannot be as confident as Gussie, so I will say it. Be careful, Harry."

He wrinkled his nose, reminding her of his aunt. "Care is too highly praised."

Patience shook her head. "How can you be so cavalier? You're heading for France, our sworn enemy. It is worth your life to even set foot on the shore."

"And there are those in England who would say good riddance."

"Stop that," Patience scolded. "You have been a true gentleman. I see that now."

He sighed. "Now who's caught up in the game? I'm an Orwell, the spawn of a pirate, a dastard, and a cheat. No one on the *ton* would ever believe I could aspire to more."

It hurt to hear him talk of it. "But I know," she countered. "Gussie knows. You must listen to your conscience, Harry."

He did not argue, turning their joined hands back and forth as if mesmerized by her touch. "And you, Patience? Do you listen only to your conscience?"

"I try," she said. And she knew what it said now. She stood on tiptoe and pressed a kiss to the firm, stubbled cheek. "Please, be careful. Come home to me."

He watched her as she dropped back onto her feet. "I will do my best for you, Patience. Never less."

She could only pray he would keep his word. For if something happened to Harry, her life would never be the same.

Harry and Julian were gone by the time she came down to breakfast the next morning. To further the ruse, they'd taken the coach and travel bags. Patience wasn't sure where they intended to leave the horses, but likely one of the smuggler's families would care for the team. That left her to play her role as Harry's bride-to-be.

Chaperoned by Lydia, she brought Beau Villers breakfast and supper in bed, staying to feed him and offer solace. She wasn't sure how he felt about her reading from the Bible to him. He would lie back and close his eyes, and she was never entirely sure whether he was sleeping or hoping she would go away. In truth, she wasn't there just to encourage him. She wanted to be certain he had no opportunity to follow Harry.

She needn't have worried. He remained waxy pale and weak, only beginning to recover as she fed him.

"Your presence is appreciated," he told her. "Sometimes I think that valet is trying to poison me."

The tall fellow slipped back into the dressing room as if wounded. It couldn't be easy being the manservant for someone like Mr. Villers. It wasn't even easy taking pity on him.

Lydia didn't agree. "You are very good with invalids," she told Patience as they left him sleeping one afternoon and retreated down the stairs.

"I have had a great deal of practice," Patience reminded her.

She had less practice waiting. She and Lydia worked with Gussie in the laboratory, trying different versions of her mother's ointment that amused Gussie and only occasionally required the house to be aired out. Sometimes Meredith joined them, leaving Fortune safely with Emma, who Patience suspected spoiled her with treats and play. Other times, Patience or Lydia kept Meredith company. But no matter what she was doing, Patience ran to the windows at the least sound outside. She also stared out her curtains for hours, Fortune curled in her lap, before finally falling asleep beside Meredith. Her prayers became focused on a single thought: *Please, Lord, keep Harry safe.*

On the afternoon of the third day, while working in the

laboratory with Gussie and Lydia, she heard a carriage passing the house. Gussie and Lydia exchanged fond smiles as she darted for the door. Sure enough, Harry's carriage had just stopped beside the stable block. She held her breath as Mr. Mayes alighted. Patience tilted her head, trying to see around him, through him. Where was Harry?

He climbed down a moment later, and she could breathe again. Indeed, she hadn't realized what a lovely day it was until Harry turned and aimed his smile her way.

Then she was running, and so was he. He met her on the lawn, caught her close.

"You did it," she murmured. "You came back."

"I would never break a promise to you," he murmured. His lips brushed her temple, soft, reverent. If only it wasn't all an act!

He drew back but kept one arm around her waist as his friend approached. Their smiling faces told her much of what she wanted to know.

"Then everything went as planned?" she asked, glad they were in the middle of the lawn where no one could overhear.

"Perfectly," Mr. Mayes said.

"It was almost too easy," Harry agreed. "We landed with a group of smugglers and came off the same way. The guards at the prison house where she was held gave us no trouble, and the soldiers stationed in the town were too busy intimidating other citizens to notice our passage."

Patience eyed him. He seemed more weary than triumphant. "You sound disappointed."

"Surprised, more like," Harry told her. "We left her with Undene and his wife in the village."

"Where she will stay until the causeway is open," Mr. Mayes added.

"Mr. Cuddlestone says that will be any day," Patience promised them. "But could you take her across by boat?"

"Too open," Harry said, starting for the house. Patience

fell into step beside him. "We'd be at the mercy of anyone who wanted to take a shot."

Patience shivered.

Harry drew her closer. "Don't worry, Patience. We're almost done with all this."

"We are?" She searched his face. "Will you stop your work?"

"Not Harry," Mr. Mayes said, slapping him on the back. "He's too important to the War Office."

Harry paused, tipping his head for the house. "Tell Gussie I'll be right in, Julian."

Julian glanced at Patience but nodded and moved to the door.

Patience steeled herself to hear what Harry had to say. He took both her hands, held them close as he had done when he'd tried to persuade her to play his bride.

"Don't ask me to lie anymore, Harry," she said, gaze dropping. "I'm finding it harder and harder to play the game."

He squeezed her hands. "So am I, Patience. I should have been focused on rescuing Yvette, but all I could think about was coming home, to you."

She glanced up. The tender look in his eyes was nearly her undoing.

"If I could persuade the War Office there was another way," he said, each word slow and hesitant, "would you be willing to stay on at Foulness Manor?"

"Stay on? As Gussie's assistant?"

"Perhaps more." He lowered his head, and she raised her chin to allow her lips to meet his, hope mingling with joy.

"Harry!"

Gussie came rushing out of the laboratory and enveloped them both in a hug, nearly knocking the breath from Patience.

"Oh, Harry, you're back. I can't wait to show you what Patience and I have been up to. And Lydia, of course. That girl is surprisingly useful." She stepped back and beamed at them both. "Well? What are you waiting for? Come inside before it starts to rain again." She seized Harry's hand and started tugging him toward the house.

"Later," Harry murmured to Patience, and she knew she would have to wait a while longer.

Still, she couldn't help smiling as Gussie explained their progress to Harry, gesticulating so wildly that the herbs rustled on the rafters. Harry caught Patience's eye and grinned, and she felt her cheeks warming. Though Gussie and Lydia outdid themselves to tell him everything, it was as if all the words bounced off a bubble that enclosed her and Harry inside. She felt a little like a bubble herself as she floated upstairs to change for dinner.

Harry had feelings for her. Harry wanted her to stay.

She came down to find Mr. Cuddlestone pacing the entry hall. He rushed to meet her as she reached the bottom of the stairs.

"It isn't right, miss. The manor was never intended for entertaining. We only have so much room. What am I to do with another guest?"

Patience frowned. "Another guest? Is the causeway open?"

"Not that I've heard, yet here she is, claiming she was invited." He lowered his voice and leaned closer. "Claiming she is related."

Something settled like a rock in her stomach. "Where have you put this person?"

He straightened. "She insisted upon waiting in the withdrawing room. I sent Wilkins for Sir Harry. I wasn't about to leave her alone downstairs."

Footfalls echoed above, and Harry came down the stairs. "What's this about another guest?"

"In the withdrawing room," Patience offered as Mr. Cuddlestone drew himself up as if to deliver a scold. "Perhaps we should go see." She took Harry's arm and led him toward the door.

A petite woman was sitting on the sofa. Even though her simple spruce-colored wool gown was unornamented, she perched with head high as if holding court. A crop of short, strawberry blond curls clustered around her oval face in the bold style favored by Caro Lamb, and her blue eyes sparkled with mischief. Her features were fine-boned and delicate.

Harry was as still as a statue beside Patience. "Yvette?"

She rose, smile pretty.

"But of course, my dear 'Arry," she said in a lilting voice. "You do not think I would languish away without you?" She turned her smile on Patience. "And you must be the *chère amie* 'Arry has been boasting of. Shall we fight a duel over him now, or do you wish dinner first?"

CHAPTER SEVENTEEN

Harry nearly groaned aloud. He was used to Yvette's teasing. She had grown up the little sister of two older brothers, who had taught her to ride and box. Her subterfuge, passing secrets from various French leaders to England, had imparted other skills. Yet even incarceration had not dimmed the sparkle that drew people to her. Perhaps that was why the guards had been so easily bribed to allow Harry and Julian to rescue her. Her charm might also be why Undene hadn't stopped her before she made her way to the manor.

Patience recovered before he did, offering Yvette a polite smile. "You are in England now, mademoiselle. Here ladies do not fight with pistols and cutlass. We wound each other with consequence while smiling."

"Ha!" Yvette grinned at Harry. "Her, I like."

Harry shook himself. "What are you doing here? You were safer in the village."

She made a face. "*Mais non*, I was like a peacock in the henhouse. Everyone remarked upon it. I am better here." She leaned back against the sofa as if making herself at home. "I have told everyone in the village that I am your cousin. You must introduce me to my new aunt."

Patience plucked at Harry's sleeve. "Much as I hate to interrupt this family reunion, we will have company soon, and we need to know what to say."

As if he agreed, Cuddlestone strode into the room. "The other guests will be down shortly, Sir Harold. What would you like me to do with this person?"

Patience turned to the butler. "My apologies, Mr. Cuddlestone. In all the excitement of having Harry home I neglected to inform you that his cousin will be joining us."

Cuddlestone stared at Yvette, who wiggled her fingers at him in greeting. "Cousin?"

"*Mais oui*," Yvette said. "Why else would I come at such a time?"

"Move Miss Villers in with Miss Thorn," Patience advised him. "I will explain the situation to them. Miss Orwell and I can share a room. And would you ask Cook to hold off dinner for another half hour?"

"Very good, miss," Cuddlestone said with a look to Harry as if to say *this is how a household should be run*. "I'll have the staff make the exchange while you are all at dinner." He bowed and left the room.

Patience turned to Harry. "Gussie next, I think. She will need to play along. We must find an explanation for how your cousin arrived, where she's been, and why she has no luggage."

She was smooth as silk. How could he not admire a woman with such aplomb?

Yvette rose with fluid grace. "I have been living on a farm in the area. I am not acknowledged by the family, you see. My father married beneath him, a French émigré, which is why I have a French accent. 'Arry in his great kindness decided to invite me for Easter." She spread her skirts. "And this is all I own."

Sadly, at the moment, the last part was true. And Undene's wife had not been happy to part with her best dress and underthings so that Yvette could bathe and change out of the filth she'd been wearing in prison.

"Plausible," Patience agreed.

"I am used to making up stories," Yvette said, but there was no pride in the statement. "Let us continue."

Harry wasn't surprised when they located Gussie in the laboratory. Some days it was all he could do to pry her loose in time for dinner. What did surprise him was that Lydia had stayed with her instead of going upstairs to change for dinner with the other ladies. Before Harry could introduce Yvette, she marched up to Gussie.

"*Ma chère tante.*" She placed her hands on Gussie's shoulders and planted a kiss on each cheek. "So very good to see you again."

"And you," Gussie said with a look to Harry.

"I met Cousin Yvette while Julian and I were traveling and invited her for Easter," Harry said. "I know it's been quite a while since we've seen her."

"It seems like forever," Gussie said with a tight smile.

Yvette released her to sniff the air. "But what do you cook?"

Gussie recovered herself. "It is a preparation designed to smooth and soothe the skin. Would you like to try it?"

"No!" Patience and Harry chorused.

Gussie blinked, but Yvette merely smiled. "Perhaps another time. I must be introduced to your guest."

"Miss Villers," Harry obligingly said, stepping forward, "may I introduce my cousin, Miss Orwell."

Lydia beamed. "A pleasure to meet you."

Yvette nodded. "And you. But Villers. It is a French name, *non?*"

The way Yvette pronounced it, it certainly sounded that way. Was that why Lydia's brother had been snooping around? Had he more ties to France than Harry had thought?

Lydia didn't seem to think so, for she shook her head. "No, Miss Orwell. I'm English through and through. But you must tell me more about yourself. Was your mother French?"

"Yes." Yvette heaved a convincing sigh. "And I miss her every day."

Lydia's eyes widened. "Did you live through the Terror? Meet Napoleon? I'd love to hear all about it."

Harry eyed her. They'd been so focused on Villers they had forgotten about Lydia. Patience seemed to think her more intelligent than Harry would have thought. Her look now was all enthusiasm as usual, but could her questions have a deeper purpose?

Yvette inclined her head. "Perhaps another time. I tire." She turned to Harry. "Could we sit somewhere quiet until dinner?"

"Of course," Patience said. "Gussie, Lydia, I took the liberty of asking Cook to set back dinner. Can you be ready in a half hour?"

Lydia nodded, starting to remove her apron. Gussie waved a hand. "Certainly, certainly. I can't wait to become reacquainted with my niece."

Leaving Lydia and Gussie behind, Harry led Patience and Yvette back toward the withdrawing room. "That went better than I'd hoped."

"Perhaps," Yvette said as they started across the entry hall. "But I wonder about your Miss Villers. She plays the innocent, yet I am certain I have heard the name Villers in France, and in high circles." Her gaze darted about as if expecting someone to pop out from behind the paintings. "Her loyalties are divided, perhaps?"

"I think it more likely we should question her brother's loyalties," Harry told her.

Patience frowned. "But do you think he has the intestinal fortitude or ability? He never attempted to follow you and Mr. Mayes. He's remained in bed most of the time you've been gone."

"Perhaps he's a consummate actor," Harry said, "fooling us all."

Yvette nodded as they reentered the withdrawing room.

"I will meet him. I will know."

"How very nice to be so sure of yourself," Patience said, following her. "It must come in handy."

Yvette shot her a look. "More politeness, I think. You will see. I will make you like me."

Patience merely smiled.

Villers arrived for dinner with Julian, who nearly stumbled across the threshold when his gaze lit on Yvette sitting on the sofa next to Patience. Harry hurried to introduce both men to his cousin. Julian recovered sufficiently to bow over her hand.

"And did I hear you were unwell, monsieur?" Yvette asked Villers when he did the same.

"A moment's indisposition," he assured her as he straightened. "Nothing would keep me from celebrating the holiday with my dear friends. I hope I may shortly count you among them."

"Such a lovely hope," Yvette said with a smile. She turned to Patience. "Did I say that right, for an Englishwoman?"

Patience's smile blossomed. "Exactly right, Miss Orwell."

"Please," she said. "You must all call me Yvette."

Villers glanced between the two women as if he wasn't sure of the conversation. Harry thought he knew. Quick study that she was, Yvette had decided to take Patience as an example and veil her threats with pleasant words. Perhaps Patience and Yvette might be friends after all.

Patience rose now. "I wonder, Beau, if you would look outside with me. I was so hoping tomorrow would be brighter. Can you tell by looking at the moon?"

"I can think of a number of things to do under a silvery moon, my dear," he drawled, but he took her arm and led her toward the window.

Clever girl. Harry took Patience's spot at Yvette's side even as Julian bent near her.

"Yvette thinks Villers might be our man," Harry whispered. "She wanted to meet him in person."

"Well?" Julian whispered.

Yvette frowned at the fellow's back. "I do not trust him. Send him away."

Harry shook his head. "Alas, I can't. Not until the causeway opens. But I'm hoping that will be soon."

The causeway couldn't open fast enough for Patience. She had never spent such an evening. She'd dined with the family at the Carroltons, but, except for the times Lady Lilith had proved fractious, Patience had been largely invisible. Tonight, she felt as if she was constantly being watched, and the least wrong word, an ill-considered movement of her hand, might spell her doom, and Harry's.

He gave no sign he was under a strain, leading the conversation along insignificant topics like the weather, changes in fashion, and the upcoming Season in London. Gussie kept frowning at Yvette, as if she couldn't decide whether to confront her with questions or dose her with formulation.

Her frown was better than Beau's calculating look. He seemed to be wondering if Yvette would taste well in a nice butter sauce. Mr. Mayes's gaze swiveled from Yvette to Beau to Meredith in turn, and only the last seemed to give him any solace. And Lydia couldn't seem to decide where to look as she alone did justice to the roast and jacketed potatoes Cook had prepared.

As dinner ended, Patience was able to take the ladies aside and explain the change in accommodations. Lydia readily agreed, and Meredith nodded acceptance. But she held Patience back as they started for the withdrawing room.

"Who is she really?" she whispered, gaze on the Yvette's back as the Frenchwoman walked with Harry.

"Someone Harry is trying to help," Patience said. "She'll leave as soon as the causeway opens."

"Which cannot be soon enough," Meredith said, mirroring Patience's thoughts. "But I wonder at your reactions this evening, Patience. Have you taken Miss Orwell in dislike?"

Patience sighed. "I would very much like to be friends with Miss Orwell. And yet…"

Meredith's mouth quirked. "And yet, cousin or no, she is pretty and exotic and clearly devoted to Harry."

"Oh, that couldn't be the reason I dislike her," Patience said, but she met Meredith's gaze, and they both laughed.

"Now, that's a sound I'd like to hear more often," Mr. Mayes said, waiting for them in the entry hall.

Patience moved closer to him to give Meredith a chance to withdraw.

But instead of retreating, Meredith held her ground. "We were just wondering about our newcomer. What do you know of her, Mr. Mayes?"

If he was chagrined that she refused to use his first name, he didn't show it. "Very little," he admitted. "Her mother was from France, I believe, a fallen countess if the stories are true. Like many aristocratic families, hers fared badly in the Revolution. I fear Miss Orwell is the last of her immediate family."

An orphan, like me. Patience drew in a breath. Perhaps Yvette's made up story was not so far from the truth. If she was all that remained of a once-proud house, had the rest of her family faced the guillotine?

"How horrible," Meredith said, once more saying Patience's thoughts aloud.

Patience nodded. "I'm very glad you could help her."

He smiled, but pleasure was not the emotion reflected in his eyes. "I had nothing to do with the matter, Miss Ramsey."

Of course! She wasn't supposed to mention that he and Harry had gone all the way to France to rescue Yvette, further proof of her ineptitude for espionage. When they entered the withdrawing room and he stalked to Harry's side, she couldn't help her sigh.

"*Did* he have something to do with the matter?" Meredith murmured, holding Patience back a little from the others.

Patience couldn't find the strength to lie to her face. "Mr. Mayes and Harry encountered her in their travels. Very likely he was kind to her. I must try to do likewise. She has obviously suffered great loss. Perhaps all she needs is our support and understanding."

Meredith smiled. "You are very good at providing that, Patience."

"Perhaps," Patience allowed. "But I wasn't the one who helped you over your worries concerning Mr. Mayes. I noticed you did not run from him this time."

"Mr. Mayes and I have spoken," she allowed, shifting on her feet and setting her skirts to swaying. "While we disagree on several points, we can at least be agreeable in each other's company."

They were, in fact, the most agreeable people that evening. Beau insisted on cards, and Patience made sure he was in the set with his sister, Meredith, and Julian, the last of which she was certain could keep the topics of conversation away from Yvette. Mr. Cuddlestone erected a second card table on the other side of the room, so at least she, Harry, Gussie, and Yvette had a little privacy.

"So, you are the lady who's been helping Harry," Gussie said in an uncharacteristically quiet voice.

Yvette regarded the cards she had been dealt. "'Arry is the gentleman who has been carrying my news to the War Office." She lay down a card.

Harry played on her card. "A small service compared to the trials of our friends in France."

"But an important one," Gussie insisted, volume rising.

"Your play," Patience reminded her, touching her foot to Gussie's under the table.

Gussie played, badly. Patience took the trick. Yvette sighed.

She only grew more restive as the evening progressed, her comments becoming terser, her movements tighter. Harry caught Patience's eye, his look concerned. As they finished a hand, Patience rose.

"Perhaps an early night after all the excitement. If the weather clears, we will have lawn bowling tomorrow and a picnic."

Lydia perked up at that, but Yvette merely smiled politely.

Harry touched Patience's arm as the others began leaving the room. "Stay a moment. We must talk."

Yvette must have heard him, for she threw up her hands. "Talk! Why do we sit and talk while people are dying!"

About to leave the room, Beau glanced back with a frown.

Harry stepped closer to Yvette. "No one is dying here, cousin."

Her eyes were stormy. "Easy to say in your pleasant house, warm and safe. What do you care about people struggling for their lives? What do you know of ridicule, rejection by your own kind?"

Harry's face fell. "Yvette."

She stared at him, fingers flying to her lips. "Oh, 'Arry. Forgive me." She turned and ran for the door. Beau stepped aside to let her go.

"Charming as always, eh, Harry?" he jibed.

Harry started after her, but Patience caught his arm. "No, Harry. Let me. You have more important matters to attend to." She nodded toward Beau, who was gazing after Yvette with a thoughtful look.

Harry nodded. "Very well. But I haven't forgotten our conversation, Patience. I promise we will return to it when the time is right."

She held that promise to her heart as she hurried after Yvette.

CHAPTER EIGHTEEN

Harry squared his shoulders as Patience hurried out of the room after Yvette. At least Villers did not attempt to stop her. After the last few hours, Harry would likely have snapped.

As it was, he made himself stroll up to the fellow. "Bit early for me. Care for a game of billiards before retiring? I'll spot you three points."

His smile was entirely too self-satisfied. "I'm more interested in another game."

Harry sighed. Not cards. The fellow would only bait him. One crack about his father would set him over the edge as well.

"I'm not sure I'm up for a fencing match," Harry joked. "And you've already beaten me soundly." He made a show of rubbing his arm.

"Ah, yes, your wound." Villers smirked. "Never fear. I don't intend to damage your consequence further. Not if you cooperate."

Harry frowned. "What are you talking about?"

He glanced out the door. Harry could see no one in the entry hall, but Cuddlestone would likely be coming through shortly to lock up for the night now that most of the guests were headed for bed.

As if he feared interruption as well, Villers drew Harry deeper into the room. "Harry, we must talk. I have an issue with you."

"Bedchamber not large enough?" Harry guessed as they came to a stop beside the dying fire. "Roast overcooked?"

"Why, Harry," he said with a shake his dark head, "what an unsatisfied guest you must think me. My time at Foulness Manor has been illuminating, and I believe, profitable."

Harry eyed him. "I won't offer for your sister. That ship has sailed."

His smile was sharp. "Nor would I wish you to offer for Lydia, not knowing what I know now." He leaned closer and lowered his voice. "I've seen you out at night."

He could not have confirmed his suspicions, not lying abed the last few days. Or had he too managed to slip out unseen?

"If you mention the matter to her husband, I will deny it," Harry informed him.

He laughed. "You should have gone on the stage. I fancy even Gussie was fooled. But I know the truth. You're smuggling. Admit it."

So, he didn't know all yet. Harry made himself shrug. "I may have purchased wine of questionable provenance, but that is no more than any gentleman seeking champagne these days must do to stock his cellars."

"How well you lie," Villers said with an admiring shake of his head. "But it seems you bought a little more than wine this time. She's no cousin of yours. I saw Gussie staring at her all evening. And that coarse dress, her lack of proper escort. I'll say this for you, Harry: you have some nerve bringing your mistress to a house party."

Harry's hand fisted, but he kept from smacking it into the fellow's leering face. The smartest thing would be to play along, but he couldn't blacken Yvette's reputation. Until all this was over, she'd have to live in England for her own safety. She'd find few friends if it was thought she was Sir Harold Orwell's doxy.

"My cousin," he said, "is a lady. She may not dress the part at the moment, but that can be rectified. Your behavior, however, is more suspect."

"As is yours," he pointed out. "But I know the value of silence. One hundred pounds, every quarter, and no one need know your secrets."

Harry snorted. "Do you think you can do anything to my reputation that hasn't already been done?"

He straightened. "Perhaps not. But if you will not think of your dear cousin, think of poor Patience. How will she hold her head up, engaged to such a scoundrel? Why, she might even call off the wedding."

He wanted to laugh in the fellow's face. Patience, bless her, knew all about him, and still she stayed by his side. But Villers was close enough to the truth that Harry couldn't allow him to learn more. He lowered his head as if ashamed.

Villers clapped him on the shoulder. "I'll leave you to think on the matter. We'll speak more tomorrow. Sleep well, Harry." He turned and strolled from the room.

He could not know it was a false threat. Most of those in the village already knew their Sir Harry was supporting the smugglers. Undene and his men even knew why. Those in the aristocracy suspected Harry of worse crimes. Yet how could he subject Yvette and Patience to the same ridicule?

One hundred pounds a quarter was a steep price. Likely Harry would have to have Julian pull some of his investments from the Exchange. Yet if he didn't pay, Villers might eventually uncover the real reason for Harry's nighttime excursions, which could make Yvette more visible as well.

At least he could rule out Villers as their assailant. Why shoot at the man you intended to blackmail? That only meant someone else was out to get Harry.

He'd come so close today to offering Patience his heart. He'd even considered refusing further work from the War Office, just for the opportunity to reclaim his reputation and marry her. He was only fooling himself. There would always be men like Villers who sought to bring him low. Patience deserved a husband whose reputation was as spotless as her own, someone who could live up to her high standards. As soon as the causeway opened, he should send her to the safety of Bath, encourage her to go on with her life.

But he no longer believed it would be easy to go on with his without her.

Patience caught up with Yvette in the upstairs corridor. The Frenchwoman turned her face away, but not before Patience saw the shine of tears on her cheeks.

"We're in here, I believe," she said, opening the door to the room that had been Lydia's.

Mr. Cuddlestone and the staff had done a good job. Patience would never have known anyone else had used the room. Fresh sheets showed on the big box bed, the cream bright against the navy cover embroidered with gold thread. Gold tassels held back the blue and red pattern of the bed hangings, and the thick blue carpet showed no sign of a recent footfall.

Patience's things had been arranged on the dressing table, her meager wardrobe hung neatly. She went to the dresser and located her nightgowns.

"This one's clean," she said, turning to offer it to Yvette.

The woman accepted it with a nod. "*Merci*. I apologize for my behavior earlier. I have not been in company I could trust for a long time."

Patience took out her own nightgown. "I cannot imagine what you've been through."

"I would not want you to imagine it," she said.

There was a rap at the door, and Emma bustled in. Her cap was askew, and one dark curl escaped to brush her rosy cheek. "Sorry, miss, miss. Too many ladies tonight, and I haven't even gone to help the mistress."

Yvette backed away. "I need no help."

Emma advanced on her. "Course you do. A lady can't sleep in her corset, can she? And don't you go cutting your laces like Miss Gussie. I can't tell you how many perfectly good strings we have to throw out when she's done with them."

Yvette held her ground, eyes turning stormy again. Patience stepped between them.

"I believe what Miss Orwell means, Emma, is that we can help each other tonight. Go to Gussie. I'll ask Harry tomorrow to find someone in the village to assist you. I'm sure you could recommend someone."

Emma stepped back. "Likely I could. Thank you, Miss Ramsey. If you're certain."

"Very," Patience assured her. "Good night, Emma."

With a last look of puzzlement at Yvette, Emma curtsied and left.

The Frenchwoman sighed. "Only two weeks in prison, and I must learn to be a lady again."

"Would you allow me?" Patience asked.

Yvette eyed her, then turned to give her access to the closures at the back of the gown. As the spruce fabric fell, dark patches sprang into view against the white of her arms, along with a leather sheath strapped to one forearm.

Patience held back her gasp. "You've been injured."

"A bit." She busied herself removing the sheath and the dagger it held. "And you must forgive the state of my corset. Madame Undene donated a dress, chemise, stockings, and petticoat, but she and I did not share the same physique."

The corset was nearly as battered as its owner, the once fine silk frayed and stained. Patience undid the lace and helped her out of it. Then she went to fetch her mother's ointment.

"This can help," she promised Yvette. "I will be gentle."

She must have been, for the Frenchwoman did not call out to stop her as she covered the bruises and chafed skin.

"How do you know to do this?" Yvette asked. "Are you an apothecary?"

Patience smiled. "No, only the companion to an elderly woman who had a number of ailments."

Yvette sighed. "She must have loved you."

"Not in the slightest," Patience said, rubbing the ointment remaining on her fingers into her own hands. "But I would never presume to compare my pitiful travails with yours."

"I can manage now," Yvette said, stepping back.

Patience turned to give her privacy. "You have no need to be ashamed of those bruises, you know. The shame is on those who inflicted them."

"*Mais oui*," she said, fabric rustling as she must have removed the chemise and donned the nightgown. "But a part of me remembers a life like this, when I had maids to dress and undress me, servants to see to my every wish. That life is gone, and I do not know what the future holds. Please, allow me to help you now."

Patience nodded, and Yvette made quick work of her ties and laces.

"We have not had a moment to discuss the future," Patience said as she pulled on her nightgown. "Harry said you must go to London when the causeway opens. What will you do there?"

She turned to find Yvette eyeing the big bed. "I will tell the fine gentlemen in the War Office everything I know," she said. "And when I am of no further use to them, they will let me go."

"To France?" Patience asked, unable to hide her shudder.

"*Non.* Not until the Corsican Monster is defeated and sanity returned. Those who flee France are not allowed to return on penalty of death. I fear I must stay in England for some time." She seemed to recover a little, for she shot Patience a smile. "But you need not worry. I will not monopolize your 'Arry."

Patience moved to one side of the bed. "He isn't really mine. Surely he told you we are only pretending to be engaged. As his supposed bride-to-be, I can make excuses for him, so he can continue his work with you."

"*C'est vrais?*" Yvette came around to the opposite side. "But the way he speaks of you, the way he looks at you. *Non*, this is no play. The man is in love."

Once more hope raised its head. "He hasn't mentioned the matter to me."

Yvette shook her head. "Men. Sometimes you must tell them what they are thinking."

Patience laughed as she climbed into bed. "I'm not sure anyone knows what Harry is thinking."

"He is open, that one," Yvette insisted, joining her. "Fearless, devoted to his country, his family. You will make him a fine bride."

She should not take such solace from the idea. "I suppose we'll just have to see what tomorrow brings."

She waited until Yvette pulled up the cover before turning down the lamp and settling back against the soft mattress.

"If you love him," Yvette said in the darkness, "do not wait to tell him. This Revolution has taught me that life is uncertain. Opportunities missed may not come again."

Andrew Marvell's poem had said the same. Patience swallowed. "I understand, but I'm not as brave as you are."

Yvette was quiet a moment, then Patience felt the bed give as she must have rolled onto her side. "I was not brave at first," she murmured. "When the mob came for my family, I ran and hid in the cellar. I did not have the opportunity to say farewell. I could not help them. But I learned, how to protect myself, how to protect others, how to use my wit and beauty to influence. It is easier to be brave when you have something or someone to fight for."

"Do you have someone, in France?" Patience asked.

She shifted again. "*Non*. My family is gone. It has been

many years, and I still miss them. I could not make friends with those loyal to Napoleon. I could trust no one. It was better to hold my heart close. But you—you have no need to dissemble. You can tell 'Arry you love him. You can accept his love. I envy you."

"Thank you, Yvette," Patience said. "Good night.

"*Bonne nuit*, Patience," she said. "And thank you for your kindness."

"It was no trouble," Patience assured her.

Indeed, the trouble would come in trying to convince herself to approach Harry and tell him how she felt.

CHAPTER NINETEEN

As soon as Harry woke and dressed the next morning, he rode out to check the causeway. A light rain was falling, but he could see the darker line of clouds to the southwest, like a wall of night heading toward him. Below, waves met the outgoing stream with violence sufficient to splash. No one would be leaving Foulness Manor today.

He intercepted Julian on the way in to breakfast and drew him into his study. But someone was there ahead of him.

Villers perched on the chair in front of Harry's desk, hands braced on his tan trousers. "Ah, there you are, Harry. I was looking for you."

Looking through the desk, more likely. Good thing the only written evidence of his activities was the notes he had already sent to Lord Hastings in the War Office.

"And I believe your sister is looking for you," Julian said, stepping aside to clear the way to the door.

With a glance at Harry, Villers rose and sauntered out.

Harry made sure he'd crossed the entry hall for the dining room before shutting the door.

"What was that about?" Julian asked.

Harry strode back to his side. "Villers intends to blackmail me. It seems I smuggled myself a ladybird."

"Smuggling," Julian pressed. "Not spying?"

"Not so far. I checked the causeway—it's still covered.

We can't rid ourselves of him. Keep him busy today, would you? Because if he insults me, Yvette, or Patience again, I won't answer for my response."

"I'll keep him away from you if I have to lose at billiards all day," Julian promised. "I just hope I have enough in my wallet to keep him interested. But Harry, if he doesn't know what you're doing, I doubt he was the one to take a shot at you."

"So do I," Harry said. "Perhaps it was an accident, someone from the village trying to warn the smugglers away from the cove. Once word got out I'd been hit, the shooter feared to come forward."

"Perhaps," Julian allowed. "But I'll rest easier when Yvette is in London."

Harry felt the same way. But her safety wasn't the only thing on his mind. He loitered in the entry hall until Yvette appeared with Patience on the way to breakfast.

"Do we leave?" Yvette asked, golden brows up.

Harry shook his head. "The causeway is still flooded. I expect another squall any time."

Yvette deflated.

Patience sighed. "Then everyone will have to remain indoors again today."

She sounded tired, and he could understand why. The bulk of the arrangements for this doomed house party had fallen on her shoulders.

"Julian has offered to keep Villers busy," Harry told her. "I can help with Meredith and Lydia."

"Gussie will want me and Lydia in the laboratory, I expect," Patience said. "Would you care to join us, Yvette?"

She smiled. "Wherever I am needed, I will go." She touched Harry's hand. "Do not fret. We triumphed over my cousin's plots, the Emperor's plans, and the Channel seas. This house party is nothing." She stepped back with a smile to Patience. "I will go eat. Remember my advice, Patience." She headed for the dining room.

"Advice?" Harry asked.

Patience had paled. "We had quite a talk last night." Her face puckered. "Oh, Harry, is it true she lost her entire family?"

"Her mother, father, and two older brothers," he said, trying not to picture it. "She was remanded into the care of a distant cousin who had thrown in his lot with the revolutionaries. He treated her as little more than a drudge until the Emperor noticed her and demanded she be made part his court. That's how she learned the secrets she passed to us. Her life was in danger every moment."

"How awful. I'll do all I can to help her ease back into a more normal life. Well, as normal as Foulness Manor can be."

He shared her smile. "I'm sure she'll appreciate it. And so will I."

She held her smile, and the silence stretched.

"Is there nothing else you wish to say to me?" Patience asked.

The tone was all politeness, but he felt the yearning under it. He'd raised her expectations yesterday, and he cursed himself for it. Until he had a name beyond shame he had no right to offer it to her.

"Only that I applaud your efforts," he said. "Your support to me and Gussie means more than you can know."

"You both deserve support," she said. "You both deserve respect and admiration as well. Surely you know that I admire you, Harry."

He could not imagine why. "I've done nothing particularly admirable since I met you. I'm a glorified messenger, and then only because my forefathers had the poor taste to league themselves with smugglers."

A frown gathered on her brow. "It's not like you to be so humble. You have sacrificed for the good of your country, just like Yvette."

"My efforts pale beside hers," Harry insisted. "Don't

make me a hero, Patience."

"Then don't make yourself a villain," she countered. She stood on tiptoe and pressed a kiss to his cheek. Then, blushing, she hurried after Yvette.

Harry fingered the spot her lips had brushed. Why did one touch from her set him to dreaming? He could imagine her beside him here at the manor, supporting the needs of the village, assisting at the church. They would travel to London, take part in the Season, convince his friend Worth to take them up in one of his balloons. They'd spend time with Wey on his island in the Thames, Carrolton at his forest hideaway. And once children came, they would teach them to be men and women of character. Patience would make an excellent mother.

The vision popped, pieces scattering like smugglers from revenue agents. He had no business dreaming of a future with Patience. Not until he was shed of his past.

And certainly not while Villers insisted on profiting from the present.

Villers caught up with Harry in the withdrawing room later that morning. Julian offered Harry an apologetic smile as he followed the fellow in. Patience, Lydia, Meredith, and Yvette were gathered in the laboratory, and Harry had been digging through the bookshelves for inspiration on how to keep everyone occupied this afternoon.

"How about a game of billiards?" Harry asked, pushing away from the shelf. "I know Julian was itching to beat your last score."

"Delighted," Villers said with a wave toward Julian. "But first I must have a word with you, Harry."

Julian glanced at Harry. Might as well get it over with. Harry nodded, and Julian left the room.

"I don't have one hundred pounds per quarter for you, Villers," Harry said.

He tsked. "Do you think so little of Patience? Or is it Yvette you find too cheap to support?"

Harry took a step toward him. "Careful, Villers. You malign the lady at your peril."

He spread his hands. "I assure you, I am only trying to help your cousin."

"But why do I require your help?" Yvette wandered back into the room. "Forgive the interruption, but I found the discussion of potions tedious." She looked Villers up and down. "What trouble do you think to spare me, Monsieur Villers?"

"Only the unkind slurs of Society," he said smoothly. "The ladies and gentlemen of London do not tolerate uncertainty well, and you arrived under mysterious circumstances."

"I do not call walking along the lane so mysterious," Yvette assured him. "I could have visited Foulness Manor at any time. It just happened to be while you were in residence."

"Because Harry allowed it." He cast Harry a coy glance. "But you will need more assistance than Harry's word if you are to be accepted into Society."

"And you offer such assistance?" she asked, head cocked.

"For a consideration." He glanced at Harry again. "And should that consideration be less than generous, I might find my way to the Admiralty. I am certain they would be very interested to hear more about your activities, Harry."

Perhaps more interested than Villers knew. Harry was almost tempted to let him try approaching the admirals.

Yvette seemed more concerned. "C'est vrai," she said with a sigh, fiddling with her sleeve as if nervous. Something sparkled in the lamplight. She sprung on Villers, thin blade in her hand.

"Worthless cur," she hissed, steel pressed under his chin. "I have vanquished smarter men than you. Did you think to malign a fine man like Sir Harry Orwell? I will dance over your corpse."

Villers' eyes nearly bugged from his head. Harry must

have looked nearly as surprised. Was this a bluff? He peered closer. Her hand trembled, and a wild light shone in her eyes.

"Yvette," he said in warning, "let him go."

"Why?" She pressed the knife deeper, wrinkling his cravat. Villers stood on tiptoe to escape the blade. "He is a snake, this one, nipping at our heels. The best way to stop a snake is to cut off its head."

"No, please," Villers warbled, wavering on his feet. "I'll say nothing. I swear."

Harry reached out and lay his hand on Yvette's, pulling it down and away from the fellow's throat. "Easy. There's no need for bloodshed. This is England. You're safe."

She shivered, as if he'd doused her with cold water, but he drew in a breath as she pulled back the blade.

"I am safe nowhere," she said, but, after a last scathing look at Villers, she turned and stalked from the room.

Villers rubbed his neck, even though the skin wasn't so much as nicked. "Mad. Utterly mad."

Harry turned to him. "Quite right. And you would be too if you'd lived through what she's witnessed. Whatever you think you know, Villers, keep silent. She's not one you want at your back. And even the Admiralty could be taken in by a pretty face."

Patience followed Gussie, Lydia, and Meredith into the entry hall. After watching Patience make a new batch of her mother's ointment, Gussie had had another inspiration. She was certain sweet flags growing in the marsh below the house would be just the thing to improve it. Lydia and Meredith had indicated interest in accompanying her to the edge of the marsh to collect samples. Of course, Patience was expected to come along, even though her thoughts were elsewhere.

Harry had been so distant today. Like Robert, he seemed

to regret having suggested his engagement to Patience might be anything other than a ruse. Was that the way with most courtships? Did all men make promises they had no intention of keeping? Surely no woman would ever wed!

Or was it her? Had she been right all along, and she had some fatal flaw that doomed her connections? Perhaps her reticence had made Harry think her unsuited to be his partner in life. She had been disappointed in her performances. How much more would he despise them?

"But, madam," Mr. Cuddlestone was protesting when she joined the others near the front door. "It's pouring."

Gussie waved a hand. "*Acorus calamus* loves water. This would be the perfect time to collect it."

Patience peered out the window. The rain fell so heavily she couldn't make out the top of the drive. "I fear Mr. Cuddlestone is correct, Gussie. We'll be soaked before we've gone a few steps."

"Sacrifices must be made for progress," Gussie insisted.

Lydia joined Patience at the window. "It is rather stormy."

"Where is your spirit of adventure?" Gussie challenged.

Yvette, who had left them earlier, came out of the withdrawing room as if pulled by their voices. "Why must we argue?"

"Because we have passion," Gussie said. "I cannot rest until my preparation is perfected. It will remove warts and blemishes, heal wounds."

"Heal wounds?" Yvette moved closer, eyes brightening. "This could be a great kindness to those fighting this awful war."

Gussie glanced around at the others. "That is what I've been trying to tell you. What's a little rain for a chance to benefit all of mankind?"

Lydia hurried back to her side. "I'll come."

"I as well," Yvette said. "Where do we go?"

Resigned, Patience returned to the group. "Gussie believes a plant growing in the marsh nearby may hold the key to her formulation."

"And we are all ready to leave the manor," Meredith put in.

Yvette turned to Patience. "But what of the ointment you used on me last night? It eased my pain and smelled like roses."

Gussie put her nose in the air. "Roses are entirely too common. I want my preparation to be original."

"I would think," Meredith put in, "that you would prefer it to be effective."

Gussie stalked up to her. "You are a guest in my home, Miss…Thorn. Do not presume to lecture me on how to manage my laboratory."

Patience wasn't the only one staring at her. "Gussie?"

As if she realized her mistake, Gussie jerked back from her, reddening. "I do beg your pardon, Meredith. It's this unending rain. I…excuse me." She hurried for the stairs.

"Shall we fetch her the plant?" Lydia asked, face puckered.

"No," Patience said. "I'll talk to her. Meredith, may I ask you to entertain Lydia and Yvette?"

Meredith shook herself. "Of course. Come, ladies. I'm sure we can find something to occupy us usefully."

Lydia nodded, and Yvette put on a sweet smile as they set off across the hall.

"You are a blessing, Miss Ramsey," Mr. Cuddlestone murmured. "I've never seen the mistress like this, not since she was a young lady trying to convince her brother to stay home." He sighed. "How she despaired of him. We all did. Perhaps you can learn what's troubling her now."

"I'll try," Patience said, and she lifted her skirts to climb the stairs.

Gussie hadn't gone far. She was pacing the corridor just off the landing. Patience could hear her muttering.

"It if isn't animal or mineral, it stands to reason it must be a plant. But which plant?"

"Gussie?" Patience ventured closer. "Are you all right?"

NEVER BORROW A BARONET   201

Gussie whirled to face her. "No! There must be an answer. Why can't I find it?"

"Meredith's suggestion agreed with mine," Patience said. "Roses and lavender are accepted healing agents. You had said you might improve my mother's ointment. Why must we look farther afield?"

Gussie turned her gaze heavenward as if seeking help from there. "Have you seen the various ointments and salves for sale, Patience? All invented by men. No one will take mine seriously if I merely employ the ordinary. We must discover something new, something important, something that will make a difference."

Patience stepped in front of her, and Gussie met her gaze.

"Is that what you want?" Patience asked. "To make a difference?"

"Why else would I go to such trouble?" She began worrying her hands in time with her steps as she paced around Patience. "Harry is doing his part to end this horrible war. You are doing your part to help him remain unseen. Why can't I help? I must be good for something!"

Patience caught her hands as she passed, steadying her. "Oh, Gussie, you have already done so much good. Where would Harry be without you? You raised him, taught him to live by his principles. You set the example of what it can mean to care."

She blinked. "I suppose I did."

Patience gave her hands a squeeze. "Yes. And he needs you now more than ever. We must safeguard Yvette until she reaches London. We must prevent the Villers from learning the truth."

Gussie nodded. "You're right. I have perhaps been trying too hard to be original."

Patience smiled. "You? Never."

Gussie grinned, the dimple on either side of her mouth reminding Patience of Harry. "And when all is well, we can discuss the introduction of more common ingredients."

"And calamus." Patience released her. "My mother used the ground root to soothe an upset stomach. I'll look in her book to see if she associated it with the skin. You may have made your discovery."

Gussie beamed. "Oh, Patience, you are so good for me. I wish you would stay on."

Harry had said the same, but she was no longer sure he meant it.

"We can discuss that later," Patience said. "For now, let's keep everyone from fretting over things they shouldn't know."

Gussie agreed, and the two headed back downstairs. Mr. Cuddlestone was hovering at the foot of the stairs. Gussie sailed right past him, but Patience offered him a thumbs up, earning a relieved grin from the butler.

Meredith and the others were in the withdrawing room. They must have decided to try a dramatic reading that evening, for Lydia and Yvette were paging through books and comparing thoughts. Meredith moved to Gussie's side.

"Please forgive me," she told the older woman. "I did not intend to direct your household or your work."

Gussie inclined her head. "And you must forgive me, Meredith. I am not myself. This house party will be the death of me."

"But *ma chère* Lydia," Yvette said across the room. "How would anyone enjoy a recitation of Roman conquests when war is so very close to these shores?"

"Historical tomes are edifying," Lydia protested. She lifted the heavy book higher. "And lo, thirty years before the birth of our Lord, Caesar did fix upon a scheme of taxation and subjugation, wreaking havoc on the peoples across the vast Roman empire." She shivered. "Fascinating."

Yvette closed her eyes, tipped her head to the side, and let out a snore.

Lydia shut the book with a giggle. "Very well. No Roman conquests. But there must be something we can declaim."

Just then, her brother strode into the room.

"Moderate your tone, Lydia. I could hear you in the game room."

Somehow Patience doubted that, but Lydia grimaced and dropped her gaze.

Yvette fluttered her lashes in his direction. "But Monsieur Villers, your sister is a darling. See how sweetly she tries to keep us all entertained. You should praise her."

"Yes, well." He shuffled his feet. "Nicely done, Lydia."

Lydia glanced up and eyed him as if she didn't believe him.

As Meredith and Gussie went to join the two by the bookshelf, Patience turned to him. "The ladies will be offering a dramatic reading for the gentlemen this evening. Your sister will no doubt have an important role."

He preened. "Well, of course. It's about time Lydia received her due."

As he was the first to criticize the girl, Patience decided not to comment on the statement. "Where are the other gentlemen? We would not want them to overhear. It would spoil all the fun. Perhaps you could keep them busy."

He sighed. "More billiards, I suppose. But very well, I'll do my part. Before I go, however, I must speak to you."

What now? Patience drew him out into the entry hall. "Activities not to your liking? Room too cool?" she guessed.

He frowned. "Why does everyone assume I mean to complain?" Before she could answer, he shook his head. "Never mind. I wanted to thank you for your kind ministrations while I was ill. You care about those around you, Patience. I find that commendable."

She managed a smile.

As if encouraged, he took a step closer. "And because you care, I feel I should warn you. I have evidence your betrothed is dealing with smugglers."

Patience searched his face. His dark eyes were alight

with glee at possessing such a scandalous secret, but sweat gleamed on his brow under the sweep of dark hair. Was he nervous? What did he expect her to do, draw a blade on him? And besides, how had he managed to spy on Harry from the sickbed? And why was he telling her now?

"I can scarcely believe it," she murmured, dropping her gaze to the carpet.

He laid his hand on hers. "I promised you I would look into the matter of his disappearances at night, and this was what I discovered. I spoke with him about it, urged him to give it up, even threatened to inform the Admiralty— merely to save him, you understand. But he laughed me off. I only tell you so as to give you time to prepare yourself for his downfall, my dear."

Downfall? He could do nothing to Harry. Surely the Admiralty knew all about his activities. Yet if Beau was willing to tell her and the Admiralty what he thought he knew, who else might he tell? Even if he only confided in Lydia, the girl's enthusiasm might lead her to blurt out the news. Harry's reputation would once more be in tatters. It was a sad fact that some men turned a blind eye to an affair. They would be less sanguine about treason.

Patience pressed her free hand against Beau's. "Please, say nothing. We cannot see Harry harmed."

His smile was kind. "Your concern does you credit, my dear. I suppose I might be mistaken. Tell me, what do you think of Harry's cousin?"

Did he suspect Yvette as well? Oh, but he was dangerously close to the truth.

Patience made her eyes as big as Lydia's. "Why, she is charming. I'm so glad Harry decided to reconcile her with the family."

Something other than kindness glittered in his eyes. "Interesting that she lives nearby yet Lydia and I have never met her."

"You have seen her, sir. She had an unorthodox

upbringing and struggles to fit in with polite society. You cannot blame Harry for not wanting to bring her into a larger group."

He shook his head with a chuckle. "You are either the most naïve woman I have ever met or the best liar."

Patience drew herself up. "Really, sir, you go too far." She started away, and he moved to block her.

"Forgive me, Patience. This whole matter distresses me greatly. Harry has been my friend, yet I find myself in a quandary. There is a war on, and good men cannot keep silent. Besides, there is the matter of the reward."

Patience frowned. "Reward?"

"Indeed. It is well known the Crown is offering one hundred pounds for information leading to the arrest of those dealing with France. Given Lydia's need for a dowry, you cannot ask me to forego such a prize."

In his world, one hundred pounds was a pittance. Lady Lilith had spent that much on two ball gowns. In Patience's world, however, it was enough to live a year frugally.

But nowhere was it enough to betray Harry.

"I'm sure some gentleman will be more than delighted to marry your sister, regardless of dowry," she told him. "Have you spoken to Lord Carrolton? He is of the age to seek a wife."

He took a step back. "As I mentioned, I know the Carroltons well. They cannot supply the life I wish for my sister."

Meaning they would not pay him a bride price nor allow him to influence them. What a grasping fellow!

Patience stared at him as his meaning became clear. "You want money from me!"

He drew himself up. "I'm sure I would never be so crass. I mention the matter only because Harry is important to you. As his bride-to-be, I thought you would want to help."

"You thought me an easy target, rather," Patience informed him. "I regret to tell you, sir, that I have nothing—

no dowry, no fortune, no family or influence. Harry and Gussie are everything to me. You threaten them at your peril."

It was a bold statement, but she meant every word. For the first time in a long time, she felt needed, important, useful. And she was ready to defend those she loved, regardless of whether they returned that love.

She had never looked particularly fierce. The shape of her face and her slender frame destroyed any chance of being menacing. But Beau Villers took one look at her, waxed white, and excused himself to hurry for the stairs.

Something strong, powerful, pulsed through her. Was this how Jane felt when she spoke her mind? How Meredith felt when she argued for a client? How Yvette felt when she bested an enemy? If Patience could do this, then perhaps she had what it took to stand by Harry's side. It was all up to her.

CHAPTER TWENTY

Confound the man! Harry stalked out of the game room, heading for the entry hall. Just when he thought he had Beau Villers safely cornered, the fellow slipped away again. He seemed intent on gathering evidence to incriminate Harry. He already knew enough to be dangerous to their plans.

But the first person he saw coming across the entry hall was a tall, slender man, whose neat but plain coat and trousers proclaimed him a servant of some sort. He must be the valet.

"Have you seen your master?" Harry demanded.

The fellow paled as if expecting a reprimand. Very likely he was used to going unnoticed by the rest of the household.

"Not lately, sir," he said, gaze downcast. "Had you need of my services?"

"No, thank you," Harry said, stepping aside to let him pass. "But if you see him, let him know I'd like a word."

"Very good, sir." He hurried past.

Mr. Cuddlestone and Wilkins were working against the far wall, coats off and sleeves rolled up. Already they had shoved the mahogany table that usually graced the middle of the hall to one side.

Harry frowned. "Are we redecorating?"

Cuddlestone straightened. "No, Sir Harry. The ladies will

be performing a dramatic reading this evening, and the mistress would like suitable surroundings." He raised his brows as if hoping Harry would gainsay his aunt.

"Did you see Mr. Villers pass this way?" Harry asked, unwilling to get between Gussie and her plans.

"A few moments ago. He looked rather indisposed."

Sick again? If only Harry could be certain it would keep him abed and out of his way.

Patience came out of the withdrawing room. "Mr. Cuddlestone, would you happen to have any extra bedsheets?"

Cuddlestone frowned. "Is there something amiss with your bed, Miss Ramsey?"

"No, no. Gussie would like to drape them over the paintings so all eyes are fixed on the performers." Her apologetic smile took in the butler, Wilkins, and Harry. Once more Cuddlestone looked to Harry.

"Whatever Gussie wants, humor her," Harry said. "It is in all our best interests to keep our guests occupied."

"Of course, Sir Harry." Cuddlestone nodded to Wilkins, who dusted off his hands, shrugged into his coat, and strode for the stairs.

Patience moved closer to Harry. Her eyes looked heavy, her shoulders tight, as if she was ready to fight the famed boxer Gentleman Jackson himself. "May I have a word with you?"

Harry nodded. Taking her arm, he led her across the entry hall to the door of his study.

"What's happened?" he asked as they stepped inside.

She raised her chin. "That odious Mr. Villers attempted to pry money from me in return for his silence. He threatened to tell the Admiralty about your work."

Harry shook his head. "Like a dog to a bone, that one. Don't worry, Patience. He already tried the same tactic with me and got nowhere."

Her color deepened. "So, he thought I would be easier

prey. The scoundrel! Can we please throw him out now?"

Harry chuckled. "Unfortunately, the causeway remains impassable. I'm tempted to send him to the inn in the village, but I don't want to leave Lydia at his mercy. He will be in no mood to be conciliatory."

She deflated. "You're right." She glanced up at him. "Isn't there any way we can keep Lydia and lose him?"

"No way short of proposing marriage, and I am spoken for, remember?"

She did not look amused. "But Harry, I cannot trust him. What if he isn't satisfied with our refusal? He could make trouble for you."

Harry shook his head. "Nothing I cannot handle. The War Office and the Admiralty keep in close contact. Surely the leaders know of my actions. With the causeway out, I haven't been able to send word about Yvette with anyone I would trust."

She shivered. "Then we're truly on our own."

He ran a hand up her arm. "But not defenseless. We'll survive this. Try to keep Gussie from rebuilding the manor for her reading, will you?"

Her gaze searched his. "What will you do?"

Harry took a step back. "I intend to have it out with Villers, once and for all."

The valet let Harry in. Shrinking in on himself, as if he feared rebuke, he backed away.

"That will be all, Tecet," Villers said. The valet quickly disappeared into the dressing room, shutting the door behind him as if wishing to distance himself from anything that might happen with his master.

Villers had already retreated to the chair by the fire, coat, cravat, and boots off, feet to the warmth and chin on his chest.

"You threatened Patience," Harry said, striding to his

side.

Villers glanced up at him. "I threaten a good many people, not that I manage to derive any gain from it."

Harry put a hand on either arm of the chair, bracketing him in place. "And that's all that brought you here? A hope you might profit from my loss?"

Villers shook his head. "You know as well as I do I'd hoped for a match between you and Lydia. She was supposed to be my ticket to the upper echelons. If she married a duke, I'd be set for life. But she doesn't have what it takes to snare a duke."

Harry straightened. "You malign your sister to no cause. She has many fine attributes."

A sneer turned up one corner of his mouth. "Oh, certainly. Bluestocking tendencies and the regrettable need to chatter incessantly. I thought surely, with your reputation, you'd be willing to take her. At least she'd have a title then. But even a penniless nobody beat her out there."

"So, failing to snare me, as you put it, in matrimony, you decided on blackmail instead."

Villers spread his hands. "It might have worked. But Patience refused to help, and you laughed it off."

"You failed to consider my reputation," Harry said. How ironic it should be the thing that saved him.

Villers sighed. "Just my luck. I finally have a secret I can share for reward, and the fellow involved is more scandalous than I am."

Harry straightened. "Am I? I seem to recall you fighting a duel last year over an unknown lady, and many have remarked at the way you push Lydia forward. If I were to swear out a complaint for blackmail, I'd probably be believed."

He sunk lower. "You might at that. Shall we call a truce?"

"I'm willing," Harry said. "But if you cross me, Villers, I will retaliate."

"Fine," he spit out. "I'll play along, stay for the holiday

as planned. But, as soon as Easter is over, Lydia and I are leaving, even if we have to swim that wretched causeway."

"My thoughts exactly," Harry said.

No one had much interest in dinner that night. Yvette, Gussie, and Meredith ate sparingly of the. mutton and candied carrots, perhaps because they were anxious about the upcoming reading. The ladies had settled upon a play and spent most of the afternoon rehearsing, Yvette and Gussie taking turns issuing directions. Like Patience, Julian seemed more interested in watching the others over dinner, and Beau, who had consented to join them, picked at his food. Only Lydia tucked in with any gusto.

After dinner, they repaired to the entry hall, Fortune having been left in Emma's care. On Gussie's orders, the place had been transformed. Sheeting draped the walls, and candles here and there sent light flickering across the fabric until the entire space sparkled. Mr. Cuddlestone and Wilkins had brought in armchairs from the withdrawing room and Harry's study and arranged them around the hearth at one end of the room. Patience took her seat next to Harry and the other gentlemen while Gussie and her troupe took up places in front of the fire.

Glancing around to make sure everyone was seated and attentive, Gussie stepped forward, eyes bright. "Ladies and gentlemen, I give you a tale of love and intrigue, courtesy of our beloved Bard."

Beau raised his brows. "You'd attempt Shakespeare?"

Gussie pointed a finger at him. "Behave, Mr. Villers, or I shall confine you to your room."

Beau leaned back and closed his mouth.

Harry winked at Patience.

With a satisfied nod, Gussie resumed her theatrical stance, head up and eyes out over the room as if one hundred people eagerly awaited the work instead of the four and Cuddlestone. "And now, without further ado, we present for your entertainment, a reading from *Antony and Cleopatra*." She stepped back next to Meredith, who held the book of plays in her hands.

Yvette took the part of Philo, a Roman solider under Marc Antony. Though she struck a determined pose, her lilting voice made it difficult for Patience to picture a brawny fighter. Then she looked up from the text to affix her audience with a vibrant blue stare as she finished her first speech. "The triple pillar of the world transformed into a strumpet's fool. Behold and see."

Beau leaned around Julian and Patience to eye Harry. If he noticed, Harry gave no sign.

Meredith took the part of Cleopatra. With her thick dark hair and flashing eyes, she was all too easy to imagine as the queen of Egypt who had enthralled countless men. "If it be love indeed," she said, gaze lighting on Julian, "tell me how much."

Julian returned her gaze, transfixed.

Lydia raised her chin, voice strong and firm in the role of Antony. "There's beggary in a love that can be reckoned."

Julian nodded agreement. Did he truly think men should be exempt from expressing their love? Small wonder Meredith had been disappointed in him.

"I'll set a bourn how far to be beloved," Meredith said with a toss of her head, as if as queen she was truly capable to setting a boundary on love.

Lydia put a hand on her heart. "Then must thou needs find new heaven, new earth."

What would it be like to be loved beyond the boundaries of heaven and earth? To have a man willing to sacrifice all just to be with her?

She waited for the next line, but no one spoke. Lydia glanced pointedly at Gussie, who shook herself and bent over the page.

"News, my good lord, from Rome," she called out.

Lydia sighed. "Grates me. The sum."

Meredith as Cleopatra interrupted, and the two characters argued back and forth, both fervent. Even Gussie watched without moving.

Harry leaned closer to Patience. "He'll never convince her of his love. Not while she doubts him."

"It is possible to love despite doubt," Patience murmured back. "The lack is in her, not him."

Harry chuckled. "You'll never make me believe it."

Gussie scowled at him, and he inclined his head in apology.

But Patience found it hard to attend. Was that the problem between them? She'd feared Harry thought her too cowardly to stand beside him, that only if she found an unknown courage could she hope to win his heart. Could it be he doubted she could care for him because he doubted himself?

The ladies finished the reading to great applause, particularly from Julian, and adjourned to the withdrawing room for refreshments before bed. Patience kept glancing at Harry, who laughed and conversed as if he hadn't a care. Had she so misjudged him?

Yvette was the first to rise, forcing the gentlemen to their feet. "Stay," she said with a magnanimous wave. "I find myself fatigued and would retire." She glanced at Patience, then quickly away, as if unwilling to impose. Yet Patience could see the darkness growing under her eyes as Yvette slipped from the room.

"Perhaps I should go," she murmured to Harry as the others resumed their seats. "She should not be alone."

He reached out and squeezed her hand. "You are very good to us, Patience."

She managed a smile before taking her leave as well.

The stairs were empty as Patience climbed them. The only person in the upper corridor was Beau's valet. He quickly bowed out of the way as Patience approached.

Funny. She'd become used to being unseen and uncared for at the Carroltons. Gussie and Harry, Mr. Cuddlestone and Emma, had made her feel part of the family. She no longer could convince herself it was all because of the false engagement.

Yvette was at the window, gazing out into the night, when Patience entered the room.

"Forgive me," she said, turning. "Sometimes I find happiness difficult."

"I know," Patience said, going to join her. "It's hard to change one's attitude, even when circumstances warrant it. Sometimes I forget I'm no longer a servant."

Yvette smiled. "And I am no longer sure what I am or could be. But tomorrow will be better, *oui*?"

"Yes," Patience agreed. "Let me help you change."

Yvette laughed. "*Non*, tonight, I play your servant first. I will bedeck you in flannel and brush out your hair. You will sleep like a babe."

Though she wasn't sure she could sleep so soundly, Patience turned to let her begin. Yvette was still brushing her hair when Emma arrived, bearing a foaming white drink in a crystal glass.

"Mr. Teacake's recipe," she said. "He claims it helps his master, Mr. Villers, sleep. Made it with his own hand, he did." She offered it to Yvette.

The Frenchwoman shook her head. "I wish nothing but thank you and Mr. Villers's man for the thought."

Emma sniffed at the brew. "I can't blame you. Doesn't smell all that good to me. Mr. Teacake was holding it in his hands when I returned Fortune to Miss Thorn and, and the little darling sneezed at it, twice! I'll return it to Mr. Teacake and come back to help." She nodded to Patience. "Thank you for arranging for more help, Miss Ramsey. Young Mary is already assisting Miss Thorn and Miss Lydia."

She had no sooner left than there was a rap at the door.

Still fully dressed, Yvette went to answer.

"Ah, 'Arry! Did you wish to kiss your bride goodnight?"

Patience's heart leaped, but she took a breath and turned to meet his gaze.

He was staring at her, eyes wide, and Patience tucked back her unbound hair.

"I wanted to make sure you were both all right," he said.

Yvette held the door wider, grin merry. "Oh, we are in very good spirits, *oui*?"

Patience moved closer. "We're fine, Harry. It was good of you to ask."

He nodded, but he made no effort to leave. With a laugh, Yvette went to the window once more, putting her back to them to give them privacy.

"You should go," Patience murmured. "If the causeway opens tomorrow, you have a long journey ahead of you."

He nodded, reluctantly, she thought. "Very well. Is there anything I can do for you tonight?"

Tell me you love me. Tell me you never want me to leave. Hold me and kiss me as if you'll never let me go.

"No," Patience said. "But thank you, Harry. Sleep well."

He stepped back, and she eased the door shut.

"You did not heed my advice, I think," Yvette said, turning from the window. "You have not told him you love him."

"No," Patience admitted. Her fingers were twisting in her nightgown; she forced them to stop. "But I begin to fear he won't believe me even if I summon the courage to speak."

Yvette cocked her head. "Why?"

"Harry's family is held in disrespect," Patience explained. "That's why it was easy for him to play the scoundrel to hide his work with you."

"But his men respect him," she protested, crossing the room. "This I have seen. And here, his staff treat him like a son."

Patience had noticed that as well. Though he had been a fatherly man, the Carrolton butler would never have spoken to the earl or his mother the way Mr. Cuddlestone spoke to Harry and Gussie. But how could she forget Beau's snide remarks?

"I take it Society has not been as kind," Patience told her. "I think it weighs on him."

Yvette was watching her. "And does it trouble you? Do you doubt him?"

Patience met her gaze. "No. Not anymore. But, doubting himself, I'm not sure he would accept my love."

"Ah." She sighed. "I suppose, my dear Patience, you will not know until you try. You must decide if he is worth risking your heart."

She had kept silent, remained in the shadows, telling herself that was her place as a companion. All this time, had she merely been trying to avoid risking a harsh word, an unkind look? Had she been so intent on protecting her heart she couldn't give it to Harry now?

CHAPTER TWENTY-ONE

It took Harry some time to fall asleep that night. It wasn't the potential danger of transporting Yvette that kept him awake, or the determination to make sure Villers didn't threaten their plans. No, it was the image of Patience, standing silhouetted against the fire, hair falling about her shoulders. He'd seen her in her nightgown before, the day he'd blundered into her bedchamber, wounded. Tonight, she had seemed softer, vulnerable, and all he'd wanted to do was pull her close and kiss her.

Perhaps he was as selfish as his forefathers. He'd thought to remove her from his life to protect her, yet he couldn't seem to let her go.

Blue sky greeted him when he rose the next morning ahead of most of his guests. He shaved and dressed himself before Cuddlestone appeared.

"Perhaps the silver-shot waistcoat instead?" his man asked with a hopeful smile.

Harry waved him off and headed for the stables.

Julian was there before him, waiting for one of the grooms to saddle his horse.

"Going to check the causeway?" Julian guessed.

Harry nodded, and the other groom went running for his horse, Rapscallion. The two men rode out a short while later. They travelled in companionable silence, the day bright and warming.

"I detected some thawing from Meredith," Harry ventured as they cantered toward the edge of the hill.

"I have hope," Julian confessed. "I intend to pursue her when we return to London. Which may be very soon."

Harry reined in beside him. The waters still crossed the road, but much less frantically, and he could see the dirt of the track in places.

"Tomorrow, if we have no rain," Harry agreed. "Now, that's reason to celebrate."

Many of the others were similarly delighted when Harry and Julian returned to the manor. Only Lydia and Patience seemed less than thrilled that the house party would soon be ending. Still, Patience rallied and took everyone out to the laundry outbuilding to dye eggs for the Easter celebration the next day. She was such a good hostess, seeing to everyone's needs, that Harry didn't have a chance to speak to her alone until later that afternoon, when they all took a turn in the gardens under the late March sun. The air smelled fresh, washed clean, and raindrops still sparkled here and there on flowers and shrubs, anointing them in silver.

"You continue to amaze me," Harry told her as they strolled arm in arm. "I'd think you'd be tired of all this by now."

"I like to be of service," she replied. Then she made a face. "Harry, we must talk. Alone."

Yvette and Lydia were walking just ahead of them. Gussie and Villers were behind, with Meredith and Julian trailing so she could walk Fortune on her leash. Normally, taking Patience aside might be challenging, but there was that false engagement to rely on as an excuse.

"I'll find a way," Harry promised.

Something zinged past him. A bee, so early in the season?

The loud crack from the trees warned him of his error.

"Down!" Harry cried, grabbing Patience's arm and tugging her to the gravel. The others fell as well, Meredith reeling in the leash to hold Fortune close.

"Why?" Lydia asked, the last to remain standing.

Gussie, on the ground near her, pulled on her pink muslin skirts. "That was a gunshot, dear."

Washing white, Lydia dropped to the gravel.

Patience was shaking beside Harry, and fear lanced him. The bullet must have been meant for him. What if it had struck her instead? He had to get her to safety.

He nodded to Julian. "Escort Patience, Meredith, and Gussie into the house. Villers, take your sister and Yvette."

"I will go nowhere," Yvette vowed.

"For once," Harry said, "don't argue. Do you want to get one of the others killed?"

Yvette paled. "*Mais non*! But I would rather go with you to chase this creature who threatens us."

Just then, Cuddlestone and Wilkins spilled from the house. Wilkins carried a long gun and Cuddlestone brandished a sword. Harry could see his grooms running armed from the stables as well.

"There!" Harry shouted, pointing to the wood. He rose to follow, but Patience caught his arm.

"No," she said. "I cannot see you hurt again."

She was white, but still, and determination etched every feature. Harry lay his hand over hers. "Go with Julian. Keep everyone away from the windows." He pressed a kiss to her cheek and sprang up to follow his staff.

Yet, once again, their search proved futile. Though they checked the woods, the outbuildings, and the path to the shore, nothing betrayed the presence of another except the silence of the area.

"Post guards around the manor," Harry instructed Cuddlestone as they returned to the house. "I don't want so much as a cricket hopping close without us knowing about it."

Cuddlestone nodded so quickly his head might have been on a spring.

Harry's guests were nearly as agitated when he joined them in the entry hall. Gussie's draperies had been removed, but the normal furnishings were still arranged against the walls. At least that left room for Julian and Gussie to pace. Villers was hunched against the hearth, as if trying to stay as far away from the door and windows as possible. Yvette stood nearby, gaze darting about as if she trusted no one. Patience sat with Lydia, Meredith, and Fortune. Even the cat looked up as Harry approached.

"We scared him off," Harry reported with his best smile. "But it's probably best that we remain inside until the morning."

Someone groaned.

Lydia glanced around. "I don't understand. Surely no one shot at us on purpose. Wasn't it just a poacher or a smuggler? Beau says there are some in the area."

Her brother straightened and cleared his throat, though he looked at no one. "I cannot help thinking that this is at least partially my fault."

Harry met Julian's gaze.

"Do tell," his friend drawled.

He rubbed his boot against the wood floor. "I tend to notice oddities—Harry's comings and goings, his whispered conversations with Mayes, the sudden arrival of his cousin. I had formed a theory in my mind, mentioned it to some of you. Perhaps I inspired others to take matters more seriously, to take action, as it were."

Yvette waved. "I have dealt with worse. You are a fly, monsieur. Easily swatted."

He frowned as if he wasn't sure whether to thank her for exonerating him or to take insult.

"I'm more likely to be blamed," Harry said. "Few too many jealous husbands."

To his surprise, Patience surged to her feet. "Enough! There are no jealous husbands. You are not a scoundrel. Someone shot at you. I might have lost you." She choked and turned away.

Harry hurried to her side. "Patience, forgive me. I never meant…"

She dashed away tears. "That is entirely the problem. You never mean anything to happen, yet it does. Someone might have been killed today. We cannot sit and pretend otherwise. We must act."

Yvette swept up to them as well. "She is right. You cannot expect me to sit playing children's games while danger crawls into England."

"What danger is crawling into England?" Lydia asked.

"Nothing," Harry said with a look to Julian.

"You have us to protect you, Miss Villers," Julian assured her.

Patience shook her head. "The time for lies is over. This could affect the outcome of the war."

Villers glanced between them. "So, Harry isn't smuggling. He's spying."

Yvette nodded. "*Et moi, aussi.* I am not an Orwell, alas. I was a lady in the Emperor's court. I have sent word to England from France, through 'Arry."

"If you breathe a word of it," Julian threatened Villers.

He held up his hands as well. "I swear! This involves the very safety of England."

Lydia stood. "No one should sit while England is in danger. Rule, Britannia!"

"Death to her enemies!" Julian agreed.

"God save the King!" Gussie cried.

Fortune meowed as if in agreement.

Meredith gazed around at them all. "Very inspiring, but perhaps myopic. We have no idea who took that shot or who was the intended victim."

"Me," Yvette said, turning to her. "Someone must have followed me from France."

"Not necessarily," Patience insisted. "Harry was shot before you arrived."

"What?" she demanded, rounding on Harry. "Why did you not speak of it?"

Harry help up his hands. "Peace! Yes, I was injured at the shore. But it was a glancing blow. It might have been aimed at...the friends with me."

"*Non*," Yvette said. "It was for you, *mon cher*. Someone wishes us to stop our work."

Julian turned to Harry. "There's nothing for it, Harry. We must catch this villain."

"But how?" Lydia put in. "We don't know who it is, what he looks like."

"If he is even a he," Meredith added.

Harry shook his head. "I applaud your enthusiasm, but, as I have been cautioned, this isn't a game. Yvette must speak with the War Office. What she knows may be vital to England's efforts to end this war. Tomorrow, Julian and I will escort her to London. Until then, we must all work to keep her safe. Yvette, you are to go nowhere, do nothing unescorted."

She eyed him. "So, you would imprison me again."

"Not just you," Patience put in. "I am not convinced Harry is any safer." She turned to Harry. "If Yvette must be guarded, so must you."

Oh, the pride of the man! Patience could not like the way Harry shifted on his feet, as if preparing to dash out into danger.

As if he feared as much, Julian positioned himself between Harry and the closest door. "She's right, Harry. You could easily be the target. If we take shifts, we should be able to keep you and Yvette safe until tomorrow."

Harry nodded slowly. "Very well. We'll make arrangements to keep us all safe."

It was a daunting thought, that danger lurked just outside these walls. And if the last few days had been tense, Patience did not like thinking about the next few hours.

Yet everyone seemed determined to make the best of things. Gussie and Lydia pulled Meredith and Yvette aside to discuss what Yvette would need to establish herself in London. Emma brought in a feather and offered it to Lydia. Her antics with Fortune won a smile from more than one person. Julian remained beside them, arms crossed, as if daring any villain to come closer. Beau clung like a shadow to Harry.

"Least I can do, old fellow," he said when Harry eyed him. "After all, I suspected the worst of you when you really had reformed. Love can do that to a fellow, I hear."

Patience waited for Harry to deny he was in love. Everyone knew the truth of his activities now. There was no need to pretend an engagement. But he merely smiled and challenged Beau to a game of cards.

Harry encouraged her to join the other women, but she couldn't make herself leave his side. If the bullet had taken a different path, she might never have held his hand again. Yvette was right. Life was uncertain. She should not delay in telling Harry how she felt.

Neither, it seemed, could Beau.

He made a show of staring at his cards, then murmured so low Patience almost missed it.

"Count on me to help, Harry. You aren't the only one working for the government."

Patience started, but Harry played smoothly. "You're not one of Lord Hastings' men."

"No." Beau almost sounded bitter. "But I do favors for the Admiralty. You must know not everyone trusts you. I was sent to watch your activities and report back. There's a courier at Folkestone I meet to relay my news or lack thereof. We have a signal."

Was that the real reason Beau had been going out at odd times? Harry seemed to think so, but he was quick to point out the flaw in the story.

"So, you would have it your attempts at blackmail were just part of the act," he murmured as he played his card, voice skeptical.

"Certainly," Beau insisted.

Despite his protest, she shared Harry's doubts. He might be working for the Admiralty, but he had been working to line his own pockets at the same time.

Whatever his reasons, however, Beau refused to leave Harry's side now. In fact, with their enforced proximity, it was impossible for Patience to speak to Harry privately. Could she declare her love in front of everyone? Wouldn't he feel obliged to accept for the moment, even if he had no lasting feelings for her?

With the male servants taking turns patrolling the grounds, Emma, Mary, and the housemaid Sally helped indoors, bringing in tea and cakes at one point, fetching and carrying so that neither Yvette nor Harry had to leave the room unaccompanied. Patience did what she could as well. After all, her life wasn't in danger.

Emma took her aside as evening approached. "Mr. Teacake says Mr. Cuddlestone wants a word, miss, before dinner."

Thanking her, Patience slipped out into the entry hall and glanced around. But the spry little butler was nowhere in sight.

She heard a footfall a moment before someone shoved a pillowcase over her head. Stunned, she froze, and strong hands pinned her arms to her sides.

"Easy now," a man whispered near her ear. "If you shout, I'll have you dead before they can reach you. Play along, as you're so good at doing, and you may live to tell the tale."

She didn't recognize the voice, but it had to belong to their enemy. Somehow, he had made it past the guards and into the house, but instead of capturing Harry or Yvette, he was taking her.

Panic wrapped around her more surely than his arms.

She fought it back.

"You're making a mistake," she whispered, but he half carried, half dragged her away from the withdrawing room. Not the stairs, then. They must be moving deeper into the house.

"I know nothing of use to you," she tried.

"Very likely," he agreed. "But you have other uses."

The very idea sent a chill through her.

He pulled up once, dragging her back against him and pressing the material to her mouth to prevent her from crying out. He seemed to be tall, if the stuttered breath above her was any indication. From beyond him came the sound of voices. One belonged to Emma, she thought. All she could manage was a grunt. It must have gone unnoticed, for no one came to her aid.

"Hush now," he murmured, steering her forward again. "Can't have you discovered before Lady de Maupassant has been disposed of."

So, he was after Yvette. What could Patience do to stop him? If she tipped him, he'd only rise again. Most of the staff were busy. Even if she could shout through the material, no one might hear her. If only she had a knife.

Yvette was right. It was easier to be brave when someone you loved was threatened.

She heard the click of a latch opening, and he dragged her over a threshold. The air felt cooler. Were they outside? The pillowcase muffled sound, smell. He pushed on her shoulders until she sat on the ground.

"Now, be a good girl," he said, binding her hands behind her. "They'll likely find you in the morning." He moved on to her feet as well.

"Please," Patience said. "Have you no family who would caution you against this? No mother who would weep to see a son brought so low?"

"Hush, I said," he hissed. "My father and mother would be proud of what I'm doing. *Vive le France!*"

She heard the latch again as he let himself out.

She wiggled. What she sat on was hard. Stretching her arms, she contacted a smooth surface. Stone, perhaps? Was she in a garden shed? But why hide her away? The villain seemed to think she could live through this, so he had taken her for other reasons than to kill her. Ransom? As dedicated to the cause of France as he claimed to be, that seemed too selfish. But perhaps he wasn't asking for money in exchange for her life.

He wanted Yvette, and Harry stood in the way.

She struggled against her bonds, but nothing gave. She tried shouting but heard no response. Where was she?

Think, Patience!

She held her breath, listening, and heard only silence. No clock ticking. Where at Foulness Manor did time hold no meaning?

Was Harry safe?

Always she came back to that. Harry's safety, his wellbeing, was all that mattered. What a fool she'd been to wait to tell him she loved him. Now images of him flashed through her mind. His slow smile when he was particularly pleased with something. That dimple as he teased. His utter devotion to safeguarding his country. His love for Gussie, even at her most demanding.

Gussie. Time standing still.

She sniffed the air, drawing it deep. Yes! It had to be. She'd become so accustomed to the scent of the laboratory she'd almost missed it through the mask of the pillowcase. There was the warm scent of roses in the air, along with the acid touch of burnt feathers, which Lydia had feared Gussie would never completely erase. She must be tucked near Gussie's work table. Which meant the pots with the latest attempts had to be just above. She tightened her stomach, leaned back, and swung her legs right, left.

There!

The work table thunked as she hit it, and she heard the

pots and mortars clattering together. A few more hits, and she ought to knock something to the floor, spreading the contents. More than one batch were redolent. Surely someone would notice the smell and remark on it. That, and if she made enough noise, she might succeed in capturing one of the staff's attention.

Before their enemy captured Harry.

CHAPTER TWENTY-TWO

In the withdrawing room, Harry gathered up the cards to deal. Meredith and Gussie had joined him and Villers at the table near the hearth for a game of whist. Lydia had picked up a tome, something about the predations of the Roman Empire, if he recalled, and sat reading. Yvette wandered about the room as if she couldn't find a place, Julian keeping an eye on her. Fortune trailed her like the tail of a kite, as if she knew Yvette needed a companion. And Harry kept watching the door for Patience.

Might as well admit it. Life was sweeter with her in it. Yet how could he ask her to share a life so uncertain, so tainted by scandal?

Emma hurried in with her usual pace, and Harry only realized her pallor when she rushed up to thrust a piece of paper at him.

"I came back from the kitchen to find this waiting on the floor of the entry hall. Oh, Master Harry, save her!"

Ice crusted his veins as he glanced down at the scrawl.

I have your betrothed. Bring Yvette de Maupassant to me at the shore at sunset, or Patience Ramsey dies.

All sound shut off. Most thought with it. Patience had been so worried he'd endanger himself. His efforts had endangered someone far more important—the woman he loved.

"Master Harry!" Emma was tugging on his sleeve. He

blinked at her, trying to marshal his thoughts.

"What is it?" Gussie demanded as Yvette, Lydia, and Julian came to join them.

Harry shook himself. "I miscalculated. It seems our enemy has entered the house."

Lydia bent and scooped up Fortune as if the cat could save them. The others at the table climbed to their feet.

Julian strode the door as if to bar it to all comers. "How, when?"

"I don't know," Harry said. "But he has taken Patience and demands that we exchange her for Yvette."

Yvette nodded. "I agree, of course. You should not lose the woman you love."

Harry shook his head. "Can you read me so well?"

She smiled. "*Oui, mon ami.* And how could you not love her? She is an English lady, and you dream of being an English gentleman. Now, what does the pig propose?"

Harry motioned them all closer and explained the situation.

"We should go to the village," Villers said. "Summon the constable."

"I cannot allow anyone else to be endangered," Harry told him, "or, inadvertently, that anyone put Patience further at risk by trying to help."

"Besides, our nemesis is likely watching the house," Julian said. "He'd know if anyone leaves."

Harry eyed him. "But he can't follow more than one person. Julian, go to the village and gather Undene and his men. Get them to the cove as soon as possible."

"Count on me," Julian said.

"Villers, take the grooms to the shore and position yourselves around the cove below the house. I believe you know the location."

He colored at the reminder he had been spying on Harry but nodded. "I'll do it."

"If possible," Harry told them all, "we'll catch him when

he arrives and rescue Patience with no threat to Yvette." He turned to his aunt. "Gussie and Meredith, explain things to Cuddlestone and Wilkins and have them stand ready."

The ladies eagerly agreed.

"What about me?" Lydia begged. "You cannot ask me to sit quietly while Patience and Yvette are in danger."

"He will not find me easy prey," Yvette vowed, fingering her sleeve once more. The thin blade leaped to her hand.

"I must find one of those," Gussie said admiringly.

"You must not," Harry said. "Your current activities are bad enough. I can smell your laboratory from here."

As if she could as well, Fortune sneezed.

Gussie raised her chin. "Nonsense. The current formulations are well covered to prevent any leakage."

"They were," Lydia agreed. "But it's possible something slipped by us. A shame I can't smell much of anything at the moment. My nose went numb days ago."

She sounded positively cheerful about the matter.

"Well, mine still functions," Meredith said, "and Harry is quite right. The scent is unmistakable."

"Fortune and I will check," Lydia offered. "It will keep me occupied. I look forward to hearing of your victory."

So did Harry.

They dispersed. Yvette watched them go a moment, then drew herself up as if ready to face whatever lay ahead.

"If you wear a cloak," Harry offered, "you won't be visible in the dark."

"This I know." She shook her head as she slid the dagger back into the sheath above her wrist. "How odd, to choose one's clothing to remain unseen by the enemy. I never thought of such things before the Revolution."

Harry touched her arm. "Stay in England when this is over, Yvette. There's not a man on Lord Hastings' force who doesn't owe you a debt, for information if not their lives."

Her smile softened until she looked little older than

Lydia. "They are fine men, and I was glad to help. But I would like to have a family again."

He could not argue there. Funny. So many times, he'd lamented his father's activities, as if his early death had deprived Harry of a family. But Gussie, Cuddlestone, and Emma had been his family, a family that would not be complete unless Patience joined it.

Determined, he led Yvette upstairs. They located a suitable cloak in Gussie's wardrobe, then collected Harry's hooded lantern and his sword. The cutlass had belonged to his great-grandfather. Gussie made sure the thing remained sharp. *A contingency*, she'd said. Somehow, he thought the original baronet of Foulness Manor would approve of what he was about to do.

The clock chimed. Only six? How could he do anything for the next half hour knowing Patience was in danger?

"He will not harm her," Yvette murmured, watching him. "Not until he knows he has me."

"All the more reason he will never have you," Harry said. Sword in its scabbard at his side, he set down the lantern and slipped Gussie's black velvet cloak about Yvette's shoulders. The folds held the faint scent of roses. Was this what Patience had been wearing the night she'd followed him?

Yvette pulled the hood up over her red-gold curls. "*Allons-y.*"

Harry picked up the lantern and followed.

As Wilkins let them out the front door with a nod of respect, Harry paused to glance about. Nothing moved in the twilight. But in the distance, something glimmered like stars—the lamps being lit in the village. Most of his neighbors would eat, talk, and go to sleep with little thought to those who risked their lives to keep them safe. His father and grandfather had been the same. He had been proud to be different. But the risk would not be worth the outcome if anything happened to Patience.

Yvette was right. Patience was everything he loved about England—her calm response to calamity, her resilience in the face of adversity, her subtle sense of humor, her beauty. He would give his life to keep her safe.

He lit a lantern and led Yvette across the lawn.

Though he listened for any sound, watched for any movement, they reached the shore without incident. He caught no sign of Villers, the grooms, Julian, or Undene and his men and could only hope they were hidden among the tall grasses. The eastern sky was already as velvety black as Gussie's cloak, which brushed the sand as softly as the waves as Yvette walked beside him.

"There," she whispered, raising her arm, and he saw a shadow gliding toward them, dark cape swirling about its long legs. He could make out no more of features or frame. Harry started forward, and Yvette caught his arm.

"Wait. He comes alone. Make him tell you of Patience."

He stilled. Of course. Another time he would have realized it first. Now every part of him tensed, like a string on a harp, ready to be plucked.

"Stop right there," he called. "Where is Patience Ramsey?"

"Safe," the other figure called. The voice was that of a man. "I will tell you her location when you send Mademoiselle de Maupassant to me."

"I refuse to send her to you until I know Patience is safe," Harry countered.

He spread his hands. "Then we are at an impasse. A shame. I do not know if your pretty bride will survive if I do not return for her shortly."

"You said she was safe," Harry said, hoping his friends and staff were edging closer.

"And so she is, for now. But I make no promises unless you hand over Yvette de Maupassant."

"Let me go," Yvette whispered beside him. "He will not get far, I think."

"He could kill you here, and we would have lost you for nothing," Harry whispered back.

Just then, another shape rose from the grasses on the right. It wore a long cloak, grey in the twilight. "*Je suis ici*," it said, a woman's voice, low and seemingly frightened.

Yvette stiffened.

"Ah, my quarry." The villain's voice thickened with satisfaction. He started to move, but another figure appeared from the grasses on the left. "*Non*, here I am."

He pulled up short, glancing between them.

A third shadow came from behind Harry, moving past him and Yvette.

"*Voilá*, Mademoiselle de Maupassant," it proclaimed.

"No, look here!" A fourth figure slipped out from behind the tree at the bottom of the cliff.

The villain stumbled back. "What is this? I warn you—I hold Patience Ramsey's life in my hands."

"And we hold yours," Julian declared, darting out from behind the closest figure. Villers and the grooms came from the opposite direction. From the grasses, Undene and his men strode out onto the sand. Their enemy backed away, then turned and ran for the waves.

"Stop him!" Harry cried, leaping forward. "We don't know what he's done with Patience!"

The cloaked figure on the right ran to stop him. "Harry! It's all right. I'm safe."

That voice! He pulled Patience close, held her tight, heartbeat loud in his ears. He sent a prayer of thanksgiving skyward.

"But how?" Yvette asked, joining them.

The other figures gathered closer as well, pulling back hoods to reveal Meredith, Lydia, and Gussie, but before they could explain, Julian and Villers returned, dragging their enemy.

"You have exceedingly poor taste in staff, Harry," Villers said. He yanked back the fellow's hood.

Harry frowned. "Your valet?"

"*My* valet?" Villers stared at the culprit. "I thought you'd hired Tecet to see to my needs while I was visiting."

The valet jerked out of their grip. "Idiots, all of you. I moved among you, and you never noticed. I nearly stopped you on the shore that night. I kept this fool out of my business with a little poison in his cup. If the cat had not dismissed the drink last evening, I would have poisoned the lady traitor as well, and no one would have been the wiser."

"I must remember to thank your pet," Yvette murmured to Meredith as Villers looked aghast.

"So, you admit to trying to kill her," Harry said. "Why?"

His smile was unkind. "The Emperor's enemies must be silenced."

"He's French, Harry," Patience said. "Or at least he is a French sympathizer."

"There are those in the War Office who would very much like to hear what he has to say," Julian said, repositioning his hand on the fellow's shoulder. "I say we take him to London with us tomorrow."

"You can take me where you like," he sneered. "I will tell you only this. My master will not rest until the traitor dies. When he learns I have failed, he will come for her."

"Take him to the house," Harry told the grooms as the ladies exchanged glances of concern. "Lock him in the laundry and stand guard. Let no one speak to him. Undene, may I ask for your help?"

The blacksmith nodded. "Whatever you need, Sir Harry." He bowed to Patience. "I'm glad to see you took no harm, miss. It was brave of you to help like that."

Patience smiled at him. "I had good examples of bravery to copy."

He nodded with a smile and turned to follow the grooms as they led Tecet back toward the house.

Julian brushed sand off his stockings. "I feel like a fool.

The fellow's been helping me dress, and I never noticed anything amiss."

Patience shook her head. "Even at Foulness Manor it seems servants can be invisible."

"As is this master he mentioned," Harry said, feeling chilled. "That means Yvette is still in danger."

There was little opportunity for discussion until they had all returned to the house. Then they had to reassure Cuddlestone, Emma, Wilkins, and the rest of the staff before Patience could slip away to change out of her potion-stained skirts. She had succeeded in knocking things over and onto herself in the process. The loss of her dress was a small price to pay for Harry and Yvette's safety.

Harry was waiting for Patience in the doorway to the withdrawing room when she came downstairs. He showed great reluctance to let her out of his sight, coming to stand beside her chair as the others found their accustomed places.

"I'm still perplexed," Julian admitted, leaning back in his chair. "How did Miss Ramsey escape? How did you all make your way to the shore?"

"Lydia and Fortune are your heroes," Patience said. "They found me tied up in the laboratory. I'd been trying to attract your attention in every way I knew."

Meredith smiled down at her pet, who sat in her lap regarding them all as she slowly blinked her copper eyes.

"The smell," Harry realized.

"Gussie's formulations," Patience explained.

"So, when I told Patience your plan," Lydia put in, "she conceived of a better one."

"Mr. Tecet wanted Yvette," Patience said. "Why not give him a wealth of them? If he was confused, that would give you time to capture him."

"And it did," Julian agreed. "Now we'll just have to

remove him to the War Office."

"What of this other person he mentioned?" Gussie asked. "I don't like the thought of another villain hereabouts."

Harry bestirred himself. "We know there are a number of French agents in England. I had thought taking Yvette to London would protect her. Now I question that."

"Will she be safe anywhere?" Villers asked, glancing around.

Meredith looked up. "I know of a situation. I'll write, and Julian can take the note on his way to town. We'll follow and await word from him. No one will think to look for her at this particular estate."

Yvette nodded. "Very well. And do not tell Harry where you take me. He will have enough to concern him here for a time." She reached out and put a hand on Harry's arm. "Once my enemy knows I am gone, you and your bride will be safe, *mon ami*."

"We should have a few days' reprieve before anyone knows you were even here," Harry agreed.

Lydia clapped her hands. "Oh, good! We can still celebrate Easter before you go."

Harry nodded, but his smile was wan. Patience could guess why. With Yvette leaving, his work stymied, the game was ending. He certainly had no need for the pretense of a betrothal. It looked as if she'd be leaving for Bath herself shortly. She ought to be delighted to start her new life. She wanted so much to be independent. Now the very thought of saying goodbye to Foulness Manor left her heavy. She would be leaving her heart behind.

Lydia glanced around at them all. "I'm so glad. I'll miss you all after we go our separate ways." Her usually bright features darkened.

Gussie patted her hand. "This has been an unusual house party, but I must say it was interesting. I wish you did not have to return to London, Lydia. You've made an exceptional assistant."

Lydia threw her arms around Gussie, knocking her back on the sofa. "Oh, thank you, Gussie! I'd be delighted to stay. I'll have Beau send all my things."

Her brother stiffened. "Lydia, don't be ridiculous. You cannot stay here. You're expected to return to the marriage mart once the Season starts."

Lydia disengaged from Gussie and raised her chin. "The marriage mart will get on just fine without me, thank you very much. I never enjoyed a minute of it. I'd much rather spend my time inventing something useful."

"Are you certain?" Julian asked as her brother gaped. "A young lady like yourself shouldn't waste away in a musty old laboratory."

"I beg your pardon," Gussie sputtered.

"I disagree, Mr. Mayes," Lydia said. "I had a lackluster showing in Society. The only man I cared about decided I wasn't good enough for him. But when it comes to advancing science and medicine, you heard Gussie. I am exceptional."

"Yes, you are," Patience agreed. "And nothing says you cannot return to Society at a later date if it suits you."

Lydia beamed her sunny smile all around. "Doubtful. Men don't like women who are bluestockings. Beau says so."

Every woman in the room aimed their scowls at her brother.

He threw up his hands. "It's the truth! Come, Lydia, you must see reason."

Lydia rose, shoulders back and gaze on her brother. The misty green of her eyes had never looked so hard. "No, Beau. You must see reason. All my life I looked up to you. I tried to be the woman you expected: pretty, happy, good-natured, and, frankly, not very bright. I think it's time I lived up to my own expectations instead."

Her brother stared at her. "And what are your expectations?"

Her smile returned. "I'm not certain yet, but I look forward to discovering the possibilities."

Patience, Meredith, Gussie, and Yvette were all smiling at her. So were Harry and Julian.

Her brother sighed. "And what am I supposed to do with myself this Season? I promised our parents I would see Lydia well settled."

"And so you have," Patience said.

Julian clapped him on the back. "Never fear, old man. I'm sure Lord Hastings would like to have a talk with you as to how you can support the war effort."

Harry caught Julian's eye. "I believe Villers has the matter well in hand."

Beau sighed again.

Gussie rose. "Time to retire. Tomorrow will be a busy day. Lydia, if the calamus does not yield the results I hope, we might try chamomile next as an additive to the ointment from Patience's mother."

"Ooo," Lydia said, rising and falling into step beside her. "And perhaps mint?"

"Yes, yes, excellent thought. I'll have Cook set some aside."

"Come along, Yvette," Meredith said, standing as well, Fortune safely in her arms. "We can discuss this placement on the way to our rooms."

Julian hurried to bar her path. "And I hope I may call on you in London, Meredith."

She hesitated, and Patience bit her lip. But Fortune put out a paw as if offering him her hand, and Meredith inclined her head. "I would enjoy that, Julian."

Julian was still grinning as he and Beau followed her from the room.

With a wink to Patience, Mr. Cuddlestone slipped out as well.

In a matter of moments, Patience and Harry were alone. For once, no rain pattered against the window. Harry's hand was warm, protective, on her shoulder.

Patience drew in a breath and stood to face him. His hair curled against his brow as if asking for her touch. His smile encouraged her to share all her secrets.

"I should leave in the morning as well," she said. "You and Gussie have no further need of me. But I cannot go without thanking you, Harry."

He raised his brows. "Thanking me? I embroiled you in a false engagement, subjected you to danger, and forced you to live through the worst house party in England's history."

She could not help her laugh. "It wasn't so bad. And a great deal of good came out of it. Gussie has an assistant who is just as eager to experiment. Beau will no longer attempt to blackmail you. He may even stop arriving unannounced and unexpected. Yvette has somewhere safe to stay. And Meredith and Julian have agreed to be friends, at least."

Harry took her hand in his. "And you, Patience. What have you gained from all this?"

Patience met his gaze. "I learned that I have an inner strength I can rely on. But most of all, Harry, I fell in love with you."

"Patience." Her name was an adoration. He bent his head and caressed her lips with his. All of her trembled at the touch. She almost pulled him back as he drew away.

"I don't know why you love me. You have seen me at my worst."

"And your best," Patience protested.

He shook his head, but he did not gainsay her outright. "You know my dreams and how far I am from reaching them. I may never see the name of Orwell restored to the ranks of English gentlemen, but I will never stop trying. Nor will I cease helping England win this war. It is a most unsuitable time to ask a woman to marry me."

She swallowed, disappointment so strong she thought

she might melt under it. "I understand."

"Do you? Because unsuitable or not, scandalous name or not, I love you, Patience Ramsey, and I am convinced life will be empty without you in it. Will you do me the honor of making our pretend betrothal real?"

Patience stared at him. His eyes were bright, his color high, and the most tender smile sat on his lips. How could she doubt him?

"Oh, Harry," she said, "yes, yes of course! Nothing would make me happier. I love you to distraction."

He took her in his arms and kissed her again. Held so close, she could dream of a future together. It seemed her baronet was not so very borrowed after all. She could imagine spending her days with him, sharing the nights, and growing old together. One thing was certain: life with Sir Harry Orwell would never be dull, and she could safely say she would never be invisible again.

CHAPTER TWENTY-THREE

Easter dawned in a rosy sunrise. Patience put on her best grey poplin gown and the wide feathered hat Gussie had purchased for her in London before they'd left for Foulness Manor. Had it only been a little more than a fortnight? She could scarcely believe it. As Yvette rose as well, Patience helped her into a blue silk gown that had belonged to Gussie. Emma had spent the evening hemming the high-waisted gown for Yvette's shorter stature.

"*Bon*," the Frenchwoman proclaimed when she glanced in the mirror, tweaking a strawberry blond curl into place. "Today, I look like a lady celebrating with friends."

"Which is what you are," Patience assured her.

Indeed, everyone seemed in high spirits as they met in the dining room. Mr. Cuddlestone carried their dyed eggs in on a platter, like a rainbow entering the room, and Cook supplied smoked salmon, pastries of various sorts, fresh fruit brought in from a local greenhouse, and other delicacies before they all moved to the coaches.

Harry looked so handsome in his navy coat and fawn breeches buckled at the knees as he led Patience in to services. Garlands bedecked the church doors, and more flowers in stone vases clustered on either side of the altar. Patience caught Gussie eyeing them as if wondering which bloom might improve her formulation. Patience was so happy she couldn't move herself to suggest otherwise.

She was going to marry Harry.

He confirmed it with the vicar after services.

"The details I promised," Harry said, handing him a piece of paper. "I'd appreciate it if you would send a copy to her home parish as well. St. John's outside Carrolton Park."

The vicar readily agreed, beaming at them both.

"Why Carrolton Park?" Patience asked as Harry walked her back to the curricle through the chiming of church bells.

"The banns are supposed to be announced in the parish of the bride and groom," Harry said. "You lived at Carrolton Park the last three years. Just think—this way Lady Lilith will have to hear your name linked to mine for three weeks, knowing the entire while that we plan to wed."

Patience shook her head. "What a considerate groom you are, Harry."

"And you, madam, are the perfect bride. I am the most fortunate of mortals."

Patience leaned closer, the feather on her hat brushing the brim of his. "There's no one around. You don't have to posture."

"I refuse to be silent," Harry insisted. "I will tell you and show you how much I love and admire you every day of my life."

And he proceeded to fulfill his promise.

That afternoon, Meredith sat in the Orwell coach, Fortune on her lap, as the team trundled away from Foulness Manor. Yvette sat next to her, hands folded properly, one of Patience's dark gowns obscuring her petite figure.

"And these Carroltons," she said, watching Meredith's hand as it stroked Fortune's fur, "they will be amenable to hiding me?"

"I believe that to be the case," Meredith said. "Lady Carrolton has been seeking a new companion since Patience left, and I do not believe she has filled the position. As Patience has noted, companions, and servants, are generally invisible. No one will look for you there."

Yvette smiled. "At least you did not try to make me a chef. I have no experience in the kitchen. A companion should be easy—just smile and nod."

Meredith kept her gaze on Fortune. "It may not be so simple. Lady Carrolton is rather exacting in her standards, and her daughter, Lady Lilith, has high expectations."

Yvette waved a hand. "I have lived in finer houses, made myself useful to the Empress when needed. This earl's family will be no trouble."

Meredith smiled. "I know no one better equipped to rise to the occasion. Fortune will, of course, have to approve of the earl."

Yvette frowned. "But why? I thought I was to deal only with his mother and sister."

"Very likely," Meredith said. "But you know the value of keeping your options open. Never fear, dear. I'm sure it won't be long before you're part of the family."

Dear Reader

Thank you for reading Patience and Harry's story. Like Harry, I find Patience epitomizes the best of English womanhood. I know she will make a difference in Harry's life, and he in hers. If you'd like to know how her friend Jane became engaged to the Duke of Wey, look for *Never Doubt a Duke*.

If you enjoyed the book, there's several things you could do now:

Sign up for a free email alert at **www.eepurl.com/baqwVT** with exclusive bonus content so you'll be the first to know whenever a new book is out or on sale.

Post a review on a bookseller or reader site to help others find the book.

Discover my many other books on my website at **www.reginascott.com.**

Turn the page for a sneak peek of the second book in the Fortune's Brides series, *Never Borrow a Baronet*, in which Patience Ramsey gets her wish for a more meaningful position as she agrees to pose as a baronet's fiancée to keep others from discovering his secret life.

Blessings!

Regina Scott

Sneak Peek:

NEVER ENVY AN EARL
Book 3 in the Fortune's Brides Series by Regina Scott

Surrey, England, April 1812

How far did she have to go to be safe?

Yvette de Maupassant peered out the window of the coach her friend Sir Harold Orwell had loaned her and saw nothing but wilderness. Well, perhaps wilderness was too strong a word for the sweeping fields and patches of woods, bright with the glory of spring. But after spending the last ten years stealing secrets from Napoleon and his sycophants and traveling among the French elite, the Surrey countryside seemed as foreign as Africa.

"And you had no one in London you could trust?" she asked her companion.

Meredith Thorn smiled from her side of the coach. She would have been at home among French society. Her lustrous black hair was properly confined under a broad-brimmed velvet hat of a lavender that matched her eyes. The ostrich plume that curled down one cheek had been teasing her pet Fortune since they'd left London four hours ago. Yvette had seen the grey cat eyeing the thing from time to time on her perch on the bench beside her mistress. She'd only batted at it three times. Such restraint!

"London was unsuitable," Meredith said, wiggling her gloved fingers against her purple poplin skirt as if to direct Fortune's copper-colored eyes away from the tantalizing feather. "Too many people. We were lucky to spirit you

into the War Office for your meeting and out again with
no one being the wiser. Your enemies will not think to
look for you at Carrolton Park."

"Because no one can find it," Yvette said, but she smiled
as Fortune pounced toward her mistress' fingers, missing
them by moments as Meredith pulled away.

Yvette scratched the plush seat, and Fortune's ears
pricked, gaze narrowing in on the movement. Ah, to have
such a life, with no more worries than where to play next.
Her life had once been as pleasant, though it had changed
forever the day the mob had come for her family.

Now the long hair her maid had faithfully brushed
each night was cut short in curls about her head like a
strawberry blond cap. It had been easier to care for when
her cousin had insisted she serve as the lowliest chore girl
in his home. In defiance, she had not changed it when
Napoleon had demanded that she be brought to his court
instead to serve his wife. How her cousin had preened that
one of his family had been close to the Empress. As if she
would ever have claimed her cousin Claude as family.

The coachman turned off the main road onto a graveled
track that plunged deeper into the wood. The shadows
lengthened this late in the day, multiplied until she felt
them reaching into the coach with greedy fingers. She
shivered and touched her wrist, where her dagger and
sheath were strapped inside her sleeve.

What, was this fear? She had played the game of
espionage, discovering secrets and sending them to Harry
in England. She had matched wits with men on both sides
of the Channel. She had been willing to risk her life to
see the Corsican Monster brought down, her hated cousin
humbled. The last time she'd known fear was when she'd
been forced to live with him after the Empress Josephine
had left the court. Claude could not touch her here. If she
did not fear him, she should not fear this earl she was about
to meet or his dismal little park. But she wasn't about to

trust him either. Time had taught her she had only herself to rely on.

The forest parted then to reveal a wide plain. Sunlight sparkled on a winding stream. Roan deer fed on the emerald lawn, glancing up complacently as the carriage passed. The lane led through wrought iron gates to an area of golden gravel. A regal multistoried home with turrets at each corner sat serenely among the simplicity, like a castle in a child's storybook.

She blinked and turned to Meredith. "This is Carrolton Park?"

Meredith smiled, gathering Fortune in her arms as the carriage slowed. "It is indeed. I understand the current earl helped redesign it when he ascended to the title five years ago. I always thought he had good taste."

"I concur." Yvette could not take her gaze off the building. The house was shaped like a U, with the open end facing the drive and spanned by a white marble colonnade. The warm stone of the rest of the house made the entrance look like a pearl in a gold setting.

Two footmen in blue livery ran down the steps to help with the coach. Following them with a more stately tread was a tall, wide-shouldered butler. Black hair slicked back, he looked down his hawk-like nose at the coach, inclining his head as the footman handed down first Meredith and Fortune, then Yvette.

"Miss Thorn," he said, correctly divining that she was the leader. "Welcome to Carrolton Park. His lordship asked that you be brought to him at your earliest convenience. Would you care to refresh yourself first?"

He spared Yvette a glance, but his gaze was more kind than condemning. After all, he thought he was looking at Lady Carrolton's new companion, not the celebrated beauty who had once been the daughter of a *comte* herself.

She had tried to look the part of a poor relation. So much of playing a role depended on attitude and clothing.

She had borrowed a plain navy gown from her friend Patience Ramsey, who was engaged to dear Harry. Miss Lydia Villers, whom she had recently met at Sir Harry's Easter house party, had been persuaded to offer a straw bonnet, though, like Patience, she did not know exactly where Yvette would be hiding.

How Patience would laugh when she learned Yvette was to take up her previous position in this very house. Yvette hid her smile and kept her gaze respectfully down as she and Meredith followed the butler toward the house.

"I think it would be best if we speak to the earl first," Meredith was saying as they crossed the flagstone-floored courtyard behind the columns. Windows on all three sides regarded them with curious eyes.

"Very good, madam," the butler said, holding the double doors open for them.

They passed into a wide entry hall, and Yvette's smile broadened. Meredith had said the earl had good taste. She was wrong. If he had had any hand in the interior design, he had exceptional taste and an eye for beauty. The walls were the color of the mist over the Channel, the floor like the waves, patterned in white marble and a stone through which blue and purple swirled, much like Meredith's eyes.

Alcoves along the walls held Grecian statues, and fluted columns held up the entry to the stairway at the back, where the banisters and balustrades were made from silver-veined marble, the walls covered in carved reliefs of forests.

The butler crossed to the door leading to what must be the north wing of the house and held it open for them. With a pang of regret, she turned away from the beauty. But the corridor proved equally wondrous. Light from the tall windows on one side made the tapestries on the other side glow like rubies, emeralds, and sapphires. Polished tables held Chinese vases and bronze sculptures. She recognized the prized Sevres porcelain in a bowl holding crimson roses. Napoleon would not be pleased to know his private pattern had been smuggled to England.

And who exactly had done the smuggling? Perhaps Harry, but surely not the earl!

Even more curious to meet the fellow, she followed the butler through the closest darkly paneled door into a withdrawing room. Everything glittered, for the bronze-on-gold pattern of the wallcoverings to the tall multi-armed standing candelabra to the gold filigree around the door and the fanciful gilt edging and button tufting on the armchairs and settee.

The man moving toward them in his simple coat and trousers did not seem to belong.

A man? No surely a giant, one of the legends of this land of the Britains. Had she stepped close enough, her nose would have bumped his breastbone. Instead, she could only gaze in surprise. The tweed coat stretched across powerful shoulders, and the tan chamois trousers encased legs worthy of the statues she'd just passed. Top it all off with a square jaw, warm brown eyes, and raven hair, and he was as impressive a specimen of a male as his house was a home.

He offered them both a bow. "Ladies. Welcome to Carrolton Park. I am Lord Carrolton, and I am delighted to be of service." He nodded to his butler. "Marbury, will you let my mother know that we will be up shortly?"

"Of course." With a dip of his head, the butler turned and saw himself out.

"Please, sit down," the earl said, striding back to the sofa near the fire. The deep voice made the request sound more like a command. "You must be tired from your travels, but I thought we should be clear on our course of action first."

What, did he think they were planning a campaign? After so many years of working alone, daring to trust no one with her secrets, she found his assumption of collusion amusing. Yvette took a seat beside Meredith on the sofa, and the earl sat opposite on a dainty chair she could not credit would hold him.

"Excellent," Meredith said, settling back with Fortune cuddled close. "You received word from London, then?"

He nodded, leaning forward until his elbows rested on his thighs, black boots pressed deep in the ruby- and gold-patterned carpet. "I was informed that Miss de Maupassant has provided critical information to support England in its efforts against the French tyrant. Her efforts have put her life in danger. My task is to hide her until someone from the War Office comes for her." His lips turned up in obvious distaste. "Is it necessary that she pretend to be no more than a servant?"

Yvette spread her hands. "I am a servant, my lord. My family was guillotined, our lands and titles stripped. I now serve a noble cause, to stop this war and restore sanity to France."

He had paled at the mention of the guillotine. Most men did. Yet he could not possibly understand the reality of it, the horror, the shouts, the dull thunk as the blade came down. Here he sat, in his beautiful home, with nothing and no one to trouble him. She envied him that.

"It is best that no one know her true identity," Meredith told him. "As I'm sure Lord Hastings told you, we've had some trouble already."

He nodded. "The spy Sir Harry caught. Hastings seems to think more are coming."

One more, if the boasts of the spy could be believed. His superior would be coming to finish the job. This new threat would meet with the same fate as his predecessor: capture and imprisonment. There were too many in England waiting for him, her included.

"We cannot be certain," Meredith said to the earl. "But make no mistake. Yvette de Maupassant is guilty of treason to the Emperor. The penalty is death. Therefore, she must disappear. I give you Miss French, your mother's new companion."

Yvette pasted on a happy smile, sat up tall, and fluttered her lashes for good measure.

The earl frowned, dark brows lowering until he looked rather formidable. Was subterfuge below him? Would he refuse her refuge after all? Had she come all this way for nothing?

Gregory, Earl Carrolton, didn't like dissembling. It seemed cowardly, disrespectful. And he'd never been terribly good at it. His square-jawed face was too open, betraying his least emotions. The few times he'd shaded the truth as a child, usually to soften the blow of bad news, his tutors or his father had caught him immediately. Now the War Office wanted him to lie to his mother, his sister, and his staff. He couldn't help his qualms.

"I cannot stress the importance of keeping Mademoiselle de Maupassant safe," Lord Hastings had written. The wily marquis led an elite band of aristocratic intelligence agents, each one hand-picked, their identities only hinted at on the *ton*. Together, they had uncovered secrets, brought down spies, and saved England from disaster time and again. That Hastings was asking Gregory to undertake even a tangential role in this work was a great honor. Gregory had been chafing at his inability to help with the war. Here was his chance to be of worth.

"Miss French," he acknowledged now, trying not to sound as doubtful as he felt about the new name. "And are you content in playing the role of companion?"

Once more she fluttered her golden lashes, blue eyes sparkling. That smile was all charm. "*Mais oui.* I assure you, it will be far easier than some roles I have undertaken."

Her lilting voice was confident, but she could not know his mother. The countess had run off three companions before Patience Ramsey had consented to stay for three years. Gregory suspected the good-natured blonde had remained because she had nowhere else to go. She had been a treasure, forever tending to his mother's many ills. But when she'd announced she'd found another position, he'd gladly let her leave. She deserved better than what they could give.

"If you have any trouble," he told Miss de Maupassant, "you must come to me."

Her smile tilted up, inviting him closer. "But of course, my dear earl."

He sat back in the chair, feeling his cheeks warm. He was never sure how to act around the fairer sex. Most of the ladies of his acquaintance acted as if they were fragile creatures. An ill-considered word, a firm glance, and they dissolved. The mincing manners employed by so many gentlemen on the *ton* seemed to please them, but the movements looked ridiculous on his larger frame. And the one time he had emboldened himself to propose, the lady had kindly let him know that he could never be more than a friend. No doubt he would have to marry one day to secure the line, but he was not looking forward to adding another lady to his already tempestuous household.

"You must treat her as you would any other staff member," Miss Thorn cautioned him, gaze pinning him in place. She had the purple-blue eyes of *Lavendula*, or at least that was how it seemed to his befuddled brain.

"Ah, but I am to be a companion," Miss de Maupassant said. "That is a special sort of staff, *non?*"

Gregory shook himself. "Yes. You'll keep my mother company from the time she wakes until the time she retires. I believe Miss Ramsey read to her, sang songs to brighten her day."

"How sweet," the Frenchwoman said.

That face was equally sweet, her bonnet and gown more practical than pretty, yet he struggled to see her being servile. "Miss Ramsey took dinner with the family and attended church services and social gatherings with my mother as well," he continued.

"We may want to forego social engagements for the time being," Miss Thorn said, hand stroking the cat in her lap. The creature regarded Gregory with copper-colored eyes, tail twitching, and he sat straighter.

What was wrong with him? Was he seeking the cat's approval now? He could fell an opponent in the boxing square with one blow of his fist, slice a sapling in half with one swing of his cutlass, urge his horse over stile and stream. He had spoken before Parliament, addressed His Highness the Prince Regent. Why did one glance from a lady, even a feline one, make him want to run back to his greenhouse and hide among the plants?

"I'll do whatever is needed to keep Miss…French safe," he assured them, palms starting to sweat.

"Excellent," Miss Thorn pronounced. She stopped her hand as she gazed down at her pet.

The cat rose and stretched high on its paws, setting the lamplight to flashing on the white blaze that ran down her chest like a stream. She stepped off her mistress' lap onto the damask of sofa's upholstery.

"This is Fortune," Miss Thorn informed him. "Fortune, meet Lord Carrolton."

She was introducing him to her cat? How was he to react to that?

As if she'd spotted a plump mouse, Fortune leaped across the space between them and landed on his thigh. He held himself still.

Fortune eyed him a moment, then rubbed her head against the tweed of his coat.

Miss de Maupassant beamed. "She likes you."

"I suspect she likes everyone," he demurred, afraid to touch the lovely creature lest he inadvertently harm her.

"No, indeed," Miss Thorn assured him. "Fortune is quite refined in her opinions. You may pet her."

It seemed this was an honor too. Gingerly, Gregory

stroked his hand down the silky fur. Fortune turned her head from side to side, and he obligingly rubbed behind each ear. Well, who would have thought?

Miss Thorn's smile spread. "It appears my work here is done."

Miss de Maupassant leaned forward, cocking her head to gaze at him out of the corners of her eyes. "But you will allow Meredith and Fortune to spend the night, *oui*? They have travelled far the last few days with me."

"Of course," he said. "And I hope you'll join us for dinner as well, Miss Thorn. I can have someone watch Fortune."

The cat glanced up at him as if she recognized her name, but her gaze seemed to chide him.

"My mother has been unwell," he said. Was he telling the cat or Miss Thorn? "The doctor advises us to keep her away from any sort of animal."

Fortune pulled back from him, hopped from his lap, and stalked off across the carpet, tail in the air. Had he offended her?

Miss Thorn inclined her head. "I understand."

That made one of them. "We keep country hours," he explained. "No need to dress. Say six?"

"Perfect." She raised her head to keep an eye on her pet, who seemed to be inspecting the standing candelabra.

Miss de Maupassant rose, forcing Gregory to his feet. "Thank you for your explanations and your hospitality, my lord. And now, you must introduce me to your mother. It has been a long day, and I have only so much charm to spare."

He nodded, but he was certain the nearly christened Miss French was wrong. She had entirely too much charm. He felt it tugging at him even now. Would his mother would take to it, or was this ruse doomed from the start?

Learn more at
www.reginascott.com/neverenvyanearl.html

OTHER BOOKS BY REGINA SCOTT

UNCOMMON COURTSHIPS SERIES
The Unflappable Miss Fairchild
The Incomparable Miss Compton
The Irredeemable Miss Renfield
The Unwilling Miss Watkin
An Uncommon Christmas

LADY EMILY CAPERS
Secrets and Sensibilities
Art and Artifice
Ballrooms and Blackmail
Eloquence and Espionage
Love and Larceny

MARVELOUS MUNROES SERIES
My True Love Gave to Me
Catch of the Season
The Marquis' Kiss
Sweeter Than Candy

SPY MATCHMAKER SERIES
The Husband Mission
The June Bride Conspiracy
The Heiress Objective

Perfection

And other books for Love Inspired Historical.

ABOUT THE AUTHOR

Regina Scott started writing novels in the third grade. Thankfully for literature as we know it, she didn't sell her first novel until she learned a bit more about writing. Since her first book was published in 1998, her stories have traveled the globe, with translations in many languages including Dutch, German, Italian, and Portuguese. She now has more than forty published works of warm, witty romance.

Like Gussie, her ideas arrive at odd times: walking down the street, shopping for lawn ornaments, and trying to get a good night's sleep. Fortune's Brides came about because her critique partner and dear friend Kristy J. Manhattan is an avid fan of cats, supporting spay and neuter clinics and pet rescue groups. If Fortune resembles any cat you know, credit Kristy.

Regina Scott and her husband of 30 years reside in the Puget Sound area of Washington State on the way to Mt. Rainier. She has dressed as a Regency dandy, driven four-in-hand, learned to fence, and sailed on a tall ship, all in the name of research, of course. Learn more about her at her website at *www.reginascott.com*.

CPSIA information can be obtained
at www.ICGtesting.com
Printed in the USA
LVHW041449110619
620864LV00003B/546/P